To Die in Spring

To Jerry, with love
In memory of my father, Ludwig Maultash

Acknowledgements

I am indebted to the following people: my husband, Jerry Warsh, for answering my interminable medical questions; my mother, Gena Maultash, for sharing with me her experiences during World War II; my children, Nathaniel and Jessica, for their help according to their talents; my writing groups for their continuing constructive criticism and support through many drafts; my editor, Marc Côté, for his faith in the book.

TO DIE IN
S P R I N G

Sylvia Maultash Warsh

A Castle Street Mystery

THE DUNDURN GROUP
TORONTO · OXFORD

Editor: Marc Côté
Copy Editor: Don McLeod
Design: Jennifer Scott
Printer: Webcom

Canadian Cataloguing in Publication Data

Warsh, Sylvia Maultash
To die in spring

ISBN 0-88882-216-2
I. Title

PS8595.A7855T6 2000   C813'.54   C00-930046-5   PR9199.3.W367T6 2000

1   2   3   4   5   04   03   02   01   00

Canadä

THE CANADA COUNCIL | LE CONSEIL DES ARTS
FOR THE ARTS | DU CANADA
SINCE 1957 | DEPUIS 1957

We acknowledge the support of the **Canada Council for the Arts** for our publishing program. We also acknowledge the support of the **Ontario Arts Council** and we acknowledge the financial support of the Government of Canada through the **Book Publishing Industry Development Program** (BPIDP) for our publishing activities.

Care has been taken to trace the ownership of copyright material used in this book. The author and the publisher welcome any information enabling them to rectify any references or credit in subsequent editions.
                                                            J. Kirk Howard, President

CHAD GADYA, by Rabbi Nathan Goldberg
© 1993 Asher Scharpstien
All Rights Reserved   Used by Permission
KTAV PUBLISHIING HOUSE, INC. Hoboken, NJ. 07030-7205

Printed and bound in Canada.

✿

Printed on recycled paper.

Dundurn Press
8 Market Street
Suite 200
Toronto, Ontario, Canada
M5E 1M6

Dundurn Press
73 Lime Walk
Headington, Oxford,
England
OX3 7AD

Dundurn Press
2250 Military Road
Tonawanda NY
U.S.A. 14150

One little goat, one little goat
That Father bought for two zuzim.
One little goat, one little goat.

chapter one

Rebecca

Tuesday, March 27, 1979

Every time Rebecca drove to the office that first week back she saw David's face in the rear-view mirror. At first it alarmed her, seeing a dead person's face. But then she realized it wasn't his face at all. It was the reflection of his face in her own eyes she was seeing. An image she carried around with her like other people carry photos in their wallets.

The sun floated pale in the sky after the long winter as she drove David's Jaguar coupe to the medical building. Spring was ironic this year. What good was the stirring of buds on maple branches to her, or the pointed daffodil shoots reaching through the soil? David would not come back this spring. She would have to stop looking in the rear-view mirror.

She turned down Beverley Street, luminous and still, in a haze of Victorian manor-houses built in the 1870s.

Immigrant semi-detached homes had sprung up in between. She always felt like she was coming home when she turned down this street. She'd spent her happiest years as an undergrad at the University of Toronto barely two blocks away. In her second year she'd met David in an art history course she'd chosen as a breadth requirement for science students. Lanky and red-haired then, he attracted her notice with his irreverent ongoing commentary about the slides of famous paintings the professor was projecting on the screen. It wasn't till he graduated that he took his art seriously. By then she was in medical school. Their lives had stretched before them then like a landscape — she thought of the muted colours, the Impressionist attention to light in his early work. If only she'd been paying attention. Maybe he would be alive. If only she'd noticed the change in his palette, it would've been a clue.

Through her windshield she could see Beverley Mansions, a series of pale brick double-houses, once grand, now renovated by the city into flats. Second Empire they were called, trying to make an impression. Their sculptured ornamental style captured the air of optimism and ambition for money in the time following Confederation. The cladding was cream yellow brick topped with mansard roofs.

The sun warmed her through the window as she pulled into the little parking lot behind the building. April was the month that bred lilacs out of the dead land. It should've been a time to re-invent herself, like the season; they had both gone through a death. The earth was accustomed to rising from the debris of winter; she didn't know if she had the strength.

In February, the Eglinton Avenue building that housed her former office had been evacuated for extensive renovations. Instead of relocating to a temporary office where she could continue to see her patients, she closed up shop altogether. It was a sudden decision that surprised everyone — including her. She had always put on a strong face, didn't show her pain, often denying it herself. But she knew she had come to the end of her rope. Her stamina and concentration were gone and she worried about making a mistake. She wouldn't jeopardize the welfare of her patients. She would have to concede that she, too, was human and couldn't always cope.

She found the vacancy on Beverley Street with her last ounce of energy, then retreated into herself, leaving Iris to set up the new office. Rebecca had never been good at that sort of thing; she'd always let David worry about colours and design. She knew she could trust Iris, who was more than an office assistant; a friend. She'd left Iris few instructions apart from some aesthetic comments about her deep loathing of the colour orange and the flat industrial paintings of Fernand Léger. Other than that Iris had had a free hand, and she'd done well.

During that first week in the new office, the languid smell of paint, the surprise at the high ceilings and wood mouldings had faded comfortably into a suggestion of fresh beginnings, perhaps a wary hope. She had the whole second floor of the building. The waiting-room, decorated in designer shades of mauve and grey, never held more than a few patients. People had probably found other doctors in her two-month absence. Iris had spent the last few weeks sending out notices of Rebecca's imminent return to practice, but her former patients were not knocking down her door. That was fine. Rebecca needed to ease into real life again. The eight weeks she had given herself seemed like eight months. She was starting her days at one, and found herself finished at six.

Behind the partition, Iris' round face broke into her usual welcoming smile when she saw Rebecca. "How are you today, love?"

Rebecca slid into the upholstered chair beside Iris, who handed her the x-ray and other test results that had come that morning. The phone rang and Iris' mother-hen voice comforted and made an appointment for a patient with a problem. Rebecca looked up to watch her. Iris was one of the constants in her life. Tall, unrepentantly bulky, Iris carried her extra fifty or so pounds with such authority under richly tailored suits and dresses that her size became an advantage. Her short blonde hair defied gravity, swept up and away from her neck in shiny controlled waves. Rebecca had been lucky to find her at that point in Iris' life when her children were grown and her divorce pending. Rebecca had been enchanted by the verve and energy manifest in the amplitude of the hips, the direction of the hair.

Apart from her parents, Iris had been the one Rebecca had leaned on the most during David's final months. Iris was the one who had done double duty in the office, arranging for other doctors to cover for Rebecca while she ran back and forth from the hospital. That last time in the office, when it became clear that all hope had run out, Iris had taken her in her arms and let her cry, gently explaining that she would have to leave her tears there because David needed her strong.

Iris was wearing a mauve suit today, matching the decor. "You start at one with Mr. Bellini," she said handing Rebecca a file. "Oh, and Mrs. Kochinsky called for an appointment tomorrow."

"Is she still seeing Dr. Romanov?"

"She said she prefers you. She not only wants the one o'clock tomorrow — she wants her old slot back, every Wednesday."

Rebecca allowed herself a momentary smile. Dr. Romanov had covered for her during her absence. Apparently he had done fine with stomach ailments and skin rashes, but had no knack for psychotherapy. She had hoped Mrs. Kochinsky would return for her weekly sessions. Though Rebecca practiced general medicine, she had realized over the ten years of treating patients that a handful of them needed to talk out their problems more than they needed sedatives or painkillers. A certain rapport with her patients was required but the decision to conduct psychotherapy always grew out of Rebecca's concern for their physical well-being. Mrs. Kochinsky refused all medication but had eagerly arrived for therapy each week like clockwork since coming to Canada from Argentina one and a half years earlier.

Rebecca stood up to retrieve Mrs. Kochinksy's file from the wall unit, leaned over to sniff the vase of daffodils Iris had arranged on the counter near her desk. Their fluted yellow centres emanated a sweet vapour filled with hope and mute possibility. Incomprehensible spring. She felt it creeping into her shrunken heart in those sudden moments when the fading fragrance of new paint wafted through the air.

She took the file and stepped into her office. A new print of Monet's *Lilies* hung on the wall. She had removed all of David's sketches and watercolours from the old office and put them into her basement. Maybe one day she would be able to look at them.

She sat down in her new grey leather chair and opened Mrs. Kochinsky's file. "Severe anxiety and insomnia. Very agitated. Rx: mild sedative. Patient refuses meds. Worries that somehow they can be tampered with. Consistent with persecutory thinking. Recommended psychiatrist, but patient reluctant."

11

Rebecca recalled the charming Polish accent tempered with Spanish. "Life in Argentina became dangerous in nineteen-seventies," Mrs. Kochinsky had told her. "After Peron died in '74, one dictatorship after another. The military. You understand. Always the military. They did what they want, they got rid of anyone they don't like. It was dangerous sometimes in streets. And you, people like you, they have special hate for psychiatrists" — she pronounced the silent p. "They pull some from hospitals, some from homes. All disappeared. Gone. They didn't trust them. Who knows why? What they don't understand, they destroy." Rebecca had taken in the stylish hair, the tasteful suit, and wasn't prepared for what came next. "Who would think they'd take *me*? What did *I* do?"

Especially difficult for Rebecca to deal with was the dream. Though described to Rebecca often, it was like a jigsaw that fluctuated with each unexpected fragment of memory, a space filled in here, another there. At first Rebecca hoped that once completed, the puzzle would lose its terror. On the contrary, the more Mrs. Kochinsky remembered, the closer she came to concluding the picture. Rebecca realized that the sum of such parts would add up to a whole that few people could bear.

Whatever details dropped out of her memory, the dream always began the same way: waking up, startled in bed. The door exploding with shouts. *¡Abra la puerta! ¡Abra la puerta!* Her face on the floor of the car, the guard's foot on her back. Mrs. Kochinsky intoned the events like a well-worn article of faith, a shadow religion that held her captive on the darkest of altars. Rebecca listened as the older woman repeated the dream in pieces that she could endure on this side of memory.

The odd thing was, when David died in September, Mrs. Kochinsky was the only patient Rebecca told, the only one she felt could understand. The older woman observed Rebecca with empathy for a while, commenting on the shadows beneath her eyes. Rebecca felt close to her then. It was a bond between them that grew like a dark flower.

Rebecca read over some of her notes from January, Mrs. Kochinsky's last visit: "Presented in somewhat agitated state. Well-dressed. Excited, unable to calm herself. Thought content disordered. Elevated BP. 160 over 100. Still upset over sister who has entered nursing home. Sister stopped speaking. Mrs. K. feels abandoned though visits almost every day. Furious with brother-in-law for quick decision to send sister away. Mrs. K. restless during session. Sleep disrupted, loss of appetite. Recommended Rx: moderate dose chlorpromazine. Still refuses meds."

Rebecca flipped through notes on Mrs. Kochinsky's previous visits. Last July her patient had missed an appointment. This had never happened before. Iris interrupted Rebecca's examination of another patient so she could take the phone. Mrs. Kochinsky muttered, between wails, that her only living relative, her younger sister Chana, had suddenly gone mad. Mrs. Kochinsky had moved to Toronto to be with Chana who had now retreated into herself, unwilling or unable to live in the world. Mrs. Kochinsky was not going to come for her appointment then or ever again, she had outlived the rest of her family. *What is there left to live for*? Chana was all she had, and now even she was gone. *I'm only alive because I'm not dead.*

Rebecca had abandoned a waiting-room full of patients and driven the few blocks to Mrs. Kochinsky's duplex to find her anything but elegantly dressed. Her patient lay in bed, wrapped in a cotton housecoat.

"Mrs. Kochinsky...."

Her eyes opened but would not focus. Rebecca checked her wrists. No blood. Then her eye caught the empty pill bottle on the nightstand. "Mrs. Kochinsky! What have you done!"

She swept up the bottle: *Chana Feldberg. Take one tablet at bedtime when needed for sleep. Valium. 15 mg. 30 tablets.*

Rebecca had waited in the busy emerg while Mrs. Kochinsky's stomach was pumped. She knew the ER nurses would be curt and perfunctory with a suicide attempt, preferring to expend their energy on patients who actually wanted to survive. They'd been waiting for a psychiatric assessment for two hours when Mrs. Kochinsky suddenly sat up in the bed, grey-brown hair fly-away, and announced she wanted to go home. Nothing Rebecca said would deter her from getting dressed. Rebecca, perturbed by the possibility that a psychiatrist might hold her for lengthy observation, accompanied her patient through the crowded ER where nobody took any notice of them.

At Mrs. Kochinsky's, Rebecca called social services to arrange for a visiting nurse. She sat on the edge of Mrs. Kochinsky's bed and looked into eyes that were vacant with pain. She took gentle hold of the limp hands. "You mustn't let them have this victory," she said, and a lot of other things she couldn't remember. Mrs. Kochinsky wept long tears as Rebecca spoke, listening more, it seemed, to the steady rhythm of her words than the words themselves. There was a primitiveness in Mrs. Kochinsky's need for the sound of someone's steadfast heart, like the need of a newborn for the beat of its mother's pulse. Rebecca was willing to be that heart, that pulse, as long as it kept Mrs. Kochinsky alive.

chapter two

Goldie

As soon as Goldie stepped onto the Bathurst Street bus she knew she was in trouble. The strangers around her stared with cold faces. The familiar palpitations began in her neck, her chest, as she determined to find the one she was looking for: it was in the eyes, the way a person held his head. This bus was why she didn't go downtown, this danger to her survival that the doctor hadn't counted on. Oh *why* had the doctor moved so far away! Goldie preferred to walk everywhere she could. The area around Bathurst and Eglinton where she lived proliferated with every kind of store. There was little she could not buy within a three-block radius of her apartment.

Today was her first appointment in the doctor's new office. If she made it. On the bus now, all her energy polarized to keep her standing in the aisle without bolting out the exit at each stop. In her head she tried to reproduce Dr. Temple's calm voice telling her that she was in Toronto, she was safe. Most of the seats had filled and more people got on. Gripping the bars, she moved further down the bus when suddenly she saw a young man who reminded her of Enrique. *Mama, you're a big girl*, he would've said. *You gotta try. It'll be all right. Besides, you look great.* She pushed Enrique from her mind.

She looked into each face to make sure she was not being followed. Most of the passengers avoided her eyes; Torontonians were so reserved. But she continued methodically row after row, face after face: immigrant women with their tightly curled hair, students with books, old men and women, their surfaces like maps of forgotten places.

Did Dr. Temple understand how hard it was for her to just go out on the street, her own familiar street, never mind all the way down to the new medical office? Goldie didn't thank the doctor for saving her when she'd finally mustered the courage to swallow the valium. She *did* thank her for caring, for understanding her pain. Ah, there was nothing else to be done; she had to go.

Now this new thing, this cousin's voice from so long ago on the phone suddenly. She didn't like to think about that time. She had escaped from Poland when she was twenty, left behind everyone she loved. Only her sister Chana survived. Poor Chana, who had ended up in a camp. Thin and frail after typhus, she finally joined Goldie in Argentina after the war. And now this forgotten cousin from Poland who had somehow escaped. The rest of her family had become dust and ashes. She owed them this much, to help the cousin find what he was looking for. They would meet soon, he said, after all these years. Where was he living now? California? They had only exchanged a few letters now and then. Maybe she could find the address he needed. Give him something of importance when they finally met. She had to work up her stamina for that kind of adventure. Maybe she would go *next* week.

Dr. Temple's voice, if she had managed to hear it at all, popped like a balloon when the young man Enrique's age stood up and looked at her directly.

"Please," he motioned behind himself. "Take my seat."

Goldie was too shocked to understand what he wanted.

"Sit down. Go ahead."

She looked into his face to see if this was a trap, but his voice was English, his manner Toronto. Not taking any chances, she nervously moved further down the aisle, leaving the young man to fall back into his seat, embarrassed.

A block below St. Clair, a short, dark-haired woman walked to the exit and stepped down on the stair. She was thick as a sausage in a cheap ski jacket over her home-made paisley dress. A group of teenagers in fashionably ragged jeans had gotten on at St. Clair and still held the driver's attention. When the woman pulled the cord at her stop, the bus careened past. The students were so noisy that it was possible only Goldie, who was close by, heard the woman shout, "*¡Abra la puerta!*" The woman began to beat her small fat fist against the glass of the door and again yelled, "*¡Abra la puerta!*"

In a flash Goldie found herself again in her apartment in Buenos Aires that night when all had been lost.

"*¡Abra la puerta! ¡Abra la puerta!*"

A cluster of fists hammered at the door of her apartment. The voices in her nightmare cried, "*¡Abra la puerta! ¡Abra la puerta!,*" and she had woken up from the dream that had once been her life. As soon as she unlocked the door, four men in plain clothes jumped inside with guns and handcuffed her from behind. They twisted her arms with such careless venom that she blinked in bewildered pain. They ran through the apartment searching for others and for this, at least, she felt relief.

"*Where is he?*" one of them asked her, the others milling about.

"*Who?*" she said.

The man threw a blanket over her head then pushed her out the door in her pyjamas. *They will get you to talk, Jewish whore.*

A gun barrel was pushed into her side as they rode down the elevator. The blanket still over her head, they threw her down onto the floor of a car. Their feet perched on her body, the gun barrel stuck in her back as they drove away.

Finally they arrived in the basement of some official building. First she was blindfolded, then, without any preamble, she was put on *the machine*. She didn't know it was *the machine* then; she merely knew her fate was catching up with her. Someone placed her on a cot, attached what she later realized were electrodes to her mouth, and pushed a button. A fire, a howling, started in her mouth. She fell into the noise headlong, forgetting her name, forgetting her face. The plague had carried off her family in Europe thirty years before; it finally remembered to come back for her. She was being punished for surviving.

Later on she found out that all the prisoners were given *the machine* on their arrival to rattle them into submission. Routine. Then to business. At the beginning the conversations went like this:

"Where is your son?"

"I don't know."

A sharp slap across the face.

"How can I help you if you don't cooperate? We don't want to hurt him. We just want to speak to him about his subversive activities."

"He has no subversive activities. He's a musician. He writes songs."

"Songs? Propaganda that describes us as animals. Lies that give comfort to the enemy."

"Students are your enemies?"

"Your son is young. Maybe he fell in with a bad crowd. We understand all that. We don't want to hurt him. Where is he?"

"Out of your reach, Mr. Interrogator. Nowhere you can find him."

The fist smashed her mouth. That stubborn mouth. Her interrogator, once interested in her son's whereabouts, now enjoyed torturing her for her own shortcomings: her uncowed demeanor, her Jewishness, her stubborn mouth that refused obedience. An uncontrollable mouth. Not that she didn't want to control it, only it was directly attached to her brain and her brain she couldn't control. With the result that her tongue, no matter how she manoeuvred it, succeeded in inflaming her interrogator to heights of sadistic rage. What was worse for an old woman — sitting in pyjamas on the wet floor of a cell, praying the scorpions wouldn't find her, or sitting in the interrogator's chair, her only human contact slamming his fist into the side of her ribs, searching for something she could not give him: herself?

After some weeks, when Goldie lay filthy on the stone floor, her pyjamas soiled from the remnants of bodily functions, her interrogator grew bolder. When fetching her from her cell, he neglected to blindfold her. She now saw he was fat, with short greasy hair. He was ageless, sexless, she would not recognize him on the street. She allowed herself a fleeting moment of hope before coming to a halt in the room. Seeing it for the first time, she was perversely satisfied with its shabbiness — it could have been a converted kitchen. She smiled to herself, surprised that she was able. She was being fried in an old kitchen. The smell was damp, musty, like long ago fried fish.

"This amuses you?"

Goldie startled at this German-accented Spanish. She twisted her head toward the source but found the figure in shadow.

"Jorge, the old whore finds her situation amusing. We must show her the seriousness of her position."

The faceless voice was German; she would hear it in her dreams long after the danger was over. Her mother, her father, her brothers, aunts, cousins, grandparents had all marched into the maw of history because of a German voice. The guttural rasps in the throat still had the power to terrorize her, the deceptively rounded vowels that could pierce a heart.

They placed her on a cot. The fat interrogator attached electrodes to her mouth with clumsy fingers. The anxiety was not on her account, she realized, but resided in the shadows with the faceless German who had, no doubt, given instructions.

The arrogant voice begins:

"Jewish cow, is it not true that you and your son are part of a Jewish conspiracy to take over Patagonia?"

Even his Spanish sounds German.

"We know everything, whore. We even know the name chosen for the new homeland: the Republic of Andinia. Does that surprise you? What is your son's role in the conspiracy?"

She hesitates.

Then someone pushes a button somewhere and the

fire starts in her mouth. She no longer knows who she is, she no longer cares. She can't stop shaking, even when they tire of this recreation. Goldie never knows whose finger actually pushes the button, but she's convinced it's the German whose voice fills her dreams.

"Excuse me, lady."

The memory of pain, the need to escape from it, brought Goldie back to the Bathurst Street bus, still on her way to the doctor's.

"Excuse me, lady."

More students had boarded, a thicket of bodies manoeuvring around her. A dark, heavy man with angry eyes was heading toward her and she knew they'd found her. He was a tall man for whom she, all five-foot-one of her, would be candy. The words in her head conquered time and space to land in his mouth. *We will get you to talk, Jewish whore.*

In a second, Goldie pushed her way roughly through some students.

"Well pardon *us*, lady."

Standing on the step, feeling the kidnapper's breath on the back of her neck, she pulled the cord continuously. It chimed every few seconds.

"Okay, lady, we get the message," one kid said. "Maybe she has to go to the bathroom."

When the bus finally came to a stop a block above College Street, Goldie hurled herself out the door and began to run. If only she hadn't worn these heels. She dashed across College Street. She'd run like this in her nightmares, aching from fear, past eyes and eyes and more eyes, in shoes that wouldn't stay on. She could hardly breathe now after two blocks. Blisters had formed on the heels of both feet. Danger lurked behind lampposts, window blinds, in the most quiescent of eyes. She would never be safe. She stumbled once, twice, finally through the blur of her exhaustion she turned to search for her pursuer.

No one.

She stopped. The overcast sky hung low over rooftops, cast shadows on the street. Like a loose-necked owl, she scanned in all directions at once to check for danger. The old houses whispered their secrets, their paint in shreds, their rails studded with rust. *I will follow you till you drop. I will get you one day. I am always there.*

So she was spared another day. She had surprised him and escaped. At least she had reached College Street. Goldie limped up to the cement island to wait for the streetcar. If she hadn't been so absorbed with the streetcar approaching in the murky distance, Goldie would, no doubt, have noticed the swarthy little man step up beside her on the island.

When she finally decided she was standing in the right place to go east on College, she turned, startled at the unexpected proximity. How had this one slipped through her defences so easily? The intruder was disguised as an Italian labourer in jeans and heavy plaid shirt, carrying a lunch pail big enough for an unassembled machine gun. How stupid did they think she was? He could have a half dozen guns in there, or knives. And handcuffs, they would need handcuffs. He had dark greasy hair like the other, but his skin was coarse and red as if he worked outside. They were so clever about these things; there was nothing they wouldn't do to fool her.

Glaring at him produced no reaction. He looked back, but blankly. These were confrontations she would rather have avoided, but she had to defend herself.

"Stupid they must think I am," she addressed the little man finally. "Stupid and blind."

The man blinked, then smiled with brown crooked teeth. "You 'a trouble, lady?"

"Me you don't fool. I know they send you for to get me. I know their dirty tricks."

The man looked around, as if an explanation might hang in the air, as if someone might translate. Failing that, he boldly proceeded.

"Ahh," he lifted his free hand (the one that would hold the gun in the lunchbox), "my hand she's a-dirty. I no toucha. You no worry."

"You don't take me so easy. Not this time."

The little man continued to smile but it was forced now. When the streetcar stopped in front of him, he motioned for Goldie to get on first.

She couldn't believe the audacity. Crossing her arms, she planted herself on the island like a tree waiting for the storm.

"I'm not so stupid like that," she said.

The man quickly climbed aboard and when inside, turned on the top step to face Goldie one last time. This was it, she thought, now comes the gun, the knife, the last pain through the heart. *Hello, Enrique.*

Before the doors folded shut, he opened his decaying mouth and replied, "You too olda for me, lady."

chapter three

Rebecca was looking over the morning's test results.
Every now and then she glanced up at the print of
Van Gogh's *Wheat Fields and Cypress* in the waiting-
room to reassure herself that none of David's paintings
had escaped the basement. She wondered whether Iris
had realized when she put up the Van Gogh how
turbulent it was, the thick heaving clouds filled with
energy, the dark trees springing from the ground like
flames. Iris chuckled on the phone as she booked an
appointment with a patient. Without warning the front
door flew open and Mrs. Kochinsky wobbled in. She
was wearing a stylish navy blazer over beige trousers
but something seemed askew, as if she hadn't put them
on straight. Or maybe it was the sweaty bangs of
greying brown hair that stuck to her forehead. But, she
still looked a decade younger than her sixty years.

"Mrs. Kochinsky!" Rebecca exclaimed. "How are you?"

"Not good!" she said and hobbled over to the waiting-room instead of approaching the counter. She dropped into one of the chairs and appeared to be trying to catch her breath.

Rebecca stepped toward her, concerned. "Are you all right?"

Mrs. Kochinsky looked up at Rebecca and absently lifted the damp bangs off her forehead with her fingers. "I'm so glad you're back, Doctor. But bus — bus ride killing me. A man...." She suddenly glanced up at Iris, who had stopped talking on the phone to listen.

"Come into my office, Mrs. Kochinsky," Rebecca said.

One of Iris' eyebrows shot up in mock offence.

Once they were seated privately, Rebecca said, "So, it's been some time since we last met. How've you been?"

The dark half-moons under her patient's eyes hinted at the anxiety, the web of paranoia she'd woven around herself.

Mrs. Kochinsky shook her head. "Not good, not good." The charming Spanish-Polish inflection. "All winter I have such trouble sleeping. The other doctor — Romanov — he no good. He don't understand. Only wants me take drug for sleeping. Maybe I don't want sleep. Because of dream. Yesterday I dream of Enrique. Oh, Doctor! I don't *want* sleep. I have nothing left. Why I should always reminder have...." She was still agitated, her chest rising and falling too quickly.

"You don't usually dream about Enrique," Rebecca said. "Why don't you tell me about it."

Mrs. Kochinsky hesitated a moment. She cleared her throat, then took a breath. "Night very dark in my dream. My husband, dead two years, sits in bedroom on chair. He say, 'They find him, Goldie. Don't wait for him. He not come back.' This scare me because I know what. Then suddenly I'm in plane. Flying. Much noise. Very dark outside. Two men — young men — sit on floor, hands tied behind. Noise from plane terrible. I shout at men: 'Wake up!' They don't move, eyes closed. Suddenly big man opens door to outside. I see clouds beside. I shout, 'Close door!' But he take one man, lift and push him out! I look — body fall through clouds, down, down into water. I scream louder. Big man don't hear me. He take other young man — I see sleeping face and suddenly I know it's Enrique. I grab his arm but like cloud, I can't touch. Big man lift like before but I push hard on Enrique's chest and finally, *finally* he open his eyes and smile last time. Then ... then man throws him down through door. I try catch my boy, but he falls. *Falls.* I can't look. I know he land in ocean...."

Rebecca waited a moment, noting how pale her patient had become. "That must've been a very frightening dream."

Mrs. Kochinsky looked up at her, brown eyes fierce. "Not just dream. Before I leave Argentina I hear talk, secret talk, about how soldiers get rid of people. They don't want bodies left. So they take prisoners up in plane. Give them drug make them quiet, weak. Then ... then," she put a hand over her eyes, "they throw them out into ocean. Still alive. *Alive.*"

Rebecca couldn't speak. Mechanically she rose and took three steps to a small sink in the corner. She pulled a disposable cup from the dispenser and filled it with water. She handed it to Mrs. Kochinsky.

"I'm so sorry," she said and sat down across from her, suddenly very tired. This was not paranoia; it had the unfortunate ring of truth.

Mrs. Kochinsky drank from the cup mechanically.

27

"My family gone. Why I should live? I'm only alive because I'm not dead."

Rebecca leaned forward toward the older woman, seeking eye contact. "Your sister's still alive. It sounds like she needs you."

Mrs. Kochinsky lifted her head, bird-like. "What I can do? I'm helpless. She just sit there, won't talk. Only sometime a word in Yiddish. We don't speak Yiddish from before war. I bring material so she can sew. She have her little machine there. You should see clothes she make for me. Beautiful dress, blouse...." She inclined her head and tapped her cheek with one hand. "Aye, you won't believe how she was good with hands. You know, in camp she had job in factory — no one can do like her, with small fast hands. She make part for weapons, little pieces metal must fit together, and if not fit, gun not work. They will shoot her. She told me religious boy come work beside her, can't do with hands. Young, clumsy. She show him, try help, but he can't. What you think? She do work for him, so they don't take him away. She lucky — they change her from factory and then she clean officers' place. Help her survive. Survive. For what?

"Now she just sit. Do nothing. Her husband happy he get rid of her." She lowered her voice. "I tell him I look after her, but he send her away. I know why he don't want me. He have office at home. Many business deals. Crooked deals. He don't want me find out. Who knows what he do there. I told her for long time *leave* him. Bad man. Did bad things in war. But was good to Chana, so she marry him. Desperate after war, no one left. And now? He don't care. I want take care for her."

"But that would've been a huge commitment, taking care of your sister. Maybe it's better this way."

"What else I have? Three mornings at bakery? He can afford pay me same like bakery. Much cheaper than nursing home. I *wanted* look after her."

Tears formed in her eyes, glistening. She wore her gently waved hair chin length, and with her straight nose and small face, she often reminded Rebecca of what Greta Garbo might have looked like at sixty. Except that, as far as Rebecca knew, Greta Garbo didn't need psychotherapy to see her through the week.

"She only one I have left." She shook her head. "I'm sorry. Man on bus — he upset me. When I get off, he follow. I run and run..."

Rebecca scribbled notes. She'd heard this before. "There've been other times when men followed you. Was there something different about this man compared to the others?"

"They all different. They send different man each time. So I won't know. But I always know. And now they got more opportunity, because I go two buses for here. Before, I walk five minutes to old office. I wish you don't move. This not safe neighbourhood."

"I understand how you feel," said Rebecca. "I know it's hard to go out of your area, but it will get easier. It'll just take time."

Mrs. Kochinsky studied her for a moment. "If you say, I believe. Look — I'll bring you knishes for Passover. Home-made. Just next week. See? I believe you."

Rebecca smiled uneasily. The emotional wall she usually kept between herself and her patients had been impossible to summon in Mrs. Kochinsky's case. The pain she had gone through, the horror, put her in a different category.

Before leaving, Mrs. Kochinsky turned to Rebecca and said, "Oh, I forget something tell you. A visitor coming for me. Cousin from California. So long when I saw him — I didn't even know he still lives. When he call, like voice from past."

Then she suddenly smiled goodbye, her mouth partly open in mute apology as if there was something she preferred not to say. It was the same smile each time she left. Apology for what, Rebecca wondered: for living, for being a casualty of war, for surviving with complications?

Iris was deep into files at her workstation when Rebecca passed by at five forty-five. "I've got my pager," Rebecca said. "I'll just be around the neighbourhood if you need me."

Iris looked down at Rebecca's feet. "What's going on?" she asked.

"I'm going to do what I tell all my patients: go for a brisk walk around the block."

Iris examined her from the feet up. "Well, the shoes are good. But you need a swanky track suit, Doc. Something with polyester to show off the slimmer you. That skirt with those running shoes...," she shook her blonde head. "You want to exercise, you gotta have the right outfit. Come shopping with me this weekend and I'll find you something spiffy."

Rebecca put one hand on her hip in protest but realized there was no use arguing. She stepped downstairs past the office of the other doctor. Lila Arons, M.D. They'd met briefly when Rebecca leased the space. A brisk handshake, the usual greetings, and they had both gone on their way.

She stepped outside the medical building, heartened by the way her feet felt in the new leather running shoes. Solid. She was ready to take on Beverley Street. The street looked as empty as the first time she'd seen it, leafy quiet in the shade of another century.

Once on the sidewalk, she dipped her hand inside

her jacket pocket to deposit the beeper. What she felt there made her stop.

"Rebecca, **Rebecca!**" David chided out of an undefinable corner of her past. His trimmed reddish beard pointed at her with irony.

She held the wrapped sugar cube up in her palm, impressed with its survival. She hadn't seen the gabardine rain jacket since last September when she had pushed it to the back of her closet together with the white cane. She had always carried something for David's carbohydrate hunger, which came on suddenly when his medication reached its peak. It was a reaction to the insulin. Common enough. Not dramatic enough for a haunting, too physical to ignore. She had gotten rid of his aftershave, his jeans, his tweed sports jackets. She had tried to sweep her life's surface clear of reminders of him but every now and then there was this self-sabotage she couldn't explain. She dropped the cube back into her pocket, but uneasily.

She moved up Beverley Street at a pace she knew was unsatisfactory, but it was all she could muster. Speed was a problem for her lately; she could do nothing quickly. Often she felt submerged in water, her body struggling just to move normally. Aunt Sally had insisted at the Shiva that what she remembered most when Uncle died was the fatigue, the dense weariness that grief deposited in the bones. Don't overdo it, Rebecca directed her solid leather-bound feet. We just want to get in shape, we don't want to win any races.

She paced herself along Baldwin Street where narrow brick houses watched behind lawns of yellow inchoate grass that would turn green inside of a month. She approached the spectacle of Spadina Avenue. Three lanes of traffic rushed on either side of the streetcar tracks that ran along the centre of the grand avenue, ready to trip the unwary pedestrian. A deathtrap for anyone dependent on a white cane. Apparently a physician named Baldwin who practiced architecture on the side had designed the street in the early 1800s with the Champs Elysées in mind. By the time Jewish merchants opened their produce stalls along the street near the end of that century, Spadina was no longer glamorous. Now modern wholesalers with their overcrowded dry goods, hardware, and poultry shops made the street garish. But because of its elaborate width, it was difficult, from one side of Spadina, to see what was on the other. A lot, thought Rebecca, like looking across to the opposite bank of a respectable river. Across the expanse she picked out the store where David had bought his art supplies. Chinese restaurants had opened on either side.

When David was alive, she had struggled with her weight — a lifetime ago when she was ten or fifteen pounds more than she liked. But her atrophied appetite satisfied her in a morbid way though she denied she was punishing herself. She hadn't given David diabetes. She just hadn't been paying enough attention to realize he was hiding his symptoms. As a physician she knew it was common to deny one's illness in the hope it will disappear. He had concealed the constant peeing, the thirst, from her. He constantly sucked on breath mints to mask the sweet ketonic breath. He didn't want to worry her. For awhile he'd fooled his mother, poor Sarah, who had survived the Holocaust but lost her only child.

Near the end, when he was in hospital, Rebecca left him alone with his mother and took the elevator down to the main floor. Sarah had no other relatives — all were lost in the camps. Though she never talked about it, and though her auburn hair and quick smile belied it, her loss defined her to Rebecca, who now found it hard to be with the two of them — one dying and the other a reminder of death. It was August and the evening air wafted so softly against her skin refreshing her, filling her with guilt. She was alive! She stood in the shadows too numb to move while traffic floated by. Voices murmured off to one side. She absently noted two interns in white coats sitting on the cement stairs leading up to the hospital. "Fellow at rounds this morning, only thirty-five. First thing he knew anything was wrong was when he went to check his eyes for blurred vision. Diabetic retinopathy. Blind now. Pyelonephritis. That's not the way I want to go! Crazy thing is, his wife's a doctor...."

She had never forgotten that conversation; never come to terms with the guilt. She knew she'd failed in her primary role. Not only had she missed the symptoms that would've been obvious if a patient had presented with them. That was bad enough. But the changes in his *painting*. How could she have ignored the reaching for the light? In a year, the subdued and muted palette that had always defined his work became transformed. His canvases deepened into cadmium reds and phthalo blues that should've set off alarm bells in her head. The dimmer his world became, the more radiant his colours. Finally they became brilliant streaks of pigment without shape. Was there anything more ironic than an artist going blind?

Near the end he would try to engage her in discussions about God. Try to get her position, as a woman of science. She mouthed the platitudes for his sake, but in reality reserved judgment. This was her deal with the Almighty: if he let David live, she would embrace Him wholeheartedly. In her prayers she stressed that David was the kindest, most unselfish person she knew and that thirty-five was too young for a good person to die.

33

She had never thought much about God before, attended High Holiday services because her parents bought tickets at a Reform synagogue. After David died, she began to ruminate on the kind of God who had seen fit to take away the best man she knew. God didn't seem to care who He made suffer, it didn't matter if one was pure of heart. The universe was a chaotic place without justice or reason.

Though she had watched patients die over the years, she had never felt that profound hopelessness till death touched her personally. It wasn't a transitory depression; it was a change in her world view. God had died, or He had lost interest in the welfare of the world. Nothing would ever be the same again.

Afterwards she had hit well below her target weight. Though she was average height, her bones were large; her back was wide, her wrists and ankles were not delicate and though the flesh had dissolved on her, she felt the solidity of her frame would see her through. She only wished she could do something about her energy level. The bustle of life here made her feel peripheral, restless.

She turned left at Dundas, mortified that walking three blocks at moderate speed was giving her a stitch in her side. Two streets away the white concrete facade of the Art Gallery of Ontario, spread over an entire city block, sat coolly on its wide steps. She moved amid the supper crowds in Chinatown in the firm knowledge that once she got to Beverley Street all would be quiet. It never ceased to surprise her: in the centre of the triangle comprised loosely of the Art Gallery, Kensington Market, and the University of Toronto, Beverley Street was as quiet as a suburb. It was like the eye of a storm; in the centre of things without all the detractions that the centre of things implied. Traffic was bad along Dundas where Chinatown and the Art Gallery tolerantly merged, and the market was a maze of one-way streets, but the heart of Beverley Street lay warm and beating quietly after a hundred years of affluence. She'd come upon a book that traced the history of old houses in the neighbourhood and had found a surprising number of Victorian styles: Georgian, Gothic Revival, Italianate, Second Empire, Queen Anne, and Richardsonian Romanesque. Some had been renovated into offices like hers, some into rooming-houses.

Her shins began to hurt as she passed the wrought iron fence of the Italian consulate filling the extensive corner of Dundas and Beverley. She was in pathetic shape. She couldn't go any faster, no matter how hard she pushed herself.

The consulate occupied a regal tawny structure built a century earlier. What was it called? *Chudleigh*, whatever that meant; her book had not said. But it represented what Rebecca wanted. She had picked Beverley Street for its other-century, traditional demeanour, its Victorian mansions still sturdy in a new age. She was looking for something solid, something that stood the test of time, something that would still be there when she looked up. Buildings that stood by serenely while the world changed were a good bet. Sure they had been renovated. That was their secret; from the inside out, the old had been made new again. Otherwise they would not have survived. That was the secret, Rebecca thought. Use the old structure for a base and add what is necessary. Change and survive. She had started from the bottom when she bought her formidable leather shoes. Iris was right. She would have to work her way up.

She was nearly home-free, her heart full in her throat, pulsing. How had she deteriorated into this shape? She blew out, then sucked in, refusing to let herself gasp. She stood on the steps of the medical building, catching her breath. Across the street Beverley Mansions caught the warm glow of the early evening sun. She heard sharp distant noises, like drawers opening and cutlery being laid down. People were coming home from work and preparing dinner. Normal people. Would she ever be normal again?

chapter four

Nesha

Friday, March 30, 1979

Nesha made the mistake of examining the photo under a magnifying glass. If it had been the original newsprint he might have been able to see something among the million grey dots. But the photocopy revealed no secrets in its pools of black and white, only bald statements he didn't know how to interpret. Yet interpret he must. He would keep trying till something spoke to him. He would be methodical as always; it was the only way he knew.

He stepped up to the living-room window that overlooked San Francisco Bay and held the photo up to the light. Starting at the bottom he read the caption, "Fowl Escape from the Market," then the photo credit: Peter Hanson/Toronto Star. His eyes moved up the page to where a duck waddled along a sidewalk, stores in the background. Finally, as a reward to himself, he let his eyes settle on the man walking in the shadow of the store beyond the duck. A spasm gripped his heart. It felt good to hate again. Like sensation coming back to a long-dead limb: a sign of life. The man in the picture was not young. Nesha looked in the upper margin at the handwritten notation: June 10, 1978. Almost a year ago. A lot could happen in a year. By now he might be dead. Wouldn't that be rich, Nesha thought, finally getting this new information and stoking up the old fires only to find out the man had died peacefully in his sleep in the meantime. He couldn't bear that. He stared at the blurred face and tried to get it to speak to him. "Are you still breathing, you bastard? Are you waiting for me?"

Once a year, before Passover, Nesha allowed himself the bittersweet ritual of taking his pistol out of the cabinet and cleaning it. It had been thirty-five years since it came into his possession and each year he brought it out like a relic, the sole concrete evidence of his youth. Only the hard steel convinced him that his past was not a bad dream. He had no mother, no father, no brothers. No photos to bring out of the drawer that could comfort him with familiar faces. After all these years it was the absence of photos he regretted the most.

He tenderly dismantled the gun into its dark steel segments. His legacy consisted of the herringbone-patterned handle, the slide, the barrel, the recoil spring. Set on a piece of cotton flannel on the kitchen table, they absorbed the light from his window. The Bay shone outside, Marin County with its upscale houses set into the hills, their glass walls flaming in the sun. But with the gun before him, sucking in the light, he was in Poland again, in the woods running between villages. Mud sucking at his feet. Branches grasping at him. If he'd only had the gun then. There would have been fear in the peasants' eyes, not contempt. He knew which ones he would've used the gun on. The big stupid one who beat him every day for a month with his hamfists. Nesha escaped one winter's night, flying through the frozen fields like a ghost, the wind taking hold of him, biting his skin beneath the thin coat. In the next village an old woman wanted him to help her feed her cows. She had a good heart most of the week but on Saturdays she got into the home-made vodka and beat him with her cane. The gun came too late to save him from those floggings. But he had been lucky, too. Not all peasants were the same. Some had pity. He was alive because of them.

A plane hummed over the Bay. He removed the magazine from the handle of the pistol and dismantled it, using a patch of cotton flannel to clean off the dirt, then rubbing it lightly with oil. He applied solvent to the interior of the barrel with a cleaning rod, then ran a fresh patch of flannel through the bore to wipe out the excess. He moved an old toothbrush along the cylinder gear, then over the grip panel of the handle, always in the direction of the herringbone pattern, to remove any dirt that managed to accumulate since the last cleaning. He didn't understand how a gun could collect dirt hidden away in a box inside a cabinet. But the Earth turned; salt air from the Pacific crept in through crevices and would pock the smooth surface of an uncleaned gun with rust.

Through the two hours that it took him to clean and lubricate the pistol, his mother's face rose before him. Each time, he pushed her back, unwilling to have his heart broken again. But as he reassembled the gun in the fading light, he blinked too long and her dark hair appeared in the distance, the usually tidy bun unravelling in strands to her shoulders as she lined up with the others. And when she turned — he would never forget — her face white and twisted with terror, all the blood drained as if she were dead already. And her eyes, as familiar to him as his own, pleading with him to run, go back to the forest, run, forget, never come back.

All at once he looked up, startled to find a ragged, bearded man watching him. It took him a full minute to recognize himself in the reflection of the kitchen window, a mirror now that the sun had set. One day, he thought, his mind would pull him back into those woods and he would never come out. He wouldn't mind. They were more real to him than the fabled Bay outside his window.

He turned on the light and finished polishing the exterior of the pistol with a lightly oiled chamois. The gun was a 9 mm Parabellum. He had done his research. The word came from a Roman proverb: Si vis pacem, para bellum. If you seek peace, prepare for war.

There was nothing he wanted as much as peace.

chapter five

Tuesday, April 3, 1979

Rebecca had barely started her second week in the new building. The scent of fresh paint lingered in the air and some of her former patients, arriving for appointments, commented on the elegance of her new office. Mr. and Mrs. DaCosta were also impressed, sitting tentatively on the edge of the nubbly new chairs while Rebecca described the surgical procedure of vasectomy. She was reassuring them that it was relatively foolproof and that, no, the likelihood was that they would have no more children, when voices rose in some commotion outside the examining room. A plaintive accented voice arrived muffled through the closed door.

"You don't understa... I must see Doctor ... life or death...."

Rebecca recognized Mrs. Kochinsky's accent but was surprised at her level of distress. What had set off her alarm bells to come running into the office the day before her regular weekly session? She had never shown up without an appointment, though she was often upset when she came. Iris would have to deal with it.

Rebecca spent ten more minutes with the DaCostas then led them back down the short hallway to the waiting-room where she spotted Mrs. Kochinsky, grey-pale, dressed more casually than usual. She was rocking back and forth on the edge of the couch. When she saw Rebecca, she jumped to her feet. Her anxiety touched Rebecca but didn't alarm her when she took it in the context of the woman's usual mental state. Beside Mrs. Kochinsky sat a young woman whose little girl had turned her back on the old lady and lay tightly curled in her mother's arms.

Iris handed Rebecca Mrs. Kochinsky's file and whispered in her ear, "She's ready to explode. I haven't seen her this bad."

The other patients, who had been waiting longer, sat stone-faced as Rebecca led Mrs. Kochinsky down the hall.

Wearing a beige trenchcoat over polyester pants, the older woman stood in the centre of the examining room wringing her hands. She nearly wept out her words, her chest heaving with exertion.

"I'm sorry — I know this not my day for appointment. But I see him. The man... He follow me here. I'm sure he there outside."

She stepped to the window that looked out onto D'Arcy Street. Pushing aside the vertical blind, she peered down, her face white with terror. "*There*. There in car, man sitting." Her finger poked the air triumphantly.

Rebecca moved toward the window and glanced out at one of the quietest spots in downtown Toronto. The facade of an alternative high school was camouflaged by mature spruce trees. In front, across the one-way street, sat a young man in a run-down silver Chevy. "How old was the man you recognized?" she asked.

Mrs. Kochinsky's hand flew up in exasperation. "I don't know. Maybe fifty, maybe sixty. What difference?"

"Look at the man in the car."

Mrs. Kochinsky bent her head toward the window again. "He's no more than twenty," said Rebecca. "There's a high school across the street. He's probably waiting for someone."

The older woman continued to look through the blinds. "Could be anywhere. There. Cars on other street. What about there?" She pointed out the corner of the window in the direction of Beverley Street. Rebecca peered sideways toward the front of the medical building. Cars were parked on both sides of the street at meters. She had picked the corner of Beverley and D'Arcy for her new office because of its tranquillity and saw nothing out the window to make her regret that decision.

"Was he the same man who frightened you last week?"

Mrs. Kochinsky's hand flew up again, this time to entreat the ceiling. Her dark eyes flashed impatience. "You don't understand! They always send different man. But this it! This man... This man last one."

Rebecca was concerned about Mrs. Kochinsky's growing propensity for panic.

"Where did you first see him?"

She jerked open the flap of her handbag and pulled out a piece of paper. "Here! Here is it!" She waved a photocopy of a picture in front of Rebecca's face.

"What is it?" Rebecca asked, trying to focus on the moving page. "May I see it?"

Mrs. Kochinsky handed her the sheet, which Rebecca glanced at, puzzled. She commented on the obvious. "It looks like a duck." Before she could examine it further, Mrs. Kochinsky grabbed it back and replaced it in her purse.

"You don't believe me," said Mrs. Kochinsky, hurt.

The image of the duck walking along a sidewalk appeared to have been copied from a news photo. Rebecca worried that her patient had lost what grip on reality she may have had.

"Can you tell me what he was doing when you saw him?" she asked.

"Waiting for me. He knew I come. I run here and he follow me. You have call police."

Rebecca placed a concerned hand on her arm. "Please sit down." When they were both seated, Rebecca said, "I can see how upset you are. Help me understand what happened before you came here. I know how difficult it is for you to leave your area. Why were you downtown?"

"My cousin from United States coming ... he ask me for shop so I look around."

"But why didn't you shop close to home, on Eglinton? Why did you come downtown?"

Mrs. Kochinsky looked confused. "But shop downtown. I have to."

It was Rebecca's turn to be confused, but she went on. "Did he touch you?"

"He come at me. But I ran." She wrung feverish hands together and leaned toward Rebecca with stark expectation. "Oh Doctor, he almost get me!"

The Greta Garbo face, the greying brown hair soft on her cheek, fought with the words. It was like a cartoon with the wrong caption. A mistake. She should have been a grandmother at home enjoying her family. Instead, she sat perched on the end of her seat, hands clasped tightly together, knuckles turning white. Deep sighs heaved periodically from her chest.

Rebecca tried to elicit cogent details that might interest the police but Mrs. Kochinsky seemed capable of relating only vague descriptions and indeterminate locations. Though she was more upset than usual, Rebecca had to put it in perspective. At last week's session, it was someone who had followed Mrs. Kochinsky off the bus when she was coming for her appointment. Rebecca had attributed the anxiety to the unfamiliar first trip down to the new office. Maybe this was the level of anxiety the poor woman was operating on now. How was Rebecca to know, as last week was the first time she'd seen her in eight weeks.

Maybe she would call Dr. Romanov again and get clearer details of Mrs. Kochinsky's behaviour during the time he was covering for Rebecca. She watched her patient now as she sat talking, her trenchcoat crumpled around her. This unscheduled visit worried Rebecca; she wondered if she could expect Mrs. Kochinsky to drop in anytime. At least she was calmer and seemed to have more control of herself.

"Feeling better now?" Rebecca asked.

Mrs. Kochinsky gave a wan smile.

"You can rest in here till you feel you're all right to leave," she said. "I'll see you tomorrow."

Rebecca closed the door and headed for Iris' desk. "Mrs. Kochinsky is taking a short rest," she said behind the partition. "Keep an eye on her and let me know when she leaves."

Iris handed her the next patient's file.

Then came a cat and ate the goat
That Father bought for two zuzim.
One little goat, one little goat.

chapter six

Tuesday, April 3, 1979

Toronto was not Buenos Aires, thought Goldie as she watched the news at eleven o'clock. It was a staid, humourless place where streets were laid out in unimaginative lines like a giant grid. A bookkeeper's city. You might not get lost in Toronto, but the trip would be tedious. Buenos Aires, now *there* was a city! As exciting as Paris, with its furtive alleyways, its wide sweeping boulevards lined with plane-trees, the women dressed like models strolling past the outdoor cafes. After nearly two years in Toronto, Goldie still missed the European feel of Buenos Aires. The city was not to blame for the nightmare of what had happened to her.

It was such a long time ago. It was just yesterday. How much older she felt now. A hundred years older, sitting in flannel pyjamas in her living-room watching the late news. At eleven-thirty Buenos Aires was just waking up. What did she care if Pierre Trudeau was heading to Calgary this week? Or that his pretty young wife was showing off their three sons to the press? He was an old goat who had found a brood mare to propagate his line. Well, why not? Why shouldn't he have sons? Maybe he would be luckier than she had been and his sons would live past their twenty-sixth birthday.

She changed the station with the remote. Another clip of that tedious *Star Wars* movie. Too loud. They were trying to whet people's appetite for the next one coming out. Something about a sinister Empire. She wished she could escape into fantasies like other people. She flicked to another channel. Maybe she could find an old movie.

That was when she thought she heard it. She flicked the mute button and strained to listen. A soft knocking came from her door. She jumped in her seat. Her heart dropped as she remembered that other knock in Argentina. "*¡Abra la puerta! ¡Abra la puerta!*"

She sat rigid while the man knocked softly, softly on her door (she was sure it was a man). Go *away*, thought Goldie, *I'm not ready yet*. She had told Dr. Temple today — she knew it would be him. This one was clever, tapping so quietly. The others had not been quiet. They had knocked and knocked. "*¡Abra la puerta! ¡Abra la puerta!*"

Soon he would kick the door down. She had seen this moment coming since the basement in Buenos Aires during that other nightmare. First the blindfold, then without preamble, *the machine*. People said they couldn't remember pain. Well, maybe one forgot the pain, but never the terror of it, never the racing heart in the night. *Where's your son, you Jewish whore?*

What was the point of surviving your children? The man at the door in Toronto was carrying the tail end of the plague that had come after her family in Poland in 1939.

For nearly two years in Canada now she had waited for the executioner. Every time she went on the street, someone was watching her. People scoffed when she told them. They didn't understand. How could they? They hadn't been tortured. Even the bakery where she worked, men came in looking for her. Oh, not openly, no. They were good actors; nobody believed her. But she knew. And she waited. Every place she had settled in had betrayed her. And now here he was at her door. Toronto was the last place that would betray her.

Safe Toronto. Safe for everyone else. Not for her. She knew he would come. She knew she could not stop him coming. And though she did not always recognize him, she *knew* him. By heart. How many years had she waited for him to reveal himself? Her body trembled now as he called through the door. She struggled to hear the words.

"I just want to talk," he said. "You wouldn't let me explain this afternoon. That's all I want, just to explain."

This afternoon. Yes, the confrontation this afternoon. And now he was going to kill her. He had just waited for the dark. She sat, stunned, on the French Provincial sofa, worn in the spot where she sat enjoying hours of old movies; *never again*.

"Let me in, please. I won't hurt you."

Lies, she knew. He would say anything for her to open the door. She would not answer, but it didn't matter. She would count the seconds she had left, standing helpless inside her own living-room. She peered for the last time at the photo of Enrique on the mantel. How had it been for him at the end? She was glad she would never know. Maybe she would meet him beyond.

Pounding on the door. Pounding as if he had a right to her life. She thought of running to turn off all the lights, but there was no time. It was too late.

She jumped as the glass shattered. The pane in the front door. He was no longer pretending. He had no more reason for lies. He was inside.

"Help!" she cried, terror building in her chest. "Help me, someone!"

It was no use. Who would hear her? Mrs. Shane from upstairs was still in Florida. Bathurst Street outside was too noisy with cars.

"Help!" she shrieked. "Help!" Adrenaline pushed the sound from her throat despite logic.

The *phone*, she thought. Get to the phone. She jumped across the living-room toward the hall. Why hadn't she thought of it sooner? She felt him behind her, a large breathing presence, as she reached the kitchen. She dared not turn but grabbed for the phone on the wall. The bear of a man lunged at her, knocking the phone from her hand. A growl of anger came from his chest as he pulled the phone cord out of the wall.

Regaining her balance, she fled back toward the front door, screaming. Someone would hear; someone would help. She just had to get outside. She was not even close when he grabbed her arm and swung her into the living-room like a rag doll.

"Help!" she yelled into the spring night. *You cannot kill me while the blossoms are swelling on apple trees*, she wanted to shout. But the sound that passed her lips became one long howl devoid of words.

Enraged, he stalked toward her, cap pulled down over his hair, eyes in shadow. Hiding his unfamiliar familiar face. His hands gestured wildly in the air, trying to quiet her down, his own voice raised. But she couldn't hear him; she was making too much noise.

Panic numbed her brain but instinctively she turned toward the living-room window. If she could break the glass, if only she could get someone's attention. She just had to reach the window. It was a mistake to turn her back on him. She realized this in a second but it was too late. She gasped as her head snapped back, forced by the cord around her neck. He was so strong he was lifting her off the ground by her neck. She scraped at the cord with her fingers, she tore at it, scratching her own skin as the breath escaped from her body. She flailed at the air with her arms, her feet, she could no longer make a sound, her mouth open to no avail as the room fogged up, began to disappear as if she and it were going in different directions. He was so strong, he was squeezing the breath from her into the fog of the living-room, her body a vessel spilling air, convulsing, leaking air like a dying balloon, until she was empty and the living-room was full.

chapter seven

Rebecca bent over a stack of patient files on her desk. This was the part of medical practice she could have lived without. Paperwork. She could spend hours filling out forms — insurance forms, Workman's Compensation forms, disability claim forms. Referrals had to be written for patients she was sending to cardiologists, internists, allergists; charts to be updated with the morning's lab test results.

She was expecting Iris to interrupt her upon the arrival of her first patient of the afternoon. But it was 1:15 p.m. before Rebecca surfaced from her papers and realized Iris was overdue.

She stepped out of her office and glanced at the empty waiting room. "Did Mrs. Kochinsky cancel her one o'clock appointment?"

Iris looked up from her papers, her spectacles part way down her nose. "I haven't heard from her."

Rebecca's eyes were drawn to the violent energy in

the Van Gogh on the wall. "She usually calls if she can't make it."

"I'll give her a ring," Iris said, opening Mrs. Kochinsky's file. She dialed the number.

Rebecca watched her face go blank listening to the futile rings. Maybe the American cousin had arrived for his visit, Rebecca thought. Maybe she'd lost track of time.

Since she always saw Mrs. Kochinsky for an hour, no patients were scheduled before two. But her two o'clock patient arrived at one-thirty and it was five-thirty before the procession of patients let up. She had been distracted all afternoon, but it wasn't until a perceptive patient asked her how *she* was feeling that she realized something was bothering her. Now, with a moment to herself, she thought of Mrs. Kochinsky flying into the office yesterday, breathless and erratic. It was only the second time she had seen the poor woman since resuming her practice. Had Mrs. Kochinsky's mental health degenerated over the winter? There was no immediate family to call. Her sister had been taken to the nursing home.

She approached Iris' desk and handed her the last patient's file. The waiting-room was empty. The Van Gogh roiled above the upholstered mauve chairs.

"Am I finished?"

"Yes, ma'am."

"No word from Mrs. Kochinsky?"

Iris shook her head.

The phone rang. "Dr. Temple's office," said Iris.

After a moment of listening, she turned to Rebecca. "It's Mrs. Morgan. She wants to renew her prescription for cardizem on the phone." One winged eyebrow climbed in disapproval.

Rebecca took the receiver. "Mrs. Morgan? Was that Dr. Romanov's prescription? Is your angina acting up, then? You're on 60 mg. No. You'll have to come in so I can check you over. Well, I understand, Mrs. Morgan, but I can't prescribe the drug without examining you. I'll give you to Iris and you can make an appointment."

Rebecca fell into the other chair behind the partition and peered over the test results of Mr. Batner's blood sugar, Miss Chow's urine.

"You look bushed," said Iris after hanging up. "Better skip the jogging today."

"I just walk around the block."

"Better watch yourself. You don't want to get any of those knee injuries."

"I'm not jogging. I'm not even running."

"Keep it that way," she said. "I need this job."

Rebecca gave her a crooked smile. But she *was* tired. Automatically she took out some charts and began to update them with the latest test results.

Iris went back to filling in the day's health insurance chits. She had taken off her tailored grey suit jacket and sat demurely in a white silk blouse. Rebecca was grateful Iris was still interested in working for her — she didn't need the money judging by her wardrobe and regular visits to an expensive hairdresser.

After twenty minutes, Iris looked up over her glasses. "I know what'll put some colour back into those cheeks. What do you say we go for some Chinese."

Rebecca grabbed her gabardine jacket and locked up. They made their way down the stairs.

"Parents coming home soon?" Iris asked, her patent leather heels clunking down the steps behind Rebecca.

"They'll be back next week for Passover."

She pushed open the back door of the converted

house. What little yard had existed was paved over with asphalt. Iris' Buick and Rebecca's Jaguar coupe stood in the waning sun. Behind the buildings opposite, a common laneway of cracked cement ran between rows of garages; their wood, grey with age, leaned in various stages of decay. Rebecca's heart dipped at the sight of the backsides of these houses, always shabbier than the fronts, always the last resting place of things that had outlived their usefulness. The houses, made up like dowagers on the street-side, with lace trim and correct sashes in place, sagged in the rear, so to speak. Rusting tools lay where they had fallen, wood buckled from the sun. Last year's chrysanthemums, desiccated, pathetic, crumbled sideways in overturned pots.

"Do you ever watch The Fonz?" Iris said as they stepped onto the sidewalk of D'Arcy Street.

"The *what*?"

"You must've heard of 'Happy Days.' It's on Tuesday nights. My kids watch it every week. The Fonz is this high-school drop-out with an unpronounceable name. He wears a leather jacket and does this funny thing with his thumbs." She demonstrated, making fists and sticking both thumbs up in the air.

"Is that the one that's set in the fifties?"

"That's the best part. Remember the clothes? Those tight sweaters! Well, you were younger than me — I was in my twenties. They're too happy — I *know* things weren't as good as that — still, it gives me a warm and fuzzy feeling watching it."

Maybe that was what Rebecca needed. A TV show with a laugh track. Couldn't hurt.

The evening sun warmed Beverley Street. They passed Lambton Lodge, the mansion built by George Brown, brick-solid with its mansard roof and the windows set in. What one would expect from the founder of *The Globe* and a Father of Confederation. Looking up to the third storey, she wondered in which room he had died from that gangrenous wound. The violence was out of place; he'd been shot elsewhere by a disgruntled employee and carried to this gentler street to die. Lambton Lodge. Even the name was soft. It was a private school now, with trendy awnings.

They walked up Baldwin Street past the narrow painted-brick homes, their chain-link fences protecting dollhouse lawns of drab brown grass. One bore a single ragged tree; another grew patio stones end to end. The house on the corner had been painted apple green and converted into the Sun Yat Sen Chinese school.

Spadina Avenue swarmed with evening traffic. It was still bright daylight but the pedestrians on the other side were faceless in the expanding distance.

"There's the El Mocambo." Iris pointed north to the tavern. Its stylized palm tree sign was a neighbourhood landmark. "Did you see the picture in *The Star* — Margaret Trudeau hobnobbing there with the Stones? In a tavern, no less. Now that girl's got a social life."

Rebecca smiled at her immaculately groomed friend and turned her attention to the street. The heat rising from the cars made the air fluid. They walked toward the push-button stop-lights where even inveterate jaywalkers waited. Trying to cross the six lanes of the street without lights was a quick route to eternity.

They began to walk on the green light, but halfway across the light changed and Rebecca dashed forward. Iris trailed behind, gingerly stepping between the streetcar tracks in her elegant heels, until she reached the other side.

A truck driver stuck his head out the window. "Hey, lady, want me to get behind and push?"

She struck a pose at the edge of the road, hand on

her hip, and yelled out, "That depends on what you're going to push *with*!"

In the Spadina Garden restaurant Rebecca picked at her meal of spicy cashew chicken in a restless silence. In restaurants lately, the food on the menu always seemed so appetizing, until it arrived. She would take a few bites then realize she was going to gag if she ate anything. She spent the rest of the time pushing food around on her plate, hoping no one would notice she wasn't eating. But she couldn't fool Iris.

"No wonder I'm getting fatter," Iris said. "I keep finishing your meals." Once it was established that Rebecca was not going to eat what had arrived on her plate, Iris speared her fork into the chicken pieces across the table.

Rebecca tried to smile. "Maybe you need to walk around the block with me."

"Maybe you need to eat more." She observed her friend across the table. "You seem distracted."

Rebecca glanced from Iris' upswept blonde hair to an old Chinese woman walking past the window. "I'm wondering what happened to Mrs. Kochinsky."

Iris jabbed her fork into the air. "If we worried every time a patient missed an appointment.... You need to take care of *yourself*. You've been looking pale lately. And you're not eating...."

"I'm alright," she cut her off.

Iris' grey eyes turned away quickly.

Rebecca leaned forward and softened her voice. "I appreciate your concern, Iris, but I'm alright. Really. It's just going to take time."

She lifted her finger in the air to attract the attention of the waitress. "Cheque, please."

Rebecca threaded her sports car in and out of rush hour traffic like an agitated teenager. She usually avoided Bathurst Street if she could but it was the fastest way to Mrs. Kochinsky's house. A truck honked as she cut in front. The little red Jaguar XJS had belonged to David; he had been the one with a sense of panache. She never cared one way or another which car she drove as long as it got her there. Hers had been one of those beige Oldsmobiles that faded into the traffic, but when he died she had surprised herself by selling hers and keeping his.

Her father liked GM cars. He had driven a long line of Chevys till he could finally afford to buy himself an Olds. His pharmacy had thrived because he never lost his sense of humour and customers enjoyed dealing with him. Rebecca's mother took care of the buying and kept the books. All in the family. Now that they had sold the business and retired, Mitch and Flo Temple had become snowbirds, migrating to California for the winter. They were finally wending their way home next week, thank God. Rebecca missed her father's bad jokes, her mother's strength and common sense. None of them felt in any condition to cook for Passover this year. David's death had sapped everyone's spirit and energy. So Rebecca had ordered a kosher dinner from a reliable caterer, mostly in deference to Susan and her Orthodox husband who were driving in from Montreal with the kids. Rebecca wished she were closer to her sister. She could've used a friend these past months. Not that Susan didn't try. She had offered herself as a shoulder to lean on, a phone number at night if Rebecca wanted to talk. But Susan had plenty on her plate already — three kids weren't enough to take care of? At least her husband wasn't too traditional to help out. Just traditional enough to require paper plates for the Seder since Rebecca's kitchen wasn't kosher. That was all right, they all liked him. But Rebecca knew she wasn't going to call Susan when she needed to cry at night.

Rebecca pulled into the driveway beside Mrs. Kochinsky's duplex. Daylight clung to the street in that long moment before dusk turns it blue. The building, like all the others along that stretch of Bathurst Street, looked quite respectable for forty or fifty years old, the exterior in good repair. She sat in the car a moment, restrained by the thought of the surprised Greta Garbo face when she opened the door.

"Is it really Wednesday already?" Mrs. Kochinsky might say. "I lost track of time."

Maybe she was out on the town with her cousin from the States. Had he been the one who'd sent the photo Mrs. Kochinsky had flashed before Rebecca's face? Apparently she'd only met him once, when he was a boy in Poland. They had exchanged some letters when she lived in Argentina but they had lost touch. Then the sudden phone call. Maybe he'd arrived, and in all the excitement of catching up, she'd forgotten what day it was. It happened. If that was the case Rebecca would admonish her gently and go away relieved. But she had to check and make sure her patient was all right.

Carrying her black medical bag, she climbed the steps to the wooden front door. She lifted the brass lion's head knocker and clanged it twice. There was no sound of stirring from inside, no one preparing to open the door. She turned the knob and was surprised to find it moved easily. As soon as she opened the door, her heart reeled. Inside the small vestibule, the door to Mrs. Kochinsky's apartment stood ajar. The glass panel, still covered by a sheer curtain, had been smashed, leaving a jagged hole. She pushed the door open and called out, "Mrs. Kochinsky?"

The place had been ransacked. She ought to leave to call the police rather than risk meeting the intruder face to face. She stood very still on the threshold, listening. The silence hung in the air. Only the desultory hum of tires on Bathurst Street and her own ragged breath interrupted the quiet. How could she leave without checking her patient?

"Mrs. Kochinsky? It's Dr. Temple." Nothing.

From the dimness of the entrance hall she could see coffee tables on their sides, ornamental cushions, vases, framed photos scattered on the floor. The kitchen lay straight ahead at the end of the hall; to the left, the living- and dining-room. Stepping over the shards on the floor, she moved forward, then stopped.

The muscles in her neck suddenly tightened. Adrenaline leaped through her chest. Mrs. Kochinsky lay crumpled, near the fireplace, like a pile of cast-off clothes.

Rebecca ran around an upturned chair to reach her, called out her name for a response. There was none. She kneeled down, her heart pounded against her ribcage. The woman's face had turned a dark congested purple. Her eyes bulged. A line had been burned across her neck, tell-tale contusions and abrasions left by a ligature. A rope, a cord, something solid wielded by someone strong. Rebecca placed her fingers flat against the woman's carotid artery. The neck and jaw were slack, the skin clammy. She shuddered at the unnatural angle of the lifeless head. The bastard had pulled so tight he had broken her neck. Crushed her like a bird. Rebecca closed her eyes and suddenly there was Mrs. Kochinsky, terrified in her office yesterday. *Yesterday*. A quiet panic took hold of Rebecca. The woman had run to her for help. Mrs. Kochinsky had trusted her. Rebecca could almost hear her: *I know you care, that's why I keep coming, I put myself in your hand*s. She looked down at her hands. She was responsible. And what had she done? Soothed her with words. Bathed her with platitudes while blinded by her own diagnosis of paranoia. No. Mrs. Kochinsky *was* paranoid. *Wasn't* she? All those times men had chased her across her nightmares, all those times Rebecca thought her patient was viewing things through her own distorted lens, perhaps it had been *Rebecca* misinterpreting, denying. Perhaps Mrs. Kochinsky had seen exactly what was there. Rebecca could hardly fathom it. She had been convinced of her patient's paranoia. And yet the woman was lying dead at Rebecca's feet.

She stood up wavering, numb with an old pain. Her last memory of David's face flashed by, white against the white sheet, his mouth loosened at the jaw, foreign, his body empty of him, the emptiness taking her over. She felt it wring her heart the same way, the old squeezing inside her chest. Surprising how much she cared for the old woman. How the bond between them had grown stronger when David died, each understanding the grief of the other. And she *needed* Rebecca so much; she said Rebecca helped her stay alive one week to the next. Then why was she dead? Why was she lying there in her pyjamas, fallen awkwardly on her side, arm beneath her back? Stay calm, thought Rebecca. Look carefully. Piece it together. There must have been a struggle. Rigor mortis still clamped part of the body tight but had released the small muscles. Mrs. Kochinsky had been dead all day, maybe all night. She seemed much smaller now than when she was alive.

A pale light filtered through the brocade curtains of

the front window, creating murky twilight an hour early. Rebecca realized the chandelier in the dining-room was on. Last night. He'd come last night. But who? She glanced around the littered apartment. Could she be sure it wasn't exactly what it appeared? Why couldn't it have been a burglar? Maybe instead of the Argentine death squad Mrs. Kochinsky anticipated every day of her life, it had been a thief caught in the act who had played out her worst nightmare. Was it impossible that she had fled persecution on two continents only to find meaningless death on the third? Yet would a thief come here? The woman was not rich. If they were looking for saleable goods, any of the houses on the winding, genteel streets off Bathurst would have yielded more.

Hovering at the edge of the living-room, Rebecca realized the side door to the apartment was open. It led to a short hall and the back staircases, one upper, one leading to the basement, then the door to the outside. This must have been the way the killer got out. He would have ended up in the laneway at the side of the house. No problem escaping unseen.

On her way to the phone in the kitchen, Rebecca passed the bedroom: everything Mrs. Kochinksy owned lay scattered on the bed and floor — cosmetics, clothes, shoes. On the dresser her leather purse resembled a dead animal, its insides pulled out. The wallet sat open, presumably empty. A robbery? A good imitation?

Rebecca stood on the threshold of the kitchen, looking for the phone. The receiver hung from the wall. Mrs. Kochinsky must have run in here, trying to call for help. The killer had torn the cord out of the wall. Then he chased her into the living-room. Trying to piece it together was giving Rebecca the creeps. He may have been gone, but the aura of his presence was strong; an evil cloud filled the apartment, it smelled of him.

Rebecca didn't want to disturb any evidence. Turning left, she stepped through the dining-room and continued into the den. Through the windows, the small backyard and garage were fading into the dim evening. The room itself seemed untouched. She found a desk in the corner. On it a phone sat beside a chocolate box filled with bills and receipts. Some papers lay to one side. The detritus of daily life. Garbage now that the inhabitant was dead. How much correspondence with art supply houses and galleries had she thrown out when David had died. All his notebooks. Wipe the slate clean. Start afresh. The clichés sounded right, but they didn't work. Envelopes for David Adler still arrived with regularity at the house. Each time she dropped one in the garbage she saw his face white against the sheet.

Using a tissue from her pocket, she draped the receiver before lifting it and dialed 911. This line had not been disconnected. The dispatcher said that police and ambulance were on their way. Rebecca wondered how quickly they would arrive, considering there was no medical emergency. While she was relaying the information, her eyes fell on the papers near the phone. On top was a card printed in Spanish outlined with a black border. She used her high school Spanish to decipher the announcement of the death of Carlos Velasco, son of Isabella, to be buried in Tablada Cemetery, Buenos Aires, in February 1977. What was this doing in a pile of current mail?

The past few years had not been good to Mrs. Kochinsky. First her husband died, then during the vulnerability of her widowhood, the regime pursued her into the torture chamber in order to catch the son who produced plodding but graphic song lyrics about bloodthirsty generals and death squads in uniform. The death of Carlos Velasco may have been history, but the card had just been received. Why else was it keeping company with Mrs. Kochinsky's latest hydro bill? It was like a voice from the past. The expression stopped Rebecca cold. A voice from the past. Rebecca remembered the cousin and the photo of the duck. Suddenly she wished she'd gotten a better look at the picture when Mrs. Kochinsky had waved it around in the office. It hadn't been among the papers near the phone in the den. The purse. Mrs. Kochinsky had brought it out of her purse.

Rebecca tiptoed toward the bedroom as if her steps would disturb someone. She could see everything from the doorstep of the small room. All the drawers from the white dresser stood open, the clothes from inside dumped in heaps on the peach broadloom. On the nightstand, strangely untouched, lay a grey doll in a striped dress, a crude shabby thing for someone as elegant as Mrs. Kochinsky. The police would be there any minute. She took wary steps toward the emptied purse on the dresser. She touched nothing but scrutinized the papers lying nearby. A few things had fallen to the floor. A chequebook, a recipe, some store receipts, a shopping list. The picture wasn't there. Crouching in a clear area at the foot of the bed, she gingerly lifted the bedskirt. There was nothing underneath. She didn't want to disturb evidence but she had to know. She poked her foot into the clothes on the floor. She inspected the piles of shoes in the closet. Nothing. It was as clear as day to her now: whoever had killed Mrs. Kochinsky had taken the picture. The inexplicable photocopy of the duck was missing.

chapter eight

Wednesday, April 4, 1979

Nesha smiled inwardly at the discomfort of the well-dressed woman seated next to him on the plane. He found, since growing his hair and beard to an unruly length, that people sitting beside him in moving vehicles were less likely to engage him in conversation. He kept himself clean but untidy, no longer able to take seriously the usual daily precepts of personal grooming. He reminded himself of Howard Hughes. Yet there had been a time, many times, before he had turned eccentric, that he had found himself on a plane beside a middle-aged woman who wanted to talk.

He had married a woman who was attracted to his melancholy. She said she wanted to help him forget, not realizing she was aiming to eliminate the trait that had attracted her in the first place. They had a son and Nesha had once considered himself satisfied with life. The son, Josh, was a good student, would be the scholar Nesha would have been — had he been given the chance. Josh had fine dark hair, like his father, that lay in loose waves around his head. Nesha feared for his son because he knew how easily the world could fall apart. Josh would tire of his father's paranoia and say, "Don't worry so much Dad, this is *America*."

Over the years Margie learned she would never be able to make Nesha forget. She knew his obsession would always take precedence over her and resentment became disaffection, then finally indifference. When Josh was twenty and had been away at school for a year, Margie decided there was no longer any reason to stay. She had had a stomachful of her husband's rage and melancholy and was ready for lighter fare. The ironic thing was that when she left, Nesha lost interest in everything, including all thoughts of vengeance.

It was still daylight when they flew over Lake Michigan and Lake Erie. For vast miles they gleamed beneath him in a kind of flat blue he had never seen on the ocean, a clear mirror of the sky, an almost blinding light in the eyes. He had looked up the Great Lakes on a map before he left and found to his relief that Toronto sat comfortably on the north end of Lake Ontario, a port city. What would he do without his precious water?

At the front desk of the hotel they eyed him suspiciously with his ragged hair and beard, but his money was as good as everyone else's. One link with his former life he had held onto was his American Express card. It reminded him he could afford to do anything he wanted, only he chose to do nothing. Until now.

From the days when he used to travel, Nesha knew which hotels had good pools. Margie had never failed to complain about the rooms but he didn't care about where he slept, as long as the pool was deep and long.

Well, he didn't have to worry about Margie anymore; let a new husband have the pleasure.

On such short notice he couldn't call around for information and had to settle for whatever there was. Late that evening, long before he would be able to sleep, he visited the indoor pool in the bowels of the hotel. The place was candy-coloured, pastel green and yellow and pink, perhaps to make one forget it was a basement. And the pool wasn't what he was used to — he took in the trendy, impractical curve — but it would do. He needed his swim the way some people needed drugs or TV — to obliterate the world, to blank out a mind that ran the same murderous pictures over and over.

Unwilling to let the old newsreel begin, he let the water take him over. He luxuriated in the kiss of the water as he plied an easy graceful breast-stroke down the middle of an empty pool. His mother wept soundlessly, her long hair unravelling from the bun. Dust whorled into the air, hid the sky. But Nesha turned away. He let the green-yellow-pink of the pool take him somewhere simpler, somewhere on a different page of history in a different millennium. This must have been the very first stroke, he thought, when hyphenated creatures slid through the primeval oceans before memory, trout-lizards and carp-toads and semi-dinosaurs, this stroke where the arms pulled the body forward by pushing the water down and away, laying open a channel as welcoming as a lover. This stroke could be sweet and soothing under an ancient sun, a movement so natural you could almost sleep in it. Suddenly the dust sifted down, down, the sun blazed a path through the dust until it became a cloud of smoke, a plume of fire in the little wooden synagogue of his nightmare. Nesha shook his head. He needed something faster.

He lowered his head and shifted his arms up into

71

the butterfly, once a knockoff of the breast-stroke, but years ago now, promoted to its own competitive category. And what a category! If this didn't kill him, nothing would. His hands traced a fast strenuous S back to his hips, then out again, back and out again at a pace that created a corridor of foam. The once voluptuous water was now violently forced open as both his legs kicked together behind him as one, like a primitive tail. He gulped and expelled air in the trough behind the bow-wave, keeping his head low and his body flat to offer the least possible resistance to the water. He didn't care what he looked like in his goggles and his long hair tied back in a ponytail.

When he had learned to swim, the breast-stroke was strictly for sissies. He had spent more time in the water than on his grades. Even then, young as he was, he recognized the water's allure: it made him forget. Like the River Lethe crossing into Hades, he learned at school; all would be forgotten on the other side. And what could be more natural. It was, after all, California. It was more like heaven than any place he could have imagined: the brightly painted, columned houses, the high sweeping vistas of the sea, the purple and turquoise and gun-metal of the water, sometimes separate, sometimes all at once, that reminded him he was at land's end, the farthest point on the continent and a million miles away from the village that haunted his dreams.

Back and forth Nesha swam the length of the hotel pool, the muscles in his body sang with pain and he knew he would have to stop soon. Pretty good for an old geezer, he thought. Forty-eight. Where did it all go? Since Margie left he'd been forced to look at himself and he didn't like what he saw. He had to hand it to her, he would've gone on like that forever if she hadn't left, then not realized how wrong things really were till he was on his deathbed. Yeah, thanks Margie, thanks for nothing. He didn't know how to love anymore, she had said. He had no love left. Well, how wrong she was. He could love. What he loved was feeling the water all around him, the water pulling at his memory, submerging it all into a deep corner of the pool. Wasn't that love?

If he could have done what he wanted when he was eighteen, he would've swum. Instead, he studied numbers. Numbers had always been magical for him and it might have worked. But the commerce and finance courses turned numbers into ciphers and sent him down to the pool at the university in search of comfort. After two years he realized he would make life easier by apprenticing himself to an accountant.

It wasn't until Nesha was married and a father that an American pup named Jastremski, coached by a breast-stroke champion, shortened and quickened the leg and arm movements of the stroke to come up with unheard-of speeds that smashed three world records. No sissy stroke then. Only fifteen years too late for him. By that time he had a house and a mortgage and several expensive cars to support. The breast-stroke became part of those deepest-sleep dreams that dissolve upon awakening.

In his heart, his painfully ledgered accountant's heart, he had always known there would be a day of reckoning. It was a matter of checks and balances, credit and liability. He had played with numbers long enough to know they were the only things you could count on.

After twenty years of marriage, Margie came to him and told him that she wanted to live. A man courting death had no use for love, she said, and love was what she needed. Once Margie left, he realized that the only reason he was getting up each morning to go to work was that he'd done it the day before. One morning he went to a Y instead. He reacquainted himself with the breast-stroke and found to his relief that like old friends, they were still compatible.

His partners noted his tardiness at work. Clients were starting to complain. Mr. Malkevich was not paying as much attention to their financial affairs as he used to, he wasn't available when they called. After so many years with their company, did they deserve such treatment? There were other firms who would be happy to get their business.

When Nesha showed no signs of "snapping out of it," the partners offered him a deal. They knew about his wife and his tragic past but they couldn't really understand what was going on. He knew they were much relieved when he accepted the deal even though they had to buy him out.

His needs were modest. The bungalow he had bought was paid for; he didn't care about fancy cars or clothes or even travelling. Where could he go where it would be different? His memories, his pain, he carried with him like baggage.

chapter nine

The uniformed young constable stationed Rebecca in the den and questioned her with official politeness, calling her "ma'am." She watched from the doorway across the length of the dining-room as the police photographer took shots of the body in detail. Rebecca folded her arms across her chest, repelled by the violation of Mrs. Kochinsky's privacy. From now on, the woman she had compared to Garbo would be a photo of a corpse in a police file accessible to anyone with a badge. While she gave the young constable particulars about her patient, then herself for the record, the forensic team went to work in their white coveralls. One man scowled as he dusted the door for fingerprints. A plump woman scraped something from the floor of the entrance hall. When the photographer was finished with the living-room, the woman cop, her long hair pulled back in a pony tail, searched on her hands and knees through the mess on the floor. All pickings were dropped by tweezers into glass vials and paper bags. "Shit" she muttered, crunching something under her leg.

"So Sharon," said the photographer aiming his camera at the dining-room buffet, its drawers hanging open. "What would you grab if you had five minutes to shop in K-Mart like this guy?"

Two men, one in tweed sports jacket, the other in a trenchcoat, walked in and stood at the edge of the living-room. Both were broad-shouldered, but where the trenchcoat was muscular, the sports jacket was stocky. He was also half a head shorter.

"This another one of those, Ed?" said the heavier man addressing the photographer. "One of those 'five minutes shopping in K-Mart' jobs?"

The constable immediately excused himself to Rebecca. "Don't touch anything, ma'am," he added. He walked back through the hall where she could no longer see him.

Rebecca watched the two men turn to greet the constable who was still out of her sight. His words were an inaudible mumble over the bustle of activity in the apartment. Both men took out pads and began to take notes after a moment of what she took to be the constable filling them in. At one point, they turned to look at the body, gestured toward something in the room, took more notes. She still couldn't hear anything. Then suddenly they turned to look at Rebecca over the distance of two rooms. The stocky detective sized her up. What struck her was the blankness of his expression. Nothing showed. While the taller man faced the invisible constable, the sports jacket disappeared into the hall. She knew where he was heading.

"I'm Detective Wanless," he said, entering the den. He showed her his identification badge. "You're the one who found the body? Dr. Temple?"

He was not much taller than Rebecca but gave the impression of size with the solid mass of his chest and shoulders, bulky beneath the jacket.

"Are you a relative?" he asked, preparing his notebook. His brown hair was thin and short on top, brushed forward over a high forehead. His large ruddy cheeks eclipsed a neatly trimmed moustache.

"No."

"What was your relationship with the deceased —" he searched his notepad "Goldie Kochinsky?" His thick fingers held the pen, waiting.

"I was her doctor."

"This was a house call, then?" His blue eyes studied her face, the pencil poised above the paper.

"Not exactly."

"Why exactly were you here then?"

The blankness of his face made it difficult for her to explain. "I was worried. She didn't show up for her regular appointment."

The blue eyes didn't change but the tone of his voice became human. "You must be one in a million, Doctor. Mine wouldn't notice if I didn't show up for an appointment. He'd go on to the next guy. Do you normally check up on your patients when they miss an appointment?"

"Mrs. Kochinsky was a special case. She came to my office yesterday very upset. She was a very anxious person."

"Why was she upset?"

"She said she'd just seen the man who was going to kill her."

Wanless arched an eyebrow. "And what did you do?"

"I made a note of it," she said. He looked up, still scribbling in his book. She couldn't read his face, though she could imagine what he was thinking. "You know, there's doctor-patient confidentiality," she said.

"There's also a murder. To me this looks like a robbery gone bad. But I need more information before I can put it to bed."

Rebecca looked around. A robbery gone bad. Someone had meant it to look that way. But she no longer believed it. "There wasn't much else I could do," she said. "Mrs. Kochinsky told me the same story almost every week. Someone was always after her. That was her problem. You see, she was coming to me for anxiety. She was suffering from post-traumatic stress disorder."

"In plain English."

"She developed persecutory thinking after being tortured in Argentina."

He whistled softly between his teeth; his eyes brightened momentarily. "Tortured! God, aren't you glad you live in Canada? You saying she thought people were after her? She was paranoid?"

"In broad terms, yes."

"So when she came to you with this latest story about the guy who was going to kill her, it was like crying wolf, is that what you mean? You didn't take it seriously?"

"It had all the same elements as her usual stories," she said. "Except that she seemed more frightened this time. And she ran in without an appointment."

"Did she describe this man? Or any of the others?"

"Only in psychological terms: he was evil, he had big dark eyes, he was powerful. I think she was waiting for someone to come from Argentina to kill her. But that would fit in with her paranoia."

"You think this Argentina story is possible? Was there a reason someone would've come for her?"

Rebecca stared at the shell that used to be Mrs. Kochinsky. "I never thought so. Yet she's dead. Who would've wanted to kill her? I know the woman was paranoid. She was a classic case, with a tightly connected system of her own truth — all very logical on the surface. But all based on a false premise. By any standards, paranoid."

"Let's start from the beginning," he said. "Can you describe for me how you found the body? From the time you came to the door. Everything you can remember."

He scribbled in his pad while she talked. It was the second time she had told her story in an hour. Only this time she mentioned the picture.

"Mrs. Kochinsky waved this newspaper photo in front of me. I didn't get a good look at it. All I saw was a duck. She was almost incoherent and I thought she was having a bad episode. But now, well, I think it might've been important."

"We'll look around for it."

"I already did. It's gone."

He looked up from his pad. "Did you touch anything?"

She shook her head. "I just looked."

"Hey, Sharon!" he cried. The plump lady cop turned around. "Get some samples off the doc here." He turned to Rebecca. "Just to eliminate your prints and fibres."

The lady cop in white coveralls approached Rebecca with her tweezers. Wanless said, "Once Sharon's finished with you, I'd like you to come down to the station to give a statement."

She didn't tell Wanless, but they would have to wait at the station. She was going back downtown to take another look at Mrs. Kochinsky's file. There were holes in Rebecca's memory. Maybe her notes would help.

Their attention was diverted by the distress of a raised voice near the front. "I saw the police cars out here, I'm only three doors down," the man exclaimed with the clipped nasal quality of a German accent. "What is going on here? Has something happened to Goldie?"

The detective in the trenchcoat waved a hand of authority at the young cop posted near the front door. The man with the insistent nasal voice was allowed into the hall. From the den Rebecca and Wanless watched a trim, well-groomed man in his sixties approach the edge of the living-room. He was dwarfed by the tall detective who obstructed his view of the body and let him go no further.

"I have a right to know what is going on," he said in his slight accent. "I am Feldberg. This is my sister-in-law's place."

Rebecca observed him with interest. The poor sister's husband. Suddenly a phrase flew through her mind like a startled bird. *Now he can have his fancy woman.* Mrs. Kochinsky's voice slurred by drugs after her sister's retreat from the world. Rebecca understood better now, with Feldberg in view, handsome in tailored grey tweed sports jacket and white shirt; thick gun-metal hair combed straight back from his forehead.

The detective in the trenchcoat lowered his voice, became inaudible from the distance. Finally he turned his bulk aside to reveal the body lying near the fireplace.

"*Mein Gott! Mein Gott!*" Feldberg stared a moment, speechless. "Who would do this to her?"

"Do you know if she had any enemies?" asked the detective.

"Enemies? She was an old lady. What kind of enemies?" He gave a heartfelt shrug. "It looks to me like maybe a robbery." He cast an eye over the havoc of the apartment.

"You said you live three doors down. Did you see anything unusual today?"

Feldberg shook his head, unable to take his eyes off the body.

"Anyone strange hanging around the building lately?"

Feldberg finally spoke. "Always punks are hanging around the stores on Eglinton. Nothing to do. It's just a block away. Go talk to them."

"Have you had any problems with them before?"

"They're drinking, using drugs, always in front of that donut shop up there."

The trenchcoat patiently rephrased the question. "Did they come down this way before?"

"I didn't see them. But where they gonna get money for their drugs? You should talk to them."

"Do you know who lives upstairs, sir?"

"Still in Florida. An old lady."

Feldberg's eyes finally looked up from the body and fell upon Rebecca in the near distance. He looked at her with curiosity and would have spoken if the detective had not motioned for him to follow.

"Are you the next of kin, sir?" Rebecca heard the detective ask, leading him toward the door.

"My wife, Chana, is Goldie's sister, but she's senile."

"And where does she reside, sir...?"

Feldberg turned to stare a long moment at Rebecca before being ushered outside, out of earshot.

Then came a dog and bit the cat
That ate the goat
That Father bought for two zuzim.
One little goat, one little goat.

chapter ten

Wednesday, April 4, 1979

Nesha restrained himself from approaching the front desk of the hotel until after dinner. "I'm expecting a package," he said to the clerk. "Malkevich."

The young man looked around under the counter. Nesha knew it was too early, that the thing couldn't get there before tomorrow, but he was impatient.

"Nothing here, sir. Sorry."

Nesha found the car he had rented waiting in the parking lot. Out of his wallet, he brought out the slip of paper with his cousin's address scribbled on it. Finally they would meet again. The prospect warmed him like none other had for years. Why had he waited so long? He unfolded the map the rental company had thrown in. There was her street. It seemed to span the whole city going north. Well, he had the house number; he would find it.

Light was slowly fading in the sky as he drove through the maze of intersections near the waterfront.

He found the street he was looking for rather quickly, since it ran directly off the lakeshore route. Turning north, he headed away from the water. Toronto was much bigger than he had expected. According to the numbers he was passing, it would be at least several miles before he reached her place.

He passed marginal quasi-lawns beyond which ugly narrow attached houses stood festooned with too many ornamental bannisters. The houses gave way to shops that glimmered beneath street lamps. He was unprepared for the orgiastic marquee lights of Honest Ed's Emporium that occupied an entire block. As he continued north, his car balked at the steep incline of the hill that rivalled some of those he had left back home. The street became residential again, first with low-rise brick apartments, then as he got closer to his destination, the houses became substantial and the lawns grew pampered.

The hill rose still higher, though gently now, as if they were climbing out of some primordial lake whose waves used to lap against these midtown shores. Traffic was light, but he could tell something had happened in the distance. Lights flashed round and round from police cruisers parked on the side of the road. A car accident probably. Or a speed trap.

He slowed down, searching for the street number. He must have been almost there. Unwilling to get too close to a police car, Nesha pulled over and counted the houses to establish where she lived. With a shock, he realized police were swarming the house he was looking for. A crowd had gathered on the sidewalk. His hands began to shake. Something had happened to her. She was elderly; maybe she'd had an accident. Then why would the police be there? An attractive woman walked out the front door carrying a medical bag.

He got out of his car and approached a middle-aged couple absorbed in the spectacle. "What's going on?" he asked.

The man turned to glance at Nesha. "I don't know what's happened to this city. Some poor old lady was murdered right in her own home." He shook his head.

Nesha's blood ran cold. The bastard had found her. What other explanation could there be? Nesha had sent her the picture on the off chance she might recognize the man. Somehow it had killed her.

Back at the hotel, Nesha found himself filled with a rancorous energy that didn't let him stand still. *Zitsfleisch*, his Uncle Sol used to call it when Nesha paced their small house as if it were a cage. Sol was long gone. Now Goldie, his only link with family. If he had arrived yesterday maybe he could've saved her. The old lady didn't know anything. Why did the bastard kill her? Nesha felt powerless before the package arrived. Once he had it in his hand, there would be no stopping him. The bastard would be finished. But meanwhile, Nesha had to control himself somehow, keep the rage from destroying him.

He made his way to the basement of the hotel like a man after a drug. People in the elevator shrunk away from his self-contained sense of purpose. He seemed frightening even to himself and hurried toward the soothing promise of water.

He dove into the pastel-coloured pool and began to swim at a pace he knew he could not keep up; his energy demanded release. He had often jumped into a pool to quell the undercurrent of his energy. Up till now the source of the turmoil had been the images buried in his mind since childhood; he had somehow hoped these would run together and blur in the water as if the chlorine could seep through his skull and cleanse his brain, bleach it into oblivion.

Nesha's torso rose and fell beneath the water, rose and fell, his arms pulling him toward racing speed. He needed to shake himself free of any doubt. He needed to fashion himself into an unswerving weapon. A seed of pain began in his stomach, he recognized its presence. He couldn't stop now but turned at the edge of the pool in the elegant prescribed way, gliding under water, and thrashed his butterfly stroke back through the lane as fast as he could.

For years he had floated on the surface of things, feinting to the left or the right whenever anything resembling emotional confrontation drifted too close. He had been more than willing to swim himself to fatigue by day and drug his mind before the TV at night, not asking any more from life than to be left alone. But now, what was he to do? Now, with the murderer looming before him and his mother's eyes after decades of silence coming back to him in dreams, the way she turned her head that last time to find him, the dark bun unravelling in strands, her face twisted with terror, and her eyes pleading with him to run, run, never come back. His heart had pounded to his own footfalls as he raced through the woods confused, terrified. Dead branches cracked beneath him like gunshots — did they hear? Were they following him? After an eternity of running he came to a clearing in the forest that seemed familiar. Hadn't it been summer when he'd been there last and a silky stream had trickled through a narrow gully? Last summer. A few months. A lifetime ago. He, his mother, and little Motele had trekked leisurely to a neighbouring village for some loaves of fresh *challah*. Now the stream had vanished and the gully was a thin line in the snow. Was this really the place he had been so carefree, so childlike? He found the birch tree where his mother had instructed him to carve all their names in Hebrew letters and then, beneath: *Next year in Jerusalem*. The ultimate Jewish rallying cry. He spat on it. None of *his* had ever made it to Jerusalem. His had become smoke rising from the ancient synagogue, the smoke thick with blood, the realization that every person who had ever loved him was gone forever. And now the murderer before him, living his life out as if he had been born in 1945 with no memory.

His guts rose in revolt against the steady diet of mash he'd been surviving on. His body thrashed through the water, in turmoil as the pain that took root in his stomach clawed at his arms and legs, knotted his calves, clutched his biceps, pulled the muscles down, down. Yet still he churned out the stroke, though a black noise thundered in his ears. He had encountered this wall of pain before and retreated from it. They said a champion had to push himself right into the pain. When he was young he thought he wasn't good enough to risk it. When he got older, he thought it was too late but now he pushed himself into the wall of it, partly to try to obliterate the picture of the murderer before him, partly to prepare his unaccustomed body to its new presence.

chapter eleven

Rebecca drove to her new office after dark for the first time. Beverley Street, empty at that hour but for the parked cars, had taken on a different cast. The stillness, the Victorian calm of the houses, suddenly seemed like a predator waiting. She pulled into the parking lot behind the building and killed the ignition. There was an overhead lamp fixed to the brick wall, illuminating the asphalt. Streetlights ranged along Beverley and D'Arcy in high arcs but in her rear-view mirror she saw only shadows stretched between the disparate pools of light.

Across D'Arcy Street the old brick schoolhouse floated behind a deep mantle of shade thrown by the mature spruce trees in the yard. The school had gone through several incarnations in its long life. Now it was an alternative high school. She wondered how tall those spruce trees had been when David attended Hebrew school there some thirty years earlier. The vision of a young David playing catch in the yard had often comforted her when she looked out the examining room window upstairs. But now, from street level, night and the memory of Mrs. Kochinsky's crumpled body transformed the corner into a bog.

She rifled through her purse in the dark until she found her keys. Only then did she step out of the car. She knew the fear, the uncertainty, would stay with her until she managed to chase it out one day, but at the moment she couldn't see her way clear to it. She hurried toward the back door, throwing the shadowy bog behind her a cautious glance.

She unlocked it and searched for a light switch on the wall before venturing inside. It wasn't there. Stepping tentatively into the dark hall, she felt her way along the door frame without success. Finally she reached across to the opposite wall and flicked on the switch. The emptiness of the hall she encountered daily was suddenly foreign to her.

As she walked briskly along the corridor and up the stairs to her office, she wondered why this couldn't have waited till morning. But she knew why. It wasn't just giving the file to Wanless. She wanted to look something up for herself. That voice from the past. She wanted to know why it was important.

She fitted the key into her door and opened it. Suddenly she stopped. A muffled sound reached her from the downstairs hall. She told herself to get a grip. Maybe it was just an echo of her opening the office door in the empty building.

She found Mrs. Kochinsky's file in the cabinet and sat down near Iris' desk. Reading through her notes on the woman's visit last week, Rebecca tried to piece together scraps of information like a jigsaw. According to Mrs. Kochinsky, a few days before the visit she had received a startling phone call from a distant cousin. Startling, it seemed to Rebecca (she could only guess since the woman's explanations were often non-linear and hard to follow) because the cousin had till then communicated only through widely spaced letters over the years. They had met only once, growing up in different parts of Poland. He survived the war, a young teenager at the time, and moved to the States. All this Rebecca gleaned from the most obscure of references in her notes.

She could see from her scribbled notes yesterday that there had been some confusion about why Mrs. Kochinsky had come downtown to shop instead of staying on Eglinton Avenue where she felt safe. What had she said? *My cousin from U.S. coming. He ask me to shop so I looking around.* Something like that. But there had been a sense of urgency about the shopping Rebecca couldn't reconstruct or perhaps didn't understand to begin with. All she knew was that Mrs. Kochinsky had been shopping when she'd been badly frightened. The man who was going to kill her, she had said. But why was he going to kill her? It had always been so obvious to Mrs. Kochinsky. The people who were after her didn't need reasons. This gap in the logic had led Rebecca to her diagnosis of paranoia. Not once, but often. And yet the woman was dead.

Rebecca closed her eyes and conjured up Mrs. Kochinsky sitting across from her. The Greta Garbo face mouthed the words but no sound came forth. Her grey-brown hair trembled with effort. Rebecca watched the mouth, willing it to speak, but it was no use. Suddenly the old woman's head turned dolefully toward the door and Rebecca opened her eyes. She had definitely heard something downstairs.

Treading softly to the office door, she turned the knob without a sound. The light was still on in the hall downstairs. She listened with the door open a crack. All at once a shadow materialized on the lighted wall.

Her nerves shot to the surface. *Keep calm*, she thought. It must be Dr. Arons coming back for something. She held her breath and watched. The shadow crept closer. Why would Dr. Arons aim at stealth? She would just saunter in and go to her office door. The shadow grew larger on the wall, then stopped. It was waiting, listening. Suddenly the shadow moved and the light in the hall went out. It wasn't Dr. Arons.

Then came a stick and beat the dog
That bit the cat that ate the goat
That Father bought for two zuzim.
One little goat, one little goat.

chapter twelve

Rebecca quickly switched off the lights in the office and closed the door, locking it. Turning to face the darkness, she felt a damp chill spread under her arms. A paltry grey light filtered in through the window of the waiting-room. She could try to climb out of it. Problem was the ceilings were rather high in those old buildings, the distance to the ground neck-breaking. And the window faced D'Arcy; beneath it a cement walkway stretched between the back parking lot and the front door. If all else failed.

In three quick steps she crossed the floor to the phone on Iris' desk. For the second time that night she dialed 911.

"I need help," she whispered. "Someone's broken into the building. Please hurry." She murmured the address into the phone.

Within arm's length stood the cabinet of medical supplies. She opened the drawer. *Feel around for it. Find it.* In the dark she flicked on the pocket flashlight she used to look down throats. Shining it in the drawer, she searched. A weapon. She needed a weapon. Okay, better than nothing: a disposable scalpel. She picked it up and poked off the protective cover, dropping it in her jacket pocket.

Behind Iris' desk, she stood listening to herself breathe, the scalpel in the palm of her hand. Footsteps began to climb the stairs. Her heart thumped against her ribcage. Someone was going to kill her. He had killed Mrs. Kochinsky and now he was going to kill her. But why?

He was climbing slowly. Waiting on every step. Closer and closer, each step louder. Finally he stopped: he had reached the landing. She gripped the scalpel in her fist, not daring to breathe. She watched the door intently, then focused on the knob. Her pulse pounded. She shone the pocket flashlight on the knob with her left hand. It began to turn, then it stopped. Her heart lurched in her throat. Again it turned until it could go no further in the lock. Several more times the knob turned quietly, discreetly. Her legs began to throb, shake. She had to keep her mind clear, not panic. Maybe he would give up when he realized it was locked. Maybe he would go away. Maybe pigs would fly.

Suddenly she heard him trying to manoeuvre the lock with something. A file, possibly. After a moment he tried it again, only this time he made no attempt at silence. The knob flashed back and forth, back and forth with a loud banging sound. He didn't care if she heard anymore. The ruse was up. He was going to get through that door one way or another.

She stepped backwards away from the door, her mind aflame. How long would it take him to get through the door, how many minutes did she have left to live?

She ran through the hall toward the farthest

examining room. Even at the back of the building the noise was agonizing. He seemed to be throwing himself at the door. She pictured Mrs. Kochinsky in her last moments, panicked, brutalized. Why didn't anyone hear? Where were those cops? She eyed the window of the tiny room, wondering if she would break her neck as easily on asphalt as on cement. Suddenly without warning, the noise stopped.

She closed her eyes to hear better. The only sound was her pulse throbbing in her ears. No, wait. Something else. A siren. She heard a siren wailing in the distance. He must've heard it too. She waited a moment to be sure, then began to creep down the hall back toward the waiting-room.

She wavered near the window of the waiting area. The ragged light that filtered in from D'Arcy Street lay ghastly on the tweedy sofas and pale walls. She stood there numb and mesmerized. She didn't know how long before a loud pounding sounded downstairs at the front door.

"Open up! Police!"

Thank God. Yet she held her breath, listening. Could he still be there, waiting by the door? He'd be a fool to stay. But how did she know what he was. Maybe he was a fool and lay in wait on the other side of her door in the darkness of the hall.

"Police!" yelled the man at the front entrance. A fainter yet steady thumping issued from the back. They had the place surrounded.

But what if he killed her before the cops could get in? What difference to her if they caught him later? No, she reasoned, this makes no sense. He's gone and it's only your own fear that's keeping you inside.

She unlocked the office door. Waited. No one jumped in. She creaked the door open.

"Police! Open up!" cried the voice outside. Fists pounded on wood. "If you don't open the door, we'll break it down."

Without stepping out of the office, Rebecca craned her neck on both sides of the narrow hall. No one.

"I'm coming!" she yelled and ran down the stairs.

A strapping young uniform stood on her doorstep pointing a flashlight waist high. His expression was unaccountably wary.

"Thank God! I'm so glad to see you," she said, acutely aware of her heart still lurching in her chest.

Suddenly the flashlight blazed in her eyes. "Put down the weapon, ma'am," said the policeman.

"What?"

She could see his eyes moving from her face to her hand. Then she remembered the scalpel. She had never let go of it.

"I'm sorry," she said, feeling the handle suddenly hard in her palm. "I'm a doctor. I thought I'd have to protect myself. I'll just...." Embarrassed, she felt in her jacket for the cover, made a show of replacing it on the scalpel, then dropped it into her pocket. "When I realized someone was in the building, it was the only weapon I could find."

"He still here?"

"I don't think so. He was frightened off by the siren. Just a minute ago."

"I'll take a look around inside," he said. "My partner's at the back."

Still numb, she watched him head down the hall towards the back door, his walkie-talkie, handcuffs, and holster all attached and protruding from the black leather belt girding his waist. He opened the rear door to let the other cop in.

"Anything?"

The other man shook his head. "All clear."

The first uniform came back and tried Lila Arons' door; it was locked. Rebecca took him upstairs to her office.

"Another minute he would've gotten through," she said. "He would've killed me."

The cop had her close the door between them to test the lock. It held fast.

"I can't find anything here," he said on the landing. "Both front and back doors were locked, no sign of forced entry. Same for the door to your office. Some scratches on the lock but could be just normal wear and tear."

He watched her the way Wanless had watched her: professionally.

"What are you saying?" she asked.

"Nothing, ma'am, except the intruder didn't leave any sign."

"Someone *was* here," she said. "I thought he was going to kill me."

"Do you have some idea who it might be?"

She shook her head. "Someone killed one of my patients yesterday. I was just taking a look at her file when this happened. You can ask Detective Wanless. He'll tell you. He's at her house now. On Bathurst Street."

"Detective Wanless. Is he Thirteen Division?"

She watched from the front door as the cop got into his cruiser and raised someone on his radio. When he returned to the building, his face was more human, easier to read.

"Detective Wanless asked me to take you to the station so you can make your statement."

"What about the man who tried to kill me?"

His lips pursed and he looked away. "You know,

we get lots of junkies breaking into doctors' offices looking for drugs. Stoned out of their minds. But you know, ma'am, those guys are careless, usually leave something behind. Especially if they're in a hurry." The cop was having trouble making eye contact. She knew what that meant: embarrassment, disbelief. He looked like he wanted to believe her.

"Well, ma'am," he said, looking behind her somewhere, "there's really no evidence of any intruder, ma'am. Detective Wanless says you had a shock tonight."

She watched the earnest policeman with horror. It was humiliating being patronized by someone so young.

"Ready to go, ma'am?"

"It's all right, officer. I have my car."

The policeman pondered her for a moment with reluctance, then tipped his hat and marched out to the squad car.

Rebecca walked along the hall toward the back door, carrying the manila envelope with Mrs. Kochinsky's chart inside. She stood staring at the knob, turned it. Opening the door, she leaned out and tried to turn the knob from the outside. It wouldn't budge. From the outside, it was locked. Then how had the man gotten in? The young cop was right — there were no marks of forced entry. She stepped outside, letting the door close. Then she realized. It closed automatically. It took a minute, and most people didn't wait. Is that what she had done earlier, gone upstairs without waiting, knowing the door would close automatically?

She stared down at the ground, suddenly astonished by the object illuminated in the glare of the overhead lamp. A branch from a spruce tree lay by the side of the steps. It hadn't been there when she had arrived. She would've noticed it; it was quite large. Unlocking the door again, she picked up the branch and laid it on the threshold just inside the door. Then she let the door go. It caught.

She looked around with a quick nervous energy, her eye drawn to the darkness directly across the street. There, in front of the school, the spruce trees rose two stories, casting deep shadows. She squinted into the murk of the branches, willing a shape to appear. A breeze picked up, wafted past her and through the spruce needles, making them sway. She shivered and ran to her car.

chapter thirteen

Rebecca spotted the flashing red lights of the police cruisers like a mirage half a mile away as she drove up the hill of Bathurst Street. Though she had expected them, the actual image of disaster they represented produced a physical response in her gut. A vague sensation of hunger rose (had she eaten that day?) then dissolved in the roiling pit of her stomach. If Wanless thought he had finished with her, he was wrong. She had become convinced of one thing — Mrs. Kochinsky had not been murdered by a thief. The robbery was a sham.

She parked a block away from the commotion and slumped back into her seat, drained from the day: the emotion, the self-searching, the fear. People had gathered on the sidewalk in small groups, facing the house. A news photographer scanned the scene with a video camera.

Large envelope in hand, she walked toward the revolving lights that stained the surrounding houses and hilly lawns a violent red. She manoeuvred her way through the whispering crowd, hoping she wouldn't have to watch herself on the news the next day. The uniformed officer standing guard at the front door of the duplex watched her duck beneath the yellow police tape and climb the stairs toward him.

"I have something for Detective Wanless," she said.

Wanless stood in the hall talking to a tall man in coveralls. Rebecca could tell who was boss by the deferential way the other man bent his head forward so Wanless wouldn't have to look up. When Wanless noticed her, his blue eyes, indecipherable as before, lingered on her face then travelled down to the envelope. The other man was explaining something. He followed Wanless' glance and stopped speaking.

"Catch you later," said the man, heading toward the kitchen.

Wanless stood waiting for her to speak.

"Someone broke into my building tonight. He tried getting into my office while I was there."

A pause while he thought it over. "Yeah, I heard. You get a look at him?"

"Just his shadow."

"Had any trouble with drug break-ins there?"

"This wasn't drugs. He was after *me*."

"Why do you say that?"

He sounded calm compared to her, rational. It made her angry. "Can't you see? He must've followed me from here."

Wanless sized her up with a look, then shifted his weight onto the other foot. "According to the report there was no sign of anyone breaking into your place, no forced entry."

She remembered the young cop on the walkie-talkie, could almost hear him commiserating with Wanless. *Yes sir, the doctor's jumpy, I'll humour her.*

"I didn't make it up."

"Did I say you made it up?" He was flipping through his notes. "You had a shock tonight. Maybe your imagination's playing tricks on you."

The sentiment, if not the words, reminded Rebecca of herself when Mrs. Kochinsky had so often tried to convey in their sessions how frightened she was.

"I've brought you something," Rebecca said, handing him the envelope. She had wondered fleetingly about confidentiality, but the woman was dead and her only relative was incommunicado. They all needed some answers.

He pulled out a thick folder filled with paper. "Mrs. Kochinsky's file?" He perused a few pages.

"I can't help feeling I've missed something," she said. "I've read over my notes and all I can see is her paranoia. Maybe someone with a fresh eye can spot what I can't. She was killed for a reason. I'm sure of that now. This ..." Rebecca waved her hand at the wrecked apartment, "this is just a diversion."

"You weren't sure before. What's different now?"

"Everything changes when your life is threatened. I know how she felt now. There are too many coincidences."

"Only if you look from a certain angle," he said, observing her critically. "I'll flip through it." He replaced the chart in the envelope. "Have you been to the station yet?"

"I'm on my way."

The April night was crisp in her mouth. And bitter. That anyone should die in spring when even the air held such promise.... Mrs. Kochinsky, who had already suffered enough.... The unjustness of it pushed her, barely aware, past the murmuring couples still waiting on the sidewalk for some news, some gossip, perhaps the taking out of the body.

She was heading for her car when she saw him. Feldberg stood on his steps smoking, three duplexes down from Mrs. Kochinsky's, as he had said. He saw her, too. Quickly throwing down his cigarette, he stepped up to the sidewalk where she would pass.

"You are the doctor? Goldie's doctor?"

"Yes."

"What a shock to find her like that. I was just going to make coffee. Would you like some?"

The statement could wait.

Feldberg's main floor apartment was laid out exactly like Mrs. Kochinsky's, but the differences in style were startling. She had filled her living-room with the curved lines of French Provincial sofas and needlepoint chairs set in a circle, creating an impression of gentle clutter. His tastes ran to modern and expensive, a pale blue leather couch beneath the bay window, a steel and leather armchair near the fireplace. Between them stood an ultra-modern coffee table of chrome and glass. On the surface a large art book lay perfectly aligned with the couch. No carpets softened the floor of blond pine planks whose pattern converged in the centre of the oblong space that housed the living- and dining-room. The lines of the floor, and their juncture, drew the eye into the dining-room, which was almost empty except for a small table and two chairs. On a corner table sat a Mayan head carved from stone.

"Make yourself comfortable, Doctor. I will start the coffee." Feldberg disappeared into the kitchen, the aroma of his cologne receding with him.

Rebecca observed the painting over the fireplace: wispy, nearly translucent figures dancing in the twilight of a romantic grove of cypress. She glanced instinctively at the signature, then smiled. Corot. Who was he trying to fool? What had David told her once? Jean-Baptiste Corot had completed four hundred paintings in his lifetime, and eight hundred of them were in North America.

From the kitchen Feldberg called out, "As you can see I'm a great lover of art. Have you heard the expression: *the air we find in the Old Masters paintings is not the air we breathe?* I deeply believe this."

Her eyes followed the pattern on the pine floor where it converged in the dining-room. The burled table top was large enough only for a few tea cups. The austere ladder-backed chairs did not invite the guest to stay long. Rather the room drew the eye to the art on the walls, where she was amused to find paintings signed by Utrillo — a scene of bleached houses pressed together in a village — Pissarro — a busy scene at the docks in some French town — and a lopsided Chagall fiddler flying over a house through a pink sky. They were very good copies. Not just coloured photographs on artboard, but brushstrokes that looked real on canvas. Was this the new technique of reproduction that David had scoffed at? All that money and taste and then Feldberg had spoiled it.

Enough schlock. She turned to the photos on the mantelpiece. Feldberg and Chana in summer clothes stood together on a sidewalk somewhere, not close enough to touch. Rebecca noted a sisterly resemblance to Goldie even in the wary half-smile for the camera. In another, a young Chana and Goldie, arms around each other's shoulders, beaming in front of a large tree. Goldie's face, small, heart-shaped, her brown hair swept up into a chic roll. And the eyes! Ironic eyes radiant with humour. How beautiful she was. They both were. No wary smiles here, no buried emotions. Then a photo caught at Rebecca's heart. Mrs. Kochinsky wistful beside a dark-haired handsome young man, his arm stretched affectionately around her. Enrique.

"A tragic family," Feldberg said entering the living-room, noting the photo in her hand. He carried in an elaborate silver tray that he placed on the coffee table. "Did she tell you of her past?" He had an admirable head of steel-grey hair for a man in his sixties. His fine bones and trim frame exaggerated the hair.

"I know about her experience in Argentina."

His back stiffened as if she'd said something personal. What had he to do with it? Perhaps there was something here to find out, but she needed to put him at ease first.

"At least she escaped from Europe before the war," she said. "Things could've been worse."

"She was luckier than me, in that respect," he said, showing Rebecca to the sofa. He sat down in the severely modern chair opposite her, crossing his legs the prim way she had seen European men do. His grey jacket was made of expensive wool, the line of the trousers creased just so. He appeared nervous though, understandable after the evening's events. His grey eyes tended to dart around quickly. Every now and then he rubbed his patrician nose as if irked by a smell.

"You were caught in the war?" she said.

He looked past her to the draped window. "At first we just ran from one town to the other, trying to stay ahead of the Nazis. Then in one of the towns, someone informed on us. Those Poles were devils. They hated Jews. And that was the end of our freedom. They took us to a camp in Poland, me and my brother."

"How did you survive?" she asked, genuinely curious.

"We were young. I was lucky I was small. My brother was bigger than me and I gave him some of my food. I knew he needed it more than me. But he couldn't take the hard labour and he wouldn't listen. I helped others to survive. They valued my advice and they lived. But I couldn't save my brother."

The nasal voice stopped and she realized he was observing her. "Did anyone else from your family survive?" she asked.

"Some cousins. They're in the United States."

"Did you go there after the war?"

He squinted his eyes, squeezed his face into a grimace. "I didn't want the States. I wanted adventure. I went to Argentina."

Rebecca recalled an autobiography by a camp survivor she had once read. It seemed everyone was trying to get into the United States after the war but only those with relatives were allowed in. She began to wonder.

"Cream and sugar?" he asked.

Once he was sipping from his china teacup, she said, "You met your wife in Argentina?"

"Argentina? No, no! We met in a labour camp in Poland. She was so beautiful, you wouldn't know, looking at her now. How she suffered there! She was never a strong woman. She survived because of me. You know why she lived? Because I got her a good job in the camp. I was there before her and I had friends. Friends were the most important thing — more important even than food. Food you could get with friends. So I pulled some strings and she didn't have to go to the factory. She went every day to clean the officers' quarters. Away from the camp, maybe five minutes walk. No danger of the quotas in the factories, or being shot by an SS out for some fun. Just cleaning up their rooms."

Mrs. Kochinsky had mentioned Chana's trauma in the camps but failed to cite Feldberg as her saviour. So he hadn't chosen Argentina for adventure but because

111

Chana could be sponsored by her sister. Water under the bridge.

"You were lucky to leave Argentina before the reign of terror there. You moved to Canada quite a while before your sister-in-law. Did that upset your wife?"

He straightened up in the chair, affronted, his eyes darting faster. "I had no choice. I had to start somewhere new. You probably heard the story about Goldie's husband, my late brother-in-law. He didn't like me. He was a hard man, a hard man. We were partners in a printing shop. I worked like a slave and one day he just kicked me out of the business. So unfair. I had to start from scratch in a new country with nothing, supporting a wife..."

He continued talking while Rebecca's mind jogged back to a memory he had let loose with his story about the printing business. It was the beginning of her relationship with Mrs. Kochinsky, the only time the older woman had mentioned her brother-in-law. Apparently her husband had taken Feldberg into the business for Chana's sake. But Feldberg had expensive tastes and proceeded to rob the business flagrantly until her husband could no longer ignore it. Mr. Kochinsky was forced to buy out the brother-in-law to save the business. He had given Feldberg enough cash to leave Argentina, where no one who knew him would deal with him, and establish himself in Canada. Rebecca vaguely remembered the bitterness in Mrs. Kochinsky's story. Could he really have thought this was the experience in Argentina Rebecca had referred to?

"You know, they were too close," she heard him say, finally. "It was unnatural. Even when we moved, it didn't make a difference. They wrote each other so many letters. Chana was always writing letters. Everything that happened, Chana had to write down.

But this, this is such a shock. I'm glad Chana isn't here anymore. Ach, I'm talking too much."

She shook her head in a non-committal way. His cologne was beginning to sicken her. "What do you think happened tonight? Your sister-in-law thought people from Argentina were still after her. You think that's possible?"

"Ahh!" He waved his hand dismissing it. "Everyone was tired of hearing what happened to her. Lots of people were tortured. You know, Chana suffered more than her when she was in the camp. How Goldie told it, she was the only one. She wouldn't forget. She always thought someone was after her. You were her doctor. Didn't you know she was crazy that way?"

"But someone did kill her."

"I'm sure it was very simple. A thief in the night. It was her bad luck he came when she was home. If he came in the day, she would be in the bakery. She wouldn't be dead. Such things happen."

"Have you told your wife yet?"

He grimaced, waving his hand with dismissal. "Ach! She's a vegetable. She wouldn't understand. I can talk to her, talk to her — she watches with those eyes. Nothing. I don't go much anymore. It's very hard for me. This is the woman I lived with for thirty-five years. I can't force myself to see her like this."

"The police will notify her, as next of kin," Rebecca said.

He shrugged. "She won't understand. They'll be wasting their time."

Rebecca looked away, recoiling with contempt. This man was still alive while David was dead.

"Mrs. Kochinsky often spoke about visiting your wife at the nursing home. Is she still at Baycrest?" Rebecca knew she wasn't.

"Baycrest!" he spat. "Who could afford Baycrest? They want you to turn over all your property to them and then they want to see your income tax return. They know how to squeeze money out of their Jews. No, I found a smaller place for Chana. Very nice, on Bathurst too, but further north. Just as nice as Baycrest. She wouldn't know the difference anyway." He sat back, smiling, in the leather and steel armchair and sipped his coffee.

Then came fire and burned the stick
That beat the dog that bit the cat
That ate the goat
That Father bought for two zuzim.
　　One little goat, one little goat.

chapter fourteen

Thursday, April 5, 1979

By half past midnight Rebecca was hurtling home along a deserted Eglinton Avenue at breakneck speed. All the traffic lights were green. All the storefronts burned their flashy neon signs into the void, turning ghostly sidewalks blue. She was going so fast she nearly missed turning off into her street.

For the past hour she had sat across from a Detective Dunhill at Thirteen Division. The station was empty except for the desk sergeant. Fluorescent lights hummed above the grey pockmarked block walls. She repeated the story of what had happened that night in a fatigued monotone, disturbed by the indifference of the man filling out the forms, the indifference of the universe.

She could have sleepwalked through the story by this time. She had not only told it to the constable and to Wanless, but had gone over and over it in her own mind, searching for answers. All the pertinent points —

her concern, the violation of the apartment, Mrs. Kochinsky like a crushed bird — were beginning to sound hollow even to her. After an hour, the detective had leaned forward and sent her on her way.

She had just gotten undressed and crawled into bed when the phone rang on her nightstand. Now what? She turned on her lamp and picked up the receiver.

"Rebecca!" her mother's warm voice crooned all the way from California. "We were a bit worried. We called earlier and you weren't there. Did you have a nice evening, dear?"

"Uh.... yes, Mom. I'm fine." There was no point in worrying them further.

"Hi, doll!" her father piped in on the extension. "You forgot to call your mother for permission to go out."

"Big shot," said Flo Temple. "Your father insisted we call till you answered. Did you go somewhere with friends?"

"Nobody you know."

"I told him it was better than you moping around at home by yourself. Are you feeling any better lately, dear?"

Rebecca'd had to convince her parents she was all right before they had left for California in December, two months later than their usual migration, but only three months after David died. Then they insisted she come down around Christmas when the office slowed down anyway. None of it had kept her from sinking into a mire of depression by mid-January. By February she knew she couldn't go on. She closed the office temporarily and Iris had sent her packing to Palm Springs, where her parents doted on her with a gentle love that kept her afloat. She couldn't worry them now.

"I'm all right, Mom. But it'll be nice to have you

back next week."

"You sound tired, dear. I don't want you to do any work for the Seder. We'll be back Monday — Daddy and I'll come over and do everything. Wait till you see the pretty Seder plate I picked up here."

"Your mother thinks if she spends enough on a Seder plate the Messiah will come to our door instead of Mrs. Cohen's."

"Who's Mrs. Cohen?" Flo asked.

"Do we have to have a Seder?" her father interrupted. "Couldn't we just have the guilt-free dinners we used to have before Susan married a rabbi?"

Rebecca smiled. Her sister's husband was an academic who taught Jewish history at McGill University in Montreal.

"You know you like Ben," Flo said. "And it won't kill you to be a Jew once a year. Besides, you need to concentrate less on food. Rebecca, tell your father to stop snacking on chips and pretzels. All that salt and fat is pushing up his blood pressure."

"What's it at?" Rebecca asked.

"It's not so bad," Mitch said. "160 over 90."

"Sometimes 95," Flo added.

"Not time to panic yet," Rebecca said. "Why don't you try some air-popped popcorn?"

"Isn't that girl a genius?" said her mother.

"If she was so smart, she'd know we left our air-popper in Toronto," Mitch said. "I got to tell you a doctor story about our neighbour. Mrs. Goldblum."

"Mitch, we don't have a neighbour Mrs. Gold...."

"Sha. I met her on the elevator when you were sleeping. So Mrs. Goldblum is maybe ninety-four and she insists on telling me this story even though I don't know her from Adam. She says she went to the doctor with this embarrassing problem. She told him,

119

'I pass gas all the time' — actually she said 'fart' — 'but they're soundless and don't smell. You won't believe this but since I've been here I've farted twenty times. What can I do, Doctor?' So the doctor gave her a prescription for pills. She should take them three times a day for seven days and then come back to see him in a week. The next week Mrs. Goldblum marched into his office, furious. She said, 'Doctor, I don't know what was in those pills but the problem is worse. I'm farting as much and they're still soundless but now they smell terrible. What do you say for yourself?' The doctor said, 'Calm down, Mrs. Goldblum. Now that we've fixed your sinuses, we'll work on your hearing.' "

Rebecca closed her eyes and smiled. Some things didn't change.

"Your father makes up a neighbour every time he wants to tell a joke."

"Your mother just won't admit she takes an afternoon nap. Mrs. Goldblum lives on the other side of the garbage chute. Honest. Besides, good medical jokes are scarce as hen's teeth. And what else can I tell our daughter the Doctor?"

"I think she's heard enough jokes for one night," Flo said. "We have to let the poor girl get some sleep. You do sound tired, dear. We'll call again on Saturday. Or if you feel like talking, call anytime."

"Can't wait to see you, doll," her father said.

Rebecca lay back in bed, exhausted, but couldn't sleep. It was comforting to hear their voices. Yet she couldn't help feeling that everything in her life had turned upside-down again. The sense of vulnerability when David died, the aloneness, stole back into her life like a phantom. She tossed and flailed in her bed. The air in the room was so close she could barely breathe.

She was suffocating in her own bed. Then she realized that the door was shut — she never closed her bedroom door, something was lurking behind it, something she almost recognized.

Suddenly someone was pounding her front door with ferocity. They pummelled and banged with unreasonable force until Rebecca checked outside the window, wondering if she could climb down the two floors to the ground. The dark outside was impenetrable. How would she get down? It would be like falling into an abyss. They were yelling something unintelligible downstairs so she opened her bedroom door to hear better. Though she knew the bedroom was upstairs, the front door had somehow moved directly across the hall and now she knew terror because it was brutally clear that she couldn't escape.

"*¡Abra la puerta!*" screamed a man's voice. "*¡Abra la puerta!*" The pounding continued.

She tried her utmost not to approach the door but something pulled her there, an old curiosity, an ancient fate.

"Who's there?" she asked, her own voice echoing in the hall.

Hard fists answered her. "*¡Abra la puerta!*"

"I know what you want and I'm not coming." Even as the words spilled out, she watched her own hands betray her and open the deadbolt on the door. *Her own hands.*

Five men with guns fell on her and pinned her arms behind her back. Everything was in shadow. "Okay, bitch, where is she?"

Terrified, she cried, "I don't know!" But on the couch, barely visible in the dark, lay a woman facing the other way, unknowable.

"Lying bitch!" they said.

Then one man stepped forward, his face still obscured by the shadows. "My colleagues are crude, doctor. They like to hurt people. Why not cooperate, just help us get the old woman the way you helped us get Goldie."

Rebecca gasped, shrieked toward the shadow-man. "It wasn't me. I loved her."

One of them was about to hit her across the face when the phone rang. They all stared at it, until one of the men said not to answer it; another said she must answer it because someone probably knew she was home. A third man picked up the receiver but said nothing. As he moved in the dark room, a slat of light from somewhere found his face. It was Feldberg.

Her eyelids burst open. The back of her neck felt damp and cool from sweat evaporating into the morning. The noise of the phone beside her was relentless.

She picked it up automatically, but she couldn't quite recall what day it was or why she felt so awful. All she remembered was the dark outline of the woman floating on the couch in her dream.

"Rebecca? Are you all right? Have you seen the paper?"

Rebecca blinked at the clock on the mantle. Seven-thirty. The woman on the couch — Rebecca knew now. It had been Chana.

"Are you awake?" said the voice.

"Oh, Iris, I'm sorry. I should've called you ... I didn't think...."

"What on earth happened?" asked Iris. "It says Mrs. Kochinsky is dead."

Rebecca knew this stretch of Bathurst Street from her adolescence when she had frequented the Jewish "Y" north of Sheppard Avenue. For several summers she and her friends had spent whole afternoons reclining around the outdoor pool meeting unsuitable boys. Twenty years later, the "Y" was still there. She was glad to be driving against traffic in the morning rush hour as she caught a glimpse of the 1960s white stone building, updated, added on to. It was sprawled on the edge of a ravine that extended from south of Sheppard all the way up past the northern boundaries of the city, a greenbelt along whose bottom groove snaked the Don River. Only a river could stop developers from paving over the grass from end to end. No matter that in some places the riverbed spanned a mere four feet. There was no way of getting around a river, its inevitable pull, like gravity, toward the lake, so one had to accept it gracefully and incorporate it into the plan. The ravine this April was still pallid, the trees bare, but there was an expectancy in the branches, a knowledge of green beneath the dormant grass that Rebecca wished she could be part of.

She had begun to feel a connection before Goldie died. She couldn't think of her as Mrs. Kochinsky anymore; she had gotten too close for that. Rebecca had been almost optimistic, as far as that went; not very far considering the state of her psyche. But it had all flattened out. No, not flattened. Sunk. Declined. She was going to have to catch herself on the decline, or someone else would. The man who killed Goldie, whoever he was. She had to find out what she could now. She was hoping against hope that Chana could tell her something. Goldie had visited her sister frequently. Maybe she'd said something about the man she thought was going to kill her.

Once past Finch, Rebecca kept her eye out for Sunnydale Terrace, the only other nursing home she knew of on Bathurst besides Baycrest Hospital. Baycrest was the model in Toronto, the queen of geriatric medicine, not a waiting-room for death like those places usually were. She hated Feldberg for his cheapness. Poorer people were in Baycrest.

The sign came into view announcing a two-storey box of a building, probably the same vintage as the "Y," only not updated. The red brick had lasted the decades well enough, but the place had a desultory look to it, sun-faded curtains stretched crookedly across the upstairs windows.

Rebecca stepped up to the reception desk where a slim dark-haired woman sat in an exaggerated upright position listening on the phone. A plump blonde in a short skirt was passing behind her.

"Excuse me," Rebecca said.

The blonde looked at her but hardly stopped moving. Rebecca had seen the look before. Professionals in hospitals saved it for people they didn't need to pay attention to. That meant everyone except doctors. There was another expression altogether they saved for doctors.

"I'm Dr. Temple," Rebecca said crisply, delighted to see the woman stop in her tracks and rearrange her face. There, that was the expression she wanted. A bit of deference. "I'm looking for Chana Feldberg."

The blonde smiled a tight polite smile as she came around the desk. "Mrs. Feldberg is up in her room. Is this a professional visit, Doctor, or are you a relative?"

"I was her sister's physician. Mrs. Kochinsky. Have the police come by to speak to Mrs. Feldberg?"

The blonde put her stubby hands together in front of her. "I was horrified to hear about what happened. It shocked us all here. The police called this morning but I explained Mrs. Feldberg's condition to them and they left it up to us to deal with it."

"And what is her condition?" Rebecca asked, getting a bad feeling from the woman's tone of voice.

"Her behaviour has regressed. We think there's some dementia involved. Maybe Alzheimer's. Most of the time she won't verbalize and when she does, it's in Yiddish. If we didn't feed her, she wouldn't eat. Even then, she'll only eat in her room, refuses to socialize. It's difficult for the staff."

There was little expression in her voice except for a slight whine.

"Have you told her about her sister's death?" Rebecca asked.

"The social worker and I believe she wouldn't understand, and in so far as she's able to understand, we feel it wouldn't be in her best interests to be told. It would just upset her."

And that would be difficult for *you*, thought Rebecca.

"I'd like to see her," she said.

The blonde glanced at her briefly, only in acknowledgement, no challenge. Rebecca knew her own authority, but suspected that the woman had reservations about Rebecca's role: was she going to tell Chana and set her off for good? Rebecca could leave after this visit and not come back. The staff had to deal with the patient afterwards. None of this was voiced but Rebecca sensed it in the stiff resentful walk of the chubby woman in front of her, rather brisk considering the heels and tight white skirt. As it happened Rebecca hadn't yet decided what she would tell Chana. She despised the power professionals reserved for themselves in making decisions for their charges, though she knew that it was sometimes necessary in cases of patient incompetence.

They stopped in front of room 201. Down the hall

a thin craggy-faced man leaned on a cane and watched them. Rebecca hated these places. Waiting for death. The blonde knocked on the door. There was no answer from inside the room, nor did the blonde expect any for she opened the door several seconds later. A tiny bird of a woman sat in a wooden upholstered chair facing the window. She turned her head in anticipation, her face somewhat animated. When she saw Rebecca, her eyes went blank, her cheeks slackened, and she turned back to the window. It was disappointment, Rebecca realized with a chill, that she wasn't Goldie.

"You have a visitor, dear," said the blonde in a raised voice. "Dr. Temple has come to see you."

No response. "Mrs. Feldberg...." The blonde raised her voice another notch.

"It's all right," Rebecca broke in. "We'll be fine."

Rebecca stepped into the room; the woman clicked the door closed.

On the wall to her right stood a desk with a portable sewing machine in the corner. Small stacks of colourful fabric stretched across the back of the desk. It all looked too neat, as if it were never touched. Rebecca imagined Goldie bringing her sister material to tempt her into activity.

Rebecca brought the only other chair close to the old woman and sat down. Chana's unwashed grey hair lay thin and flat against her tiny head. Her skin was nearly transparent, the skull beneath poking through. She had once been beautiful, Rebecca knew from her photos. Now her eyes sunk amid features that mingled with bone. She stared out the window but appeared to see nothing. Rebecca followed her eyes toward Bathurst Street and beyond. Across the road, extending as far as she could see, were cemeteries, both Jewish and Christian. Some joke, she thought. The universe was filled with jokes like these. That Rebecca was here at all was a joke. What could this ghost of a woman possibly tell her? Especially since Rebecca couldn't speak Yiddish.

"I'm Dr. Temple," she said. "Your sister's doctor." She wondered if Chana had regressed beyond the ken of English or whether she was just more comfortable using Yiddish.

Though Rebecca had spoken quietly, the woman was startled, her hands beginning to tremble. That was when Rebecca noticed the doll in Chana's lap. An uncomfortable pang of recognition went through her. The doll was a match to the one in Goldie's bedroom, made of coarse grey cotton and striped clothes.

"What an unusual doll. May I see it?" Rebecca asked, holding out her palm.

Without expression, Chana grabbed the doll tightly, and pressed it close to her breast, bringing the other hand up as a shield.

"Then again," Rebecca said. "I can see it from here."

"You know, your sister Goldie has one of these dolls in her bedroom." No reaction from Chana.

"Your sister tells me she comes to visit you. When was the last time she was here?"

Chana stared out the window, her expression unchanged. Rebecca had gotten a basic response from her before. Maybe the woman was capable of more.

"When your sister was here, did she talk about a man? A man who frightened her? Did she say anything about him? What he looked like? This is important, Mrs. Feldberg."

The woman's eyes remained fixed but they suddenly shifted from the window to the bed. That was progress, thought Rebecca. Now the woman was avoiding her. Rebecca followed her gaze to the bed. Perhaps Chana was communicating. On the flowered comforter near the pillow, a dozen more misshapen cloth figures in the same prison stripes lay camouflaged amid the vibrant colours of the bedclothes that, Rebecca imagined, Goldie had picked for her sister.

"Could I see one of those?" Rebecca asked softly.

When there was no response, Rebecca stood up and stepped across the floor. She glanced back at Chana hoping for permission. The old eyes were empty. Rebecca bent over slowly, giving Chana time to voice any objections. None were forthcoming and Rebecca picked up a doll.

"*Kinder*," a dry voice croaked.

When Rebecca looked up, Chana's small eyes watched her. Good, thought Rebecca, at least a response. *Kinder*. Children.

"*Kinder*," Rebecca repeated, hoping for more. But Chana seemed all talked out.

Rebecca turned the doll in her hand, marvelling at the primitive simpleness of the thing, very much like a grey sock with arms and legs sewn around. Some brown yarn tacked on for hair, a few stitches for eyes and mouth. Not much uniformity. The object must've been to crank out a population of inmates but she hadn't stuck to a pattern. Each one seemed a new beginning, each an individual. The doll in Rebecca's hand wore rough trousers, but a number of figures on the bed wore skirts, all of the same striped fabric. Chana must've sewn each of them along a bitter journey backwards into some depth of memory. Her sewing table appeared abandoned. Perhaps she'd sewn these in the early stages of her illness. Rebecca knew that the trauma suffered by victims in concentration camps was a wound that never healed. These figures were clearly images from that period. Had the regression halted there, in that time of nightmare?

Rebecca glanced at Chana, whose bony face could have been one of the pitiful multitude staring out from behind barbed wire in the photos she'd seen of camp survivors. Rebecca's eye was drawn to the doll whose head poked out above Chana's hand. Something was different about it. Beneath the yarn hair, the head was tightly covered with red gauze, the eyes and mouth stitched over it. Rebecca peeked back at the bed. She focused on each doll till she found two more with red-covered heads.

"*Kinder*," Chana said.

"*Kinder*," Rebecca repeated. She wanted a closer look. "May I?" she said, as a formality.

But as soon as she picked up the two red dolls, Chana began to moan. Rebecca glanced at her, surprised.

"*Nisht kinder!*" she wailed "*Nisht kinder!*"

"All right," Rebecca said. "I'm sorry." She put them down but near the edge of the bed where she could examine them. One doll was a match to the one Chana held, only male to her female, both heads covered with red gauze. The other doll was definitely different. Its trousers were not striped like the other males, but black, worn with a black jacket and cap. This was a uniform. She screwed up her eyes to try to decipher the irregular object sewn onto the end of its arm. A greyish form, probably a gun. What was the significance of these dolls, especially the three with their sanguine, forbidden heads?

Goldie used to describe to Rebecca the elegant clothes Chana sewed for her. It was hard to fathom that the same hand that had created Goldie's wardrobe had fashioned these crude representations. Yet what was the point of fathoming? Chana was lost somewhere within herself, unable to give Rebecca directions. Whatever Goldie had told Chana was lost

with her, the words rattling around somewhere amid
forty-year-old memories.

chapter fifteen

Thursday, April 5, 1979

Nesha opened the door of his hotel room and waited, one hand leaning against the frame, the other grasping a can of Coke. The front desk had called to say a courier had arrived with a package for him. Something from his accountant. Could they send the guy up? They sure bloody well could. How long had he been waiting for this?

Down the plush distant hall, someone in a black baseball cap bobbed up and down at a gallop. A young East Indian man stopped at Nesha's open door, eyeing the scraggly hair, probably writing off any possibility of a tip. He read the name off the front of the package.

"Mr. Malkevich?"

"Yep."

He gave Nesha a form to sign then handed him the padded envelope.

The man was about to fly but Nesha reached into

his pants pocket and brought out an American five dollar bill.

The dark eyes widened beneath the cap, then narrowed into a smile. "Thanks, man."

In the room, Nesha took his penknife and slit open the top of the padded envelope that he had taped so firmly shut in San Francisco. He pulled out all the extra paper and crumpled junk mail filling out the empty spaces that would have given shape to the object he wanted to render shapeless.

Finally he drew out the Luger, a hard bit of reality poking out of his dream of the past. He held it flat in his palm, entranced by the silky cold of the steel. This was no ordinary gun. With his connections he could have arranged to buy something in Toronto. But this was the gun he wanted. The symbolic value was worth all the effort. He had called in a favour from a former client. The man had Nesha to thank — at least, Nesha's experience with the intricate workings of the IRS — for the accumulation of capital that helped him expand his business. Evading taxes was a democratic right. It also helped him afford the small plane that flew Nesha's package over the U.S. border, avoiding customs. A Canadian courier company had taken it from there.

He had taken care of the Luger these long years, cleaning, swabbing, polishing his dark token of hope with only one thought: justice. Justice for his family. And for how many others? He had waited patiently for the right time to bring out the gun. This was the right time.

The immanence of a confrontation left him winded. It had been thirty-eight years since he'd been that little boy. Thirty-eight years since he'd last seen his mother, his little brother. He gripped the textured butt, his heart racing, flying with excitement. He looked up into the mirror, half expecting to find that ten-year-old boy. He hardly recognized the face he saw there. It was like watching himself from the outside. His eyes had grown round and stark. Together with the greying beard, the hair, he looked quite mad. For once this displeased him.

If he was going to succeed, he needed to become part of the scenery, to blend in with whatever background his prey had become accustomed to. He would have to think about that. Turning himself around in front of the mirror, he worked to position the barrel comfortably inside the waistband of his pants in the middle of his back. It was time.

He took the photocopy out of his suitcase. He needed his magnifying glass to read the name of the store in the smudgy backdrop behind the duck. The Toronto phone book, thicker than he had expected, lay in the hotel dresser. Leafing through the parchment-thin pages he found the name he was looking for. He located the address on the street map he had taken from the rental car. The place was not far, as distances went. He would scout it out first by subway, maybe by streetcar. He would find it, all the while warmed by the constant bulk of the metal pinned near the small of his back.

He was surprised at how cold it was in Toronto the first week of April. The sun gave off a milky thin halo of light, hardly what he would call spring. It had been warmer in San Francisco in the winter.

The subway he rode north to Queen's Park was brisk and clean. Climbing the stairs to the surface he found, in the shelter of a glassed-in corner, a hot dog vendor with his portable stand and a middle-aged woman in an expensive ski jacket selling daffodils. The Cancer Campaign. An excellent cause. He, himself, was planning to eradicate a deadly cancer. He only had to find it, the rest would be easy. He shifted his back to reassure himself with the weight of his weapon, his own answer to medicine.

The wide intersection roared with the tumult of six lanes of cars flying north and south on either side of sculptured stone boulevards; the whine of trolley cars rolling east and west. A short distance north, the six-lane artery split to ring around a massive rose-coloured structure, gracefully Victorian and surrounded by lawns. The seat of the provincial government, according to his Toronto guidebook. He pulled out the street map and tried to orient himself. Keep going west.

He passed large ivy-covered houses that had been converted and taken over by the university; here and there some boxy, slightly newer buildings housed the departments of botany, engineering, and architecture. Students did not linger here. All the young men and women were in a hurry, carrying their books to the next appointment. If he remembered correctly, they were probably writing exams. Many were alone, but none as alone as he. Nobody on earth knew where he was. (Maybe Louis could have made a wild guess; Louis, who had been there when the whole thing started again, in the Wiesenthal Center.) Nobody else. All he had to worry about now was God. And he did worry about God, God the instigator, God the creator of species that ate each other, of people who killed others for treasure as arcane as a Yankees jacket. God the sadist. What else could describe a being that set up a system where the large were forced to hunt the small for every meal. It was better to think of God as dead than to think of Him as evil. In either case, life was meaningless. Those who didn't see it were just fooling themselves.

Uncle Sol had been just such a fool. What did he

used to say? When God closes one door, He opens another. That little lesson had been lost on Nesha. Doors had only closed for him. What about this door? This door would be the shadowy entrance that led him into the abyss. Louis had been the gatekeeper. When he heard Louis' voice, Nesha had hoped it was a call for contributions. Nesha's brain had arranged fortresses around itself, prepared for onslaught. He remembered standing before Louis in the Center, what — a week ago? The man's mouth dropped open, framing a pink "O" beneath his trim moustache. Nesha saw himself mirrored in the other man's eyes: overgrown beard and hair, jeans, sneakers. Every year he had come to the Center to search for news of the man, and every year he had grown more ragged, whereas Louis had been a constant: compact and well-groomed, hair clipped short. Louis had left him alone in the room but Nesha couldn't keep the excitement to himself when he finally found a scrap, a hint of what he had been looking for; couldn't help showing Louis with shy triumph what he had found. He could hardly fathom it had been only a week.

Nesha shook California off and turned down a street with desperate lawns and dingy porches. The two-storey near-shabby Victorian houses were painted like the ones at home, but the colours were different. The gingerbread trim was white, but here the brick was painted solid red or green, strong unyielding colours to keep out the cold of the Canadian winter. In San Francisco houses like these were coloured pastel blue or yellow or pink, sometimes all at once, reflecting the dreamy seascape of the Pacific.

As he got closer to his destination, students thinned out and were replaced by shoppers. Some ragged men shambled near the ethnic shops, trying to catch a sympathetic eye for a handout. Many in the crowd were Asian. He could easily have been back home in San Francisco's Chinatown.

A small elderly Chinese woman in trousers and drab winter jacket stood near a stall arranging apples. She looked up as he passed by and held one out to him, a large red Delicious. He stopped, charmed by this gesture, shy and aggressive at the same time.

"Is it always so cold in Toronto?" he asked, pulling some change from his pocket.

She began to chatter in some mysterious dialect, prodding the apple closer to his chest. As she opened her mouth into the strange shapes of her language, he could see she had almost no teeth. Biting into the apple, he nodded appreciation, and moved on.

All at once, he stopped, mesmerized by the shops across the narrow street. He drew the photocopy of the duck from his pocket and compared, though he knew as soon as he saw it. He had found what he was looking for. He had arrived at the location of the cancer and now it was just a matter of rooting out the centre. He had the instrument ready. Like a surgeon, he had the tool for the job. He threw the half-eaten apple into a carton of trash and looped his arm behind to stroke the comforting bulge beneath his jacket with tentative fingers.

chapter sixteen

Thursday, April 5, 1979

Bubie's Bakery was on Eglinton, one and a half blocks from Mrs. Kochinsky's duplex. Rebecca used to come here for bread when she still had an appetite, before David died. Before she had lost the insulating flesh on her bones. She was always surprised when she came across herself unexpectedly, like this morning in the paper. She had unfolded it and scanned the front page till she found the headline: "Senior Strangled in Own Home/Police Follow Lead." At first she didn't recognize herself in the photo, a grim, distracted shot. It was Mrs. Kochinsky's duplex, the front yard skirted by police tape, that caught her eye. Then her own face, grey and blurry in the foreground. She couldn't say it was a bad likeness of her, only one she would have preferred to keep shut away in a mirror in the privacy of her bedroom where she could still convince herself she was alive and well. She pictured the killer scrutinizing the photo. It would just make it that much easier for him. At least the reporter had gotten very little information from the police. Her name was not mentioned, nor any important details of the crime. She supposed she ought to be grateful.

In the bakery two elderly women in white uniforms stood behind the counter serving a few customers when Rebecca entered. The satisfying aroma of baking bread swelled from the back in a pervasive cloud.

"Can I help you?" one of the women addressed Rebecca in a Yiddish accent. Her stylishly short hair was dyed reddish brown; her eyes sparkled.

"I'm looking for Rosie," said Rebecca across the glass shelves of rolls and pastries. Which of the two would it be?

"That's me," said the woman surprised. "I'm Rosie."

"I'm Goldie Kochinsky's doctor, Rebecca Temple."

The sparkle went out of her eyes. "She's sick, God forbid? I yesterday wondered where she is. I tried phone her...." She stopped, seeing something in Rebecca's face.

"You haven't read the paper?" said Rebecca.

The woman wavered on the spot, her round face turning pale. "Newspapers I don't read. Too depressing." She motioned Rebecca to move toward the back door where they could speak directly over a counter rather than across shelves of kaiser buns and danishes.

"If it's in the papers, it must be bad."

Rebecca told her as gently as she could, if one could relate a brutal act in any terms but violent. She hated being the bearer of bad news, though as a doctor she was thrust into that role too often.

Rosie held onto the counter for support.

"Rose," the other server called out, "there are customers here!"

Suddenly in the doorway leading to the back, a large

lumpy man in an undershirt smeared with flour appeared. Displeasure with Rosie turned into puzzlement as he watched her lead Rebecca past him into the back.

"Oy, this is no good, I gotta sit down." Rosie held her stomach as if she suddenly had a bellyache, then collapsed into a floury chair. Her eyes clouded over; a tear drifted quietly down her cheek.

"I don't understand," she said, her voice cracking. "Goldie's dead? Murdered in her house? No, I don't believe it. I don't believe it." She sat doubled over a moment, tears dropping on the tile floor mixing with the flour.

Finally she sat up with a deep sigh. "Why would someone do this?"

"You have any idea?"

Rosie wiped a tear then flapped her hand through the air. "She could drive you crazy, but to kill her..."

"Did she tell you about her past? Where she came from?"

"Ach! The background, very bad. Terrible things she went through. *This* drove her crazy. Sometimes I remember, a customer walk into store and she runs to the back. 'He's here for me,' she says. 'He's gonna get me.' The guy walk out. Nothing." Rosie tapped her index finger against her temple. "I felt sorry, but what I could do?"

"Did you see her Tuesday?"

Rosie thought. "Only in the morning. She worked till maybe lunch. Then she went somewhere. Downtown, I think."

"Wasn't that unusual?" Rebecca asked.

"Sure. I was surprised. She had to go on the bus."

"Did she say where she was going?"

"To be honest I didn't pay attention. She was telling me while I was serving a customer and ... well, I loved her but she could drive you crazy with her stories."

Rosie got up abruptly and took a few steps to a corner where her purse leaned against the wall. She retrieved her wallet and from it she handed a photo to Rebecca. In the photo, Rosie and Goldie stood in the bakery, shoulder to shoulder, happily grinning at the camera. Rebecca felt a pang of loss.

"You know, must've been a store," Rosie said, ruminating. "The place she went Tuesday. I remember something. I know sounds funny, but I think the name was after a river."

So she hadn't just gone shopping. Rebecca recalled the confusion with Goldie's English the day the poor woman had run into the office. Rebecca had heard a verb where Goldie had meant a noun. The cousin had asked her *for* a shop, a particular shop, not to *go shopping*, as Rebecca had understood.

"A river?"

"You know, in the name. A famous river."

"You mean like the 'Mississippi' Shoe Store?"

Rosie stared at her bleakly. "I'm sorry, I only trying to help."

"I'm not making fun of you," said Rebecca. "I'm just thinking out loud. Would it make any difference if I told you the place was within walking distance of Beverley and Dundas?"

She shook her head. "You know more than me."

"She came to me very frightened Tuesday afternoon," Rebecca said. "All I know is she walked to my office from wherever she was. She was killed that night."

"She came to you before she was killed?" Rosie watched her horrified and perplexed. The unstated question: Why didn't you do something?

A lump formed in Rebecca's throat. "Could I

borrow this photo?" she asked. "I'll get it back to you."

Rebecca felt the woman's uncomprehending eyes follow her as she left the store.

chapter seventeen

Rebecca drove home along Eglinton Avenue with Rosie's voice ringing in her ears: She came to you before she was killed? She came to you...? It was barely 9:15 a.m. and Rebecca was already tired.

She had a few hours before her first patient, scheduled at one. She thought of flipping through the Yellow Pages to look for the store Rosie had mentioned — if it was a store — but she didn't know where to begin. She couldn't look up restaurants or furniture or garden supplies. All she knew (and that was probably too strong a word for it) was that there might be a river in the name of it, whatever it was. A river. How many rivers did she know the names of? The Mackenzie, the Missouri, the Thames....

From habit Rebecca's eyes searched out the watercolour on the wall of the den. The only painting of David's she hadn't taken down to store in the basement. It had been hard to come across them at every corner of the house. Now it was just hard in the den. David had painted her in profile sitting with her ankles tucked beneath her on a green verge of grass by the lake. The picture was bathed in the kind of golden light the sun might deliver on a late afternoon in summer. He had told her she was like the sea when he made love to her because she was all around him, she was everywhere, and he had to submerge himself in her even if he drowned. She hadn't the heart to take this one down.

Okay, the river. She stepped over to the bookcase in the den and retrieved an atlas. Happily, there was a page on world statistics: the largest countries, the highest mountains, the most populated cities, and among this fascinating lot, the one she needed — the longest, ergo best-known, rivers. Only she couldn't imagine how anyone would work them into the name of something in downtown Toronto. The Nile What. The Amazon Something. The Yangtze Such and Such. And there were columns of them, rivers she had never heard of, rivers she had forgotten about. There was no easy way to find what she was looking for. She would just have to get on with it.

She was putting on her jacket when the phone rang.

"Rebecca? Are you all right, dear?" said the Polish-accented voice. "I saw your picture in the paper and I got worried."

That awful picture of her coming out of Goldie's place. "I'm fine, Sarah; thank you." Rebecca didn't want her mother-in-law to worry; she was still getting over the death of her son.

"Was it someone you knew?"

"A patient of mine."

"I'm so sorry. What a terrible thing. Is there anything I can do to help?"

"I'm fine, really." Sarah was an elegant, cultured woman who loved art and had imparted that love to her son. She had been responsible for David being the man he was and Rebecca would always be grateful to her for that. But his death, instead of bringing them closer together, had formed a wedge between them, each reminding the other of their loss.

By 10:15, Rebecca was driving along College Street at a snail's pace in the right hand lane. While she read the names of each shop on both sides of the street, drivers who found themselves behind her honked and veered to the left to pass. Gino's Hardware, College Gifts, Margo's Donuts and Coffee Shop. Drier than dry. No hint of river, lake, or stream.

A few blocks east of Bathurst, she made an illegal U-turn and drove back along College Street, reasoning that Mrs. Kochinsky wouldn't have been able to run to the office from further afield. Rebecca turned down Spadina and suddenly came to a full stop. While traffic whizzed around her, she sat just north of a street that intersected Spadina and led into Kensington Market.

She felt as if she were poised on the edge of a time warp. The market, its chaotic goods stacked and sprawled on the sidewalks under sun-faded awnings, looked like it could toss her back fifty years. The genteel veneer of Beverley Street, barely two blocks away, may as well have been on the moon. She blinked at the crisply painted sign several stores down the side street: Atlantic Seafood. What if Rosie didn't know an ocean from a river? What if her translation from the Jewish was slightly off? Rebecca parked and set out on foot.

She stood at the corner facing the noisy clutter of the narrow street jammed with small shops and cars. Pungent smells of butchers and fishmongers and God knows what else trailed into hints on the air. She approached Atlantic Seafood. Iridescent layers of whitefish, red snapper, and perch glimmered on beds of crushed ice outside the store. The effect was esthetic, spoiled only by their blank eyes, empty as glass.

Inside the store, two dark Mediterranean-looking men stood wiping down the cutting boards behind a counter piled with shrimp and snails.

"Can I help you?" one of the men asked.

She reached into her shoulder bag and pulled out the photo she had taken from Rosie. "I'm trying to find my aunt," she said, showing him the picture. "The one on the left. She may've come in here on Tuesday. She was wearing a beige trenchcoat and polyester pants. She had ... she has an accent."

The man reached across the counter and took the photo, showing it to his partner. "I don't know, lady. Lots of people come in here. I don't know if I'd remember. Why don't you go to the police?"

Rebecca looked at their faces. There was no guile; they didn't know and they didn't care. "Are there any other fish stores in the market?"

"You kidding?" he said, handing her back the photo. "Probably five on every street."

Outside Rebecca squeezed by sidewalks that shrank around stalls of fresh fruit and vegetables and spices by the pound. A skinny cat slunk into an alley to forage through the garbage. She passed stores that sold *schmatas* and handbags and gifts from the Orient. Lucky for her, the other fish stores bore names like Joe's Fish, Kensington Fish, and Ontario Seafood.

Down the street a truck was being unloaded. As little room as there was on the sidewalks, at least people could move through. The same couldn't be said for the road where cars parked along one side left a single lane for the one-way traffic. The delivery truck was parked half on the road, half on the sidewalk, effectively blocking the only lane open. A line-up of cars that had turned down the market street could go nowhere, their exhausts humming with poison. Pedestrians managed to squeeze by single file. As Rebecca approached, a man inside the elevated back gate of the truck flipped a huge side of beef onto the waiting shoulders of another, standing on the road. Sinew-red with the leg still on, it looked alive, as if it would jump down and walk away if the man let go. He started toward her, carrying it slung between his head and shoulder the way one carries a child high above a crowd. She stopped and gasped as he carried the thing toward her. Pale cushions of fat bloated the surface of the meat; blood from the flesh grazed his hair, his collar. In her panic she retreated into some shoppers, then swung across the street between the cars.

Standing on the opposite sidewalk she stared across at the butcher's. The morning sun glanced off the metal of the sign. In the window David hung by his feet upside down, his back to her. She began to run. The cold wind chilled the sweat off her neck and she thought of Goldie. She imagined Goldie running, running through the streets just as Rebecca was running now. From what? From herself? Shoppers moved aside from her as if she were crazy. As if she were Goldie. Rebecca was nearly back to Spadina again when she realized the shops had ended abruptly, giving way to the sudden high grey wall of George Brown College, a building wildly out of place here, too linear, too simply rendered in the complex spring sun.

Then she saw it. The noise from the cars on Spadina was suddenly deafening. She had found her river and it flowed loud. Not more than three shops in from Spadina stood Blue Danube Fish.

Then came water and quenched the fire
That burned the stick that beat the dog
That bit the cat that ate the goat
That Father bought for two zuzim.
  One little goat, one little goat.

chapter eighteen

Standing at the window Rebecca could see a darkened hovel of a room whose green-grey walls did not reflect light but absorbed it. A solitary fish lay on the newspaper-clad counter just inside the window, a feeble attempt at advertisement. Behind the heavy wooden counter to the left, a woman lurked in the shadows.

The smell overpowered Rebecca as soon as she opened the door. She stood on the threshold to let her eyes and nose adjust. The place reeked. A woman stood behind an ancient, crusted counter, filleting a fish as if she could do it with her eyes closed, slow but steady. The back of her black hair hung down to her shoulders; the rest was gathered off her face into an elastic at the crown, revealing a widow's peak. Despite the teenage hairstyle, the woman was middle-aged. Her eyes were badly pencilled, her prominent cheekbones ruddy.

"Can I help you?" she asked.

A handmade wooden tub filled with water stood off to one side. Nearby a makeshift partition of plywood painted the same green-grey. In the corner was a closed door.

Moving closer, Rebecca noticed the woman's apron was muddy with old blood. She held up the photo of Goldie. "Did you see this woman on Tuesday?"

The fishmonger stared at the photo. Her arms were plump, waiting, as she held the knife. "Why d'you wanna know?"

"I'm trying to trace her movements."

The woman had outlined her eyes in black pencil as if they were circles. She pursed her lips while examining the picture. "She missing?"

Rebecca barely paused. "Something like that."

"She was just coming in when I went for lunch," said the woman, starting to work the knife again. "I didn't talk to her or nothing. Max must've served her."

"What time was that?"

"Twelve. Maybe twelve-thirty."

"Did she seem upset?"

The woman shrugged. "Only saw her for a second. Didn't really notice." Her eyes dulled; as far as she was concerned, the conversation was finished.

Rebecca heard a shuffling behind the partition door. "Could I speak to Max?" she asked.

The woman's head came up. She eyed Rebecca up and down, half turned her head toward the closed door. "He's not here."

"Could I have his number? It's important that I speak to him."

"Look, Max is busy. He's always busy." The woman's forehead had turned as red as her cheeks. "If it's your mother or something, maybe you should go to the cops."

"Actually, it's my aunt...," Rebecca began.

"Well, leave me a number. Maybe he'll call you."

Without warning, a tall man emerged from the back door. His dark greying hair curled at the nape of his neck. He wore a navy blue turtleneck that sharpened the blue of his eyes. He was not young, but had aged gracefully.

"What's all the commotion, Mona?" he said, irritated. His accent was German.

Mona's body turned stiff, awkward, almost angry. "I didn't want to bother you, Maxie." She pointed her thumb at Rebecca.

He turned to look at Rebecca and his handsome face rearranged itself. His high forehead relaxed beneath the wavy hair; the lines moved up instead of down. His eyes became the colour of calm water. She was both puzzled and flattered by the frank stare.

Mona cleared her throat abruptly. "She wants to ask about her aunt."

"How can I help you?" His accent had softened.

"I need some information," Rebecca said holding up the photo. "This woman came in here on Tuesday."

He stepped forward, not taking his eyes off Rebecca, then delicately took the picture from her hand. He looked briefly at it. "I'm afraid I don't recall her."

Rebecca glanced at the woman with the pencilled eyes. "I was told she came in here and that you served her."

They both turned to Mona, who flushed. "I musta made a mistake. I'm not sure it was her. Maybe it was somebody else."

Max shook his head at her feeble attempts. "Never mind," he said. Then turning to Rebecca, "We better straighten this out. Won't you come in the back?"

Mona's jaw was set as Rebecca followed Max behind the wall. He walked self-consciously in front, a well-built man whose age was not quite definable,

153

shoulders wide beneath the cotton turtleneck.

The room behind the wall ran the width of the store. To the left, a door exited into a laneway that was visible through a window. Wooden crates were stacked against the opposite wall. Max turned right on entering, leading her to a desk covered with papers and several books left open face up on their hardcover spines.

Across from the desk and chair stood four-foot-high bookcases stuffed with oversized art books. Red velvet draped the tops of the cases at eye level. Set in a row on the cloth were finely wrought objects that surprised Rebecca: a filigreed spice box in the shape of a miniature house; a brass Chanukkah menorah whose row of nine tiny candle holders Rebecca recognized from her childhood when her mother lit the candles on the holiday. A large silver goblet. And of all things, a Seder plate.

He pulled his own chair out from behind the desk and motioned her to sit down. Clearing a space on the desk, he perched on the edge of it.

"Let's get one thing straight," he said. "I know this woman is dead. Mona may not read the paper, but I do. Who are you, and why did you come here?"

"My name is Rebecca Temple. I was the dead woman's physician. I seem to be the only one interested in her murder. The police think she was killed during a robbery."

"You don't."

"I think someone meant to kill her. I just don't know why. You are…?"

"Max Vogel. I'm afraid I can't help you. She was barely coherent when she came here."

"What did she want?"

"Information. I couldn't give it."

"What information?"

"Just some questions about someone I know. It was nothing."

"Who was it?"

His eyes went blank. "I wouldn't like to say. The man is blameless except for raising the suspicions of a disturbed woman."

"But the woman is now dead. Perhaps her suspicions were not unfounded."

"Nevertheless, I will not say."

"I think the police might be interested in you after all," she said.

Something behind his eyes shifted. "You are a strong-willed woman. Alright. I will speak to this person today. I'll get any information I can and tell you. Is that satisfactory?"

"I'd like to know his name."

"I can't take responsibility for maligning an innocent man. If he is agreeable, I will tell you his name, but first I must speak to him."

She could see he wasn't going to budge.

Leaning over, she picked up a remarkable silver goblet. The stem was fashioned to look like a fish leaping out of water. Four little silver fish heads were arrayed around the bowl of the goblet. "You have some extraordinary things here. Are they for fun or profit?"

His brow relaxed at the turn in the conversation. "This is a very good piece you have in your hand. German, eighteenth-century, probably Nurenberg. It's one of a kind. I'm afraid I don't keep up with the market value."

"You're a collector," she said.

His lips turned up in a charming, self-deprecating smile. "I'm far too humble to be called a collector. I merely seek knowledge about the artifacts entrusted to me."

He selected his words carefully, speaking them in a voice both nasal and throaty, a not unappealing combination.

"What was the cup used for?" she asked.

"Now you've asked the right question. The decoration is exquisite, no? But the true value of the cup lies in its history. It was used by some Jewish neighbours of mine during Passover as Elijah's cup. You know the story?"

Rebecca smiled. "The cup is filled with wine and left in the middle of the table while everyone eats. At the end of the Seder someone gets up to open the front door. Usually my sister and I went. We were letting in the prophet Elijah so he could come in to drink from the cup. We all watched the wine to see if it moved."

The memory tugged at her heart. Her family was so scattered now.

"These are all exceptional pieces. Where did you get them?"

"I will tell you everything. But it's a sad story. Would you like some coffee meanwhile?" He motioned to the filter coffee maker on a small table behind the desk.

The ironic intelligence in his eyes intrigued her. She had forty minutes before her patients started arriving. "I'd love some," she said.

While the coffee dripped through the filter, she asked, "How long have you and your wife had the store?"

"Mona?" He pursed his lips together. "Mona's not my wife. I bought the shop from her parents years ago and she decided to stay on. She knows the business better than I do." His blue eyes sparkled with humour. "I can see why you would get that impression though. She behaves like a wife." His mouth curved up in a little smile. "Poor Mona."

"She handles customers in the store while you

work in the back?"

He handed her a mug of hot coffee then sat back down on the desk with a mug of his own. His darkly greying hair rose in a delicate wave from his high forehead. "I was not, I think, meant to be a fishmonger."

"How did your collection start?"

He adjusted himself on the edge of the desk. "I like to think that it chose me rather than the other way around. You see, without wanting to, I benefited from the misfortune of others. These treasures were given to me in gratitude by the wealthy Jews who owned them. For my help. They couldn't take all their possessions with them, you understand, though I didn't want to accept them under the circumstances. I finally did, otherwise they would've been lost or destroyed."

"You're German," she said.

"Swiss."

"From...?"

"One of the smaller towns not far from Zurich. You wouldn't know it. My parents had a fish market."

"Wasn't Switzerland neutral during the war?"

"Ah. Well, you see I travelled often to Germany for the business. To keep in touch with our suppliers and so on. There was an apartment in Hamburg I stayed in when I was there. It belonged to Jews. I saw what was happening there. I offered my help. I had some connections because of the business. I knew people. I knew where to get a forged passport. I knew who could falsify documents so I arranged phony papers for the Jews who owned the apartment. A family with three children. They left the city and took only what they could carry. They insisted on giving me what they left behind. I never heard from them again. I don't think they survived. But through them I met others. All the Jews were scared. I couldn't help everyone, of course. The

157

Gestapo would've caught on. But I did what I could. These people were running for their lives. They couldn't worry about their candelabra. So, instead of leaving everything for the Nazis who inherited their apartments, they gave me tokens of their gratitude. It would have been churlish of me to refuse, don't you think?"

"You're not Jewish," she said, struck by the irony that this gentile man collected Jewish artifacts while she, a Jew, had never given them a thought. His head tilted on an angle observing her; he seemed amused at her reaction.

She looked at her watch. "I'm afraid I have to go." She stood up. "Here is my card. If I haven't heard from you by tomorrow about your mystery man, I'm afraid I'll have to call the police."

His eyes fixed on her. "You will hear from me."

She made her way back to the partition door where Max took his leave of her. She nodded politely at Mona who busied herself cleaning the counter and studiously ignored Rebecca as she headed out the front door.

She stood on the sidewalk taking deep breaths of the fresh air. Several cars pulled into the covered parking lot across the street. Near one of the pillars a man stood watching her. Grey sweat pants, sweatshirt, blue baseball cap. Beneath his visor he'd watched her emerge from the store. As if he'd been waiting for her. Was this the shadow in her office? He seemed smaller than the killer she expected. He was nervy, out in the light like this. She wasn't going to run from him in broad daylight.

She looked him in the eye — at least into the darkness beneath the visor — and made to cross the street. Suddenly he jumped into the parking lot behind some partition or car. Gone into the tumult of the market. Some killer.

158

Maybe she was getting jumpy. Maybe the poor guy was just a jogger and she was getting paranoid. She wasn't going to turn into Goldie.

chapter nineteen

Nesha watched the store with unflagging attention. He had found some steps to sit on nearby and pretended to read the paper. The barrel of the gun felt hard and bulky in the small of his back. He was dizzy with hatred, but what had he expected? The news photo was dated 1978. He'd gone into the store and recognized no one. He'd tried the adjoining store — nothing. He couldn't just show the storekeepers the photo of the bastard. They could be friends, or relatives. They'd open their mouths and the pig would be long gone. But then, anything could've happened in a year. He could have retired.

Maybe he was puttering around in his garden after a respectable business career, having lived a quiet life for thirty-five years, unmolested, when he had buried so many. He had helped bury a civilization. They were all gone, Nesha's own family was gone, and only an archaeologist could investigate the ruins. This was what he had become. A scholar fascinated by the extinct. A gravedigger sifting through rubbish heaps.

The problem with such scrutiny was that it required a constant examination of the heart and that was a part of him he kept under wraps for self-preservation. Some memories, like the one of his mother's pinched face turned and searching for him, needing to call to him yet not daring to, were wounds his heart had grown a callous over, thicker with each year till one wall of his heart was quite immobile. So that now, when he thought of her, he could touch the petrified skin instead of her face. This was the way he had intended to live out the rest of his life, a callous in his chest under his ribcage; it was the least painful way. How long could one live with a sword through the heart?

That was before he'd found the news photo. Everything changed then. All the pain suddenly crystallized into rage and, to his shock, it felt good. He felt more alive at this moment than he had for decades. Even sitting on the cement stair, he was aware of the milky April sun trying to warm the air. His blood sang through his veins.

The chill of the morning reminded him of spring in Poland, though he hadn't thought of that for a very long time. Since last week, the discovery of the file, he could think of nothing else: visions of that frosty morning had returned with a vengeance, a swooping of the scythe that he had taken pains to forget. Sometimes he could almost make himself believe he had imagined it. The years of working in a reasonable grey office with columns of numbers that never refused him, never disappointed him, made him forget he was an orphan. A branch of a tree of Israel, only the tree had been cut down and burned to ashes. So how had the branch survived? By rooting itself in the ground of another place, somewhere the earth didn't smell of blood. It had been the most natural of things, to forget. But in his heart, his painfully ledgered accountant's heart, he had always known there would be a day of reckoning. It was a matter of checks and balances, credit and liability. He had played with numbers long enough to know they were the only things you could count on. Now he had to dip into the real world and hope he could find his prey without losing himself.

And what about Goldie? Justice for Goldie. Another innocent casualty. She would never see the spring. He mourned for her but from a distance; in his heart as well as literally. He could do that because he didn't remember her. He'd been too young when they had visited each other in Poland. Goldie and Chana were already fashionable young women when he was still in short pants, maybe seven or eight. They were cousins, children of an older uncle, but he always called them aunts because of the age difference. He was glad to keep the sadness at bay. Yet the photo they published of her in the paper tugged at what was left of his heart. He recognized that pale blonde of women of a certain age. When his wife had gone blonde one day in her forties, he was surprised. To her it was a turning point, not because of the change, but because till then, he had noticed nothing about her.

"You've dyed your hair," he had said that fateful day.

"I've been dyeing my hair for years," she had said.

It turned out she had been dyeing her hair brown to cover the grey. It had gotten greyer and lighter until there was more light than dark, and the sensible thing to do was to go blonde. Confronted with the stark change, he finally noticed. Only by then it was too late. Now, ironically, he noticed women's hair. The older ones were blonder, like Goldie, because they were white underneath.

He only thought about Margie maybe ten times a day now. Not bad considering he hadn't seen her for three years. Or was it four? If it was only three, she'd worked pretty fast to find herself a new husband. A friend from the office, the only one who kept in touch, had called last week to invite him to a Seder and given him the latest gossip. Okay. So good luck to her. Probably a normal guy this time. She'd make damn sure of that. Could he blame her for eventually gagging on the kind of grief he lived with? The grief that hadn't allowed him to celebrate a joyous occasion like a Seder for years. After all, how could he take part in a festival that honoured God for His miracle in Egypt? If God could part the Red Sea to rescue the Jews from slavery, where was He when Nesha needed a miracle?

This time of year was always painful for him. It had happened in April, six days before Passover. His mother had been busy cleaning up the house for a week. Everything had to be spotless before the holiday began. All the cupboards had to be cleaned and wiped free of crumbs, the Passover dishes prepared to replace their everyday crockery. God, he could still see her stooped on the floor with her head in a cupboard, wet *schmata* in her hand. So many times he wanted to crawl back into that picture and stay there forever.

He remembered in younger years singing "*Chad Gadya*/One Little Goat" after the Seder every Passover. A simple Messianic little folk-song in which a father bought a baby goat for his child. Nesha always pictured a son. But the goat was eaten by a cat that was bitten by a dog that was beaten by a stick that was burned by fire that was quenched by water that was drunk by an ox that was killed by a *shoichet*, a ritual slaughterer, who was killed by the Angel of Death who, finally, was slain by the Almighty Himself. Blessed be He, said the text. Only the Messiah, whom God had sent, could kill Death, hence the Jewish yearning for his coming. Nesha never sang that song again. The primitive wheel of punishment, in which the executioner himself is executed, no longer held any charm for him. He never understood why God waited all that time to slay the Angel of Death. God always came too late.

Tonight, a million miles from that little boy, he would gather the four memorial glasses filled with wax that he'd brought with him from San Francisco. He would light them in his hotel room at sunset as he had lighted them every *Yahrzeit* for decades. They would burn for twenty-four hours, then he would begin another year alone.

Sunnydale Terrace was a low-rise institutional kind of building on Bathurst Street in the north part of the city. There had been only seven nursing homes in the Toronto phone book. It didn't take long to call and find out where she was. Why had he lost touch with his two cousins, the only ones left of his family? He supposed it was the difference in their ages. They had written periodically from Argentina. When Chana moved to Canada there'd been a flurry of letter writing. Months before Josh's bar mitzvah, Nesha had phoned Chana for the first time and invited her to come. She'd been excited on the phone and he was sure she would make the trip to San Francisco. Then they'd received a modest cheque in the mail with her unexplained apologies. He phoned again to find out how he had been so wrong about her intentions. She sounded diffident this time, almost nervous, whispering into the receiver. Apparently her husband told her they couldn't afford the trip, and besides, she said, he didn't like family affairs. Nesha offered to send a plane ticket if she wanted to come by herself; she could stay with them for a week if she liked. He remembered her gasping at the other end. "Oh, I couldn't do that. Leo wouldn't let me...."

He'd spoken to Goldie only once on the phone, several days before leaving San Francisco. Was it just last Thursday? It seemed like last year. When asked about Chana, Goldie told him she was in a nursing home. Goldie was still furious with Chana's husband for depositing her there. "I told him, ach! I look after her half day if he look after the rest. Just half day. Terrible man. He don't want. Easier sent her away. Now she suffering."

A wide scraggly lawn separated the front of Sunnydale Terrace from the four lanes of suburban traffic that sped by. On the other side of the road was a series of cemeteries, some Jewish, some Christian, all of them fenced in spiked metal to separate the dead from the living and protect them from each other.

The reception area was not ungenerous, furnished with wine-coloured sofas, their material thin and dirty on closer inspection, and tables and chairs that looked too orderly to be much used.

Nesha waited before the empty reception desk, part of a cubby-hole that backed into an office. "Excuse me?" he addressed the air.

When no one answered, Nesha raised his voice. "Anybody here?"

A very wide middle-aged woman with permed dark blonde hair appeared behind the desk, irritated. "Please keep it down, sir. This is the residents' quiet time."

He glanced at his watch: 2:40 p.m. Must've been afternoon nap time.

"I'm looking for Chana Feldberg," he said.

"Are you a relative?" she said, looking over his baseball cap and leather jacket. He could imagine her face if she could see the ponytail inside the cap, or if he still had his beard. At least he'd had the foresight to bring a packet of daffodils as an offering.

"She's my aunt."

"You haven't been here before." Her head tilted with suspicion.

"I'm visiting from the States," he said. "I'm staying at the Harbourfront Hilton. You want some I.D.?" He pulled out his driver's licence and made a show of displaying it.

She blinked with annoyance. "Gloria!" she called behind her. "Take Mr. — " She turned to him.

"Malkevich."

"Take Mr. Malkevich up to Mrs. Feldberg's room."

A younger woman with mousy brown hair appeared out of the depths of the office. "Come this way, Mr. Malkevich," she said, heading toward the elevator.

There were only two floors in the building, but Nesha followed. In the elevator, the woman kept her eyes on the floor number overhead. "Mrs. Feldberg doesn't talk anymore. Only sometimes in Yiddish. It's terrible what happened to her sister. But she doesn't understand."

The woman knocked once on the door of room 201, then opened it without waiting. In a raised voice reserved for children and the mentally impaired, she said, "My dear, you have a visitor."

Chana half-turned her head, barely glancing at him, satisfied, it seemed, that nothing behind her could be of interest. She returned to stare out the window as if she were watching her favourite TV show. She had a good view of the cemeteries from here. He wondered if it bothered her, contemplating the uneven earth where one day soon she might lie. He took off his cap, letting his ponytail fall onto his neck. The mousy brunette

167

sniffed, satisfied with her opinion of him, then left.

He approached Chana's chair, surprised at his own shyness. Her mere presence was pulling him back forty years to the house in his small Polish town, his mother, the contented memories of a ten-year-old that were obliterated by what came after. The last time he'd seen Chana she was in her early twenties, closer to his mother's age but elegant with long smooth brown hair.

This woman in the chair was tiny, on the point of disappearing. What little was left of her hair was white and pressed flat against her head. By his calculation she was not more than sixty-five. She looked closer to eighty. She had survived the camps but couldn't escape the ravages of the body. Would his mother, if she had lived, have succumbed so early to some unstoppable disease?

"Aunt Chana," he murmured. "It's Nesha. Do you remember?" He drank in the worn pointed features of her face. Did he see his uncle there? Her expression remained unchanged, no movement in the chair.

"My mother was Rivka. Your father's sister. Your father was my Uncle Yitzhak."

Then he remembered what the woman had said in the elevator about the Yiddish. Something had happened to Chana since he'd last spoken to her, some years before. She seemed to have retreated into herself with nothing left but the language of her youth. He hadn't spoken Yiddish in thirty years, not since cousin Sol died. Nesha started to sweat. To him Yiddish was a distant dam holding back the flood of his memories. Once he touched it, cupped his tongue around its intimate cadences, the dam would be breached and the ordinary days of his youth would flood in and drown him with his mother's silky face, his brothers playing in the square, the neighbours chatting along the muddy street. All of it waiting for him to open his mouth in the *Mameloshen*, the mother tongue. Okay, what do I have to lose, he thought. I have nothing left.

He pulled up a chair and sat down next to her. "*Meema Chana*," he whispered. Then he tried it out loud. "*Meema Chana. Du mir gedainkst?*" His Yiddish probably wasn't perfect after all these years, but she didn't seem to notice. She didn't notice anything. "*Rivka iz gevein mein mameh. Farsteyst?*" Nothing.

She remained immobile staring out the window, while his heart flinched within him at the familiarity of the words, children's words stored up and waiting. He had come this far. "*Meema Chana, du bist mein eyntsik familye. Du bist mein meema.*" It felt strange addressing an old woman he hadn't seen in forty years with the familiar *Du*. Yet not so strange. Her small eyes, the shape of her cheekbones reminded him of his uncle, even his mother, if he looked hard enough. What wonder, his mother in Chana's face.

He laid the bunch of daffodils in the old lady's lap. In her hand, he saw a small rag doll, roughly made. Now she was the child and he the adult. Despair rolled over him in a wave; the dam had broken when he wasn't watching. He crossed his arms over his stomach and leaned over in the chair, his head close to his knees, rocking, rocking.

"*Kind*," she said softly.

He looked up, astonished. She watched him with eyes like his mother's. Her brown-spotted hand floated in the air near his head. "*Kind ... bist ...*," she murmured.

Tears filled his eyes; he was overwhelmed with loss. He took her feather-light magical hand and brought it to his lips, his head echoing with his mother's soft words of petting and comfort. The air diffused into another time, grew bittersweet with memory and longing as he knew it would.

"*Di denkst azoi?*" he said, looking once more into his mother's eyes.

"*Kind,*" she breathed, the pressure of her bony hand like a bird's.

He drove back downtown in a haze, drained, at the same time enervated by his connection with Chana. Why couldn't he have come before? Why couldn't he see Goldie once before she died? They were all that was left of his past. All except the murderer. The invisible man. The needle in a haystack. How did one go about finding a needle in a haystack, he thought, stepping into the elevator in the hotel. Look under N for needle? For Nazi?

He bought a can of Coke from the machine on his floor. The caffeine and sugar jolt kept him going when his energy level dropped in the late afternoon. He sat down with the Toronto Yellow Pages and flipped through. What was he looking for? He came to *Restaurants*. One of the pages listed them under ethnicity. There were three restaurants under the *German* heading. Not much of a presence in the city.

He picked up the White Pages and looked under *German*. German Bakery, German Consulate, German News, German Translators. He dialed the number of the German consulate.

"*Deutsches General Konsulat.*"

"*Guten tag.* I'm new in Toronto and was wondering if there is a community centre or club where I could meet other German immigrants?" People told him he had a wisp of an accent; now he introduced gutturals into his *r*'s and pronounced *w* like *v*.

"Well, we don't usually recommend such places over the phone." The man clipped his words in a hurry, all business; maybe a line of people were waiting in front of his desk. "But there is an Austrian club that is quite popular. The Edelweiss on Beverley Street. Below College."

Nesha examined his Toronto map book and found Beverley Street. Just a few blocks from the market. Easy enough. He searched for himself in the mirror. His grooming would have to go a step further. Taking his scissors he began to clip at his hair until all the straggly ends lay on the floor. He ran wet fingers through what was left, folding it behind his ears. A little more fashionable. Now he looked artistic, rather than vagrant.

It was still too early to go to a club. The Coke hadn't touched the profound fatigue he felt settling in his bones. The emotional charge of Chana's presence had depleted all his energy. He lay down on the bed and fell into a deep sleep.

The lake was dark outside his window when he woke up. He couldn't quite remember where he was, until he saw the four *Yahrzeit* candles in their little glasses waiting on the round table near the window. He lit the wicks and, for a few minutes before he left, watched the tiny flames transfigure the walls with flickering memory.

He drove up Spadina because it was familiar, then turned right on Dundas till he reached Beverley. A few blocks north, the Edelweiss Club hovered on the east side of the street. The building had seen better days, a narrow structure squeezed in between a small office building on one side and a semi-detached house on the other. Edelweiss was printed in an arc of large Gothic letters above the door.

He didn't know what he was expecting, but the inside of the club wasn't it. No one greeted him at the entrance. There was a strong smell of onions and meat as he climbed the few steps into what looked like a ballroom. A wrought iron railing fenced in a round carpeted area set with square tables and white tablecloths. The centre was left uncarpeted, the wood floor scuffed but waxed. Only one table was occupied; two men talking quietly. Nesha stood awkwardly for a moment, glancing at the two in the hope they would greet him. Then a man in a white shirt and tie appeared quite suddenly before him.

With a courtly bending of the head he asked, "Do you come for dinner?"

Nesha looked around at the nearly empty room. "It's very quiet here."

The man's nearly bald head shone beneath the 1950s chandeliers. "Oh, you want company. Come back tomorrow night. Saturday and Sunday, too. The place will be full with people. We'll have music and singing. Accordion music. Very nice."

Nesha looked at his watch. It was nearly eight and his stomach was growling. "You serve dinner here?"

"Yes, sure," the man said, pretending offence. "Tonight we have roast beef and potatoes. Very nice. It comes with apple strudel for dessert."

Nesha sat down at a table and waited. When the man came back with the obligatory beer, Nesha said casually, "I must ask you. I'm new in town and I'm looking for someone. A friend of my father's. His name is Johann Steiner. Maybe he's been here?"

The man examined Nesha, at the same time appearing to think. "The name is not familiar, but I don't know everyone who comes here. Why don't you look in the phone book?"

"I tried that. You have no idea how many J. Steiner's there are."

Nesha was only half way through the beer when the balding man brought out his roast beef and potatoes, well done with some gravy. While he ate, he practiced questions and answers, none of which satisfied him. Whatever he said, he was taking the risk that Steiner would get word of it and run for cover. On the other hand Steiner might never have set foot in the place. He had to take the chance.

The man appeared after Nesha had finished dinner. While clearing the dishes, he said, "How about some coffee?"

Nesha pulled out the photo he carried around with him. "I'd really like to find my father's friend. They were close in the Old Country, and now that *Vati* is gone, I would love to meet him again. Here. Take a look. Maybe you'll recognize him."

The man scrutinized the muddy photo with the duck, then looked at Nesha with new eyes. "Who are you?"

"Look, I don't want any trouble. My father ... they were together in the war. Buddies, you know? You can ask him. Waldhausen. He'll remember. Ernst Waldhausen."

The man checked Nesha over, the harshness in his eyes fading. "He doesn't have that name, Steiner."

Nesha shrugged. "A lot of people changed their names. What is he calling himself?"

The man shook his head slowly.

"Will I see him if I come back tomorrow night? Or Saturday?"

He shook his head again. "He makes appointments. Business appointments."

Bingo. Adrenaline shot through Nesha's chest. "What kind of business?"

"He buys, he sells."

"Well, give me his number and I'll make an appointment."

"You give me *your* number and I will pass it to him."

"Fine," Nesha said. "Only I'm staying at a hotel and I don't know the number. I'll call you tomorrow and give it to you."

chapter twenty

That afternoon Rebecca focused all her concentration on attending to her patients. It was therapeutic to solve other people's problems, feel she was really helping someone. More than once she became gratefully lost in the puzzle of a patient's illness. At the end of the day, though, her own predicament awaited her.

Soon after the last patient had closed the door, Iris threw on her jacket. "I gotta get going. My kids are coming for dinner tonight. Kids! They're both over thirty and I'm still calling them kids." She turned to Rebecca. "Why don't you come over for dinner? I'm cooking up a storm." She stood a moment, watching Rebecca, her hazel eyes concerned. "You all right?"

Rebecca glanced up from the file she was reading. It was a question Iris had asked many times over the past six months. Rebecca must have had a grim expression on her face.

"I'm fine," she said.

"Dinner?" Iris repeated.

Rebecca smiled sheepishly. "Thanks, Iris, I'll take a

rain check."

Iris hovered near the door, the perfect waves of blonde hair blurred in Rebecca's peripheral vision. "Really, Iris, I'm fine. Have a nice dinner."

Rebecca heard the door close, then sat a moment, mesmerized by the evening silence. Dr. Lila Arons, from downstairs, had gone home on time tonight. Rebecca was alone in the building. She wondered what Iris was making for dinner. Rebecca had been over a few times but always felt awkward with Iris' grown children, who were too polite to refer to David's death except obliquely, and then an embarrassed pause would hang in the air till Rebecca or Iris broke the silence.

Suddenly she was aware that the present silence, the silence in the building, had been broken. Footsteps sounded downstairs. No, someone was coming up the stairs. The noise echoed in the empty building. Rebecca stiffened. She wasn't expecting anyone. Should she lock the door? She jumped up, realizing she couldn't get to the door in time to lock it before the man — she was sure it was a man — reached it. She flew into her inner office, adrenaline pumping. What were the chances the killer would be so brazen? She stood by the phone, hating her own vulnerability. If she screamed, would someone hear?

"Dr. Temple?" A man's voice rose in uncertainty.

Her breathing was shallow. She listened, but wasn't sure what she had heard.

"Dr. Temple?"

She recognized the accent then, and tried to still her heart. When was she going to stop panicking? She took a breath, then walked into the hall with a purposeful stride.

"Mr. Vogel," she said. "What a surprise. I thought you were going to phone."

He looked around the office. "I took the chance you would still be here. Are you alone?"

She ignored the question, wishing Iris had stayed for a few more minutes. Or maybe he had waited for Iris to leave. She had to stop imagining monsters everywhere. The racing of her heart made that impossible. He looked very civilized, with his blue turtleneck tucked into navy wool pants.

"I hope I didn't frighten you when I came in."

Was it that obvious, she wondered. "What have you found out?"

His pale blue eyes observed her. "Something reassuring," he said. "The man's innocent. He was occupied with something in a public place the night of the murder. He has witnesses. And he cannot explain the poor woman's inquiries about him. You must admit she was a disturbed woman. You mustn't take seriously what she said if she wasn't quite right — here." He pointed to his temple.

"Then you can tell me the man's name."

He glanced around the office. "I would think this would be good news. That the man is innocent. Perhaps you should move on. It may even be that the poor woman *was* killed by robbers."

"Mr. Vogel..."

"Max. Please."

"I must speak to the man. If you won't tell me who it is...."

Vogel raised his palm in some sort of defeat. "There is a place you can find him. A club. I'll give you the address, but I promised I wouldn't give away his name. And, of course, you must not mention me."

Rebecca ate her dinner in the kitchen looking out the

patio doors at the garden. It looked no different from last spring when David could still see enough to clear the dead leaves off the crocuses and grape hyacinths that would soon unfold their purple hearts. Tulips and tiger lilies came later. He had organized the garden so that something would always be blooming. There were the perennials that returned each year: yellow black-eyed Susans that spread in clumps, red hollyhocks against the fence, and forget-me-nots a heart-rending blue in unexpected corners. Near the end of May he would plant little annuals that would blossom and spread till the first frost. That was before he had gotten ill and lost his sight. Tears welled in her eyes at the irony: the garden he had created would come alive each year while he was gone forever.

She knew this was a road of thought she didn't want to travel down again. She got dressed to go out.

El Dorado glittered in the night of College Street, its marquee outlined by a necklace of flashing bulbs. Nothing subtle there. Rebecca parked at a meter several blocks away, locked her doors, and set off in the direction of the club. She passed small hardware stores, dress stores, and food shops closed for the night. As she opened the door to the club, she turned momentarily and in the distance caught sight of the man in the sweatsuit who had watched her in Kensington Market the day before. Stopping automatically, she peered into the milky haze born of too many light bulbs tearing the dark. The outline of the man flickered down the street then burned up in the volley of the flashing lights like a moth. She had to get hold of herself.

She stepped into a dimly-lit hallway, aware of the music arriving in distorted echo through the ceiling. The restaurant on the first floor was nearly empty. A carpeted stairway straight ahead was flanked by a sign: "Upstairs, Thursday to Sunday, The Gauchos with Isabella Velasco." Isabella Velasco. The black-edged card, the dead son in Buenos Aires. Interesting coincidence.

Rebecca's eyes adjusted to the light and she realized there was a balding, angular maitre d' in a black suit standing in the restaurant, watching her. His sour face prodded her to follow the music.

chapter twenty-one

The stairs were carpeted in an orangey-red that reminded her of Spanish tiled roofs and the satin dresses of flamenco dancers. She stood in the doorway of the club, halted by the smoke and the noisy rhythm of the music that set the floor vibrating. Middle-aged couples clung to each other in the centre of the dance floor, gliding to some tango. The sultry beat was being produced on the opposite side of the room by a band of trumpet, guitar, and drums, and Isabella Velasco. Her voice insinuated itself along the melody of some song about rain, while her fingers punctuated the journey, her hands opening and closing to click her castanets like little clams. A long black dress, slit to the thigh on one side, hugged her bony figure. Her dark hair was pulled tightly off her face. She was not young. A well-preserved forty-nine, as she swayed to the rhythm.

Rebecca took a moment to observe the room. It looked like a club for homesick Latins: a rigid toreador, with charging bull, had been painted across the wall behind the band. David would not have approved. The two figures were naively drawn and the colours flat and childish. Near the entrance hung several paintings of, presumably, the Spanish countryside, as well as the requisite rendering of a señiorita in lace mantilla. A set of bull's horns and a sword were suspended in one corner.

She couldn't keep standing in the doorway. How was she going to find the man Vogel talked about? Rebecca took off her trenchcoat and hung it on the rack in the hall. She caught a glimpse of herself in the mirror and was surprised to see how pale and unhealthy she looked even in the subdued light. Her dark hair was more unruly than usual after the run outside. She smoothed it down with a quick hand then applied some lipstick to give her at least a semblance of life.

To the left of the entrance was a bar. Two men sat drinking at the far end, laughing over something. Rebecca took a deep breath, then entered the noise and smoke. She found herself a stool at the empty end of the bar. The noise, she realized, was loud music alone rather than a combination of music and chatter. There were not enough people in the room to make an appreciable noise but the band more than made up for it. She was surprised they would bother with a band on an evening when only four tables were occupied by maybe fifteen people.

After ordering a glass of wine, she turned so she could see the band. Isabella Velasco's voice caressed the room in a sensuous Spanish. *Hay lluvia*.... It was raining.

After a minute a sleek dark man in his forties boldly sat down on the next stool, facing her. Maybe she should have expected this. It had been so long since she was single that she had quite forgotten the procedure. She was in no mood for it now. He lit up a cigarette, then offered her the package.

"I don't smoke," she said.

"Very smart." Hispanic accent. Sure of himself. His angular features, his dark hair, salted with grey, gleamed in the reflected light of the bar.

He turned his head to exhale a long column of smoke away from her. At least he was polite. "I haven't seen you here before."

"I guess that's because I haven't been here before."

"And you are here alone? A beautiful woman like you?"

He was going through the motions but she didn't quite buy it. The attitude seemed more reflex than real intention. Despite the warm approach, there was something cold about him. His black eyes studied her as one hand played with a gold cigarette lighter on the counter. The barman placed a glass of whiskey in front of him without a word. A regular. A candidate for the mystery man.

"She's very good," Rebecca said, glancing at the sultry, severe woman growling out her song.

"You like our Spanish music?"

"Its very moody."

He smirked. "For an English it is moody. For a Spanish it is passionate."

"Maybe it's the singer who's passionate."

Without looking at the stage he said, "All Spanish singers are passionate. It is in the blood." He stared at Rebecca as if Spanish blood and passion were unimportant for the moment. Crushing his cigarette in an ashtray, he slid off his stool.

"You would like to dance?" It wasn't a question. He stood in front of her, his hand out, not tentative at all. There was a dangerous charm in the well-defined cheekbones, the sharp nose. His expensive suit clung sensually around his waist.

A couple heading toward the dance floor turned

183

toward them. "*Buenos noches, Capitán,*" said the man, nodding with more than respect.

*Capitán.*This must be her man.

"Pardon my manners. I am Manuel Diaz." He bowed his head slightly, very elegantly.

"Capitán Diaz," she smiled. "Rebecca Temple."

It had been a long time since she had danced and she gave herself credit for nerve. The straight calf-length skirt she had worn gave little leeway for the strides that the tango required of her. He led her easily, holding her at a polite distance. His eyes half-closed in the rhythm of the dance, but he was alert, watching her under heavy lids. She hadn't been held by a man since David and she wasn't ready. Just the proximity was unnerving, the pressure of the man's fingers on her back. Maybe a murderer's fingers. The music died away. He led her back to the bar.

"You're a military man?" she said, in the lull between the music.

He waved away the suggestion. "A title of respect. In South America, where I come from, soldiers have the most respect. So when I come here, they call me *el Capitán.*" He stretched his hand out like a priest indicating his flock. "This is my place. When you give orders, you must have a rank." He motioned to the bartender for more drinks. Another glass of wine appeared before her.

He was certainly in charge. But he seemed to have more power than ordering changes in the menu or setting the price of Tia Maria.

"Then you know Isabella."

He lit up another cigarette. "I know everybody here."

"She was acquainted with a patient of mine. Goldie Kochinsky." She watched his reaction.

His eyelids rose slightly. "You are a doctor." Then he shook his head, furrowing his brow in the appropriate response. "It is terrible what happened to the old woman. We were all shocked. It is what you expect in Argentina, where I come from; not here."

"Did you know each other in Argentina?"

"The old woman? No."

"You know what happened to her there?"

He blew out a long stream of smoke, observing her. "You mean her kidnapping. I heard something. It was a terrible time. It was bad for everybody."

"Did you know the men who tortured her?"

He watched her for a moment. "I knew men in the junta. I didn't ask them what they did. The trick was, not to know too much."

"So. You were not involved?" His waiting eyes prodded her to add, "In the junta?"

He tapped impatiently on his cigarette. "I'm a businessman. I don't kill people."

"What kind of business are you in?"

"Import-export."

"What do you import and export?"

"Anything I can buy low and sell high. Nothing you would be interested in, Doctor."

"Then you managed to escape the terror when you were in Argentina."

"I was lucky. The old woman was not." He shrugged.

Rebecca wasn't going to get any more information out of the *Capitán* than he wanted to give her. He turned toward the band where Isabella was purring out a suggestive version of "The Girl from Ipanema." "What about Isabella?" she said. "She knew Goldie in Argentina."

"Isabella hated the old woman because she was

weak. She told the junta where Isabella's son was hiding and they killed him."

"I don't believe that."

"I don't blame the old woman. She didn't want to die. So she gave up a name." His tone was too casual for the information. He was accustomed to government-sponsored murder while it still appalled her.

The song ended. Someone turned on a Latin version of canned muzak and the band headed toward the bar. Isabella held her head stiff, her gait self-consciously haughty. She looked even older close up, the lines around the edges of her mouth and darkly lined eyes visible through her pancake make-up.

She smiled coyly at Diaz. "*Buenos noches, Capitán.*"

He nodded formally. "*Maravilloso*, your performance, as always, Isabella." There was no feeling in his voice, merely rote. He touched Rebecca's arm lightly. "This is Dr. Temple. She was Doctor to Goldie Kochinsky."

Isabella turned to look at her for the first time.

"Tell her that you forgive Goldie for what she did," Diaz said, sipping another glass of whiskey that the bartender had automatically poured.

He was toying with them both, thought Rebecca.

The woman searched her face for a clue to the mystery, but found none.

Rebecca jumped in. "I'm sorry if this brings up painful memories for you, but on Goldie's desk there was a notice of your son's death dated 1977. Do you have any idea why it was there?"

Isabella turned toward the room. "Come, let's sit," she said, motioning to an empty table. "I must get off my feet."

At the table, both the *Capitán* and Rebecca watched her, waiting. Her neck arched higher, the severe bun black against her skin; her eyelids drooped. "It was like an anniversary. I sent the card every year. So she wouldn't forget." Isabella took a gulp of what looked like vodka. "She killed my son, but now that she is dead, I must forgive her."

The *Capitán* smirked, every now and then nodding recognition toward those greeting him from a distance.

"Why do you think she was responsible?" Rebecca asked, trying to ignore him.

"Because he is dead and she knew where they were. My son, her son, together in a safe house. Only a few close friends knew where. She was the only one who was tortured. They grabbed her because she was weak and they can smell weak. The junta were afraid of their songs — the boys sang songs in protest. Here it would be nothing, nobody would notice. But there, they killed people who opposed them. When they tortured her, she gave in."

"Isn't it possible someone else told?" said Rebecca. The *Capitán* smirked again. He was enjoying this.

Isabella finished her drink. "It doesn't matter anymore. She is dead. Why do you care?"

"Someone killed her. I'd like to know why."

Isabella lifted her glass high, motioning to the bartender. "It was a robbery, I heard. These things happen."

"I believe it was something more."

The Capitán no longer smiled. "You shouldn't get involved," he said, crushing out his cigarette, pretending lack of interest. "This is not a job for a doctor. You must have more important things."

What was he hiding, she wondered. Who was he really?

"I hope I haven't upset you," she said, pleased with his reaction.

His nostrils flared but she couldn't take complete credit for his displeasure since he stood up at that moment to greet someone at the door.

Isabella stood up, both arms extended, her shoulder blades taut. "Leo," she sang. The man embraced her, kissing her the European way, on both cheeks.

"My dear lady, ravishing as always."

He turned toward the table and smiled at Rebecca. "Why, Doctor, what a delightful surprise!" said Feldberg. "How nice to see you again so soon."

Then came an ox and drank the water
That quenched the fire that burned the stick
That beat the dog that bit the cat
That ate the goat
That Father bought for two zuzim.
One little goat, one little goat.

chapter twenty-two

"It's a small world," said Rebecca.

The *Capitán* nodded a greeting and sat down.

Feldberg smiled with bared teeth. "You see," he addressed her. "Here we try to recreate a little bit of Buenos Aires." His hand showed her the room as if the feeble rendering of the toreador on the wall, the painted señorita, the bull's horns, had transfigured a rather perfunctory space into something more.

As he sat down, Isabella rolled her eyes. "Ay! Buenos Aires! How can you compare? All along the streets people sit laughing, singing till four in the morning. Strangers *talk* to each other, people are friendly. You can *discuss*. Not like here. Nobody talks to you here. You could be dying in the street, people would just step over you." Unsmiling, she looked to Rebecca for an answer.

"I've heard people say Toronto is a cold place for a stranger," Rebecca said. "But if you're in trouble here, people will help. The city may be cold, but the individuals aren't."

A few strums from a guitar made Isabella turn toward the men in the band who had gone back to their places. Feldberg and the *Capitán* rose as she stood up and passed by, lithe and bony.

As soon as the music resumed, Feldberg approached Rebecca's chair. "Would you like to dance, Doctor?"

The *Capitán* watched her with half-lidded eyes and lit up another cigarette.

While Isabella sang, Feldberg manoeuvred Rebecca deftly around the other couples sharing the dance floor. His arm gripped her waist with firm assurance, his own back straight and dignified. Rebecca took deep breaths in the opposite direction to avoid the noisome sweetness of his scent.

"So how do you like our little club?" he asked.

She nodded approval and hoped he wouldn't push for a real answer. "It's the *Capitán*'s place?"

Feldberg's smile stiffened a bit. "He runs the day to day in the club. I manage the rest. And of course, the building is mine. He rents from me." With this, his old smile resumed.

"Then you're old friends," she said. His lips pursed with displeasure. She'd expected as much. "You knew each other in Argentina?"

"Slightly," he said.

"And he knew Goldie too?"

"*Goldie*?" The contempt he injected into his voice distorted his face. "He didn't know Goldie."

"Was he in the military?"

Feldberg appraised her, then said, "No. He knew people; he had connections if he needed something. But he himself, no."

As if to evade further questions, Feldberg began some faster, fancier dance steps. She tried to follow, but fumbled.

"Don't think so hard about what you are doing, Doctor. Let yourself go. Is that the expression? You Canadians are too self-conscious. You don't know how to enjoy yourselves."

The song rose to a sudden crescendo, then lapsed into a trembling beat.

"You've known Isabella a long time?" she asked.

"We're both expatriates from Argentina. Away from home, so to speak. It's hard to make people understand who never had to flee their country. And her past is tragic. So many tragedies. The world is filled with sad stories, Doctor."

The words came too easily. All the sad stories were someone else's. Life went on.

"You believe Goldie betrayed her own son?" she asked.

He shrugged. "It doesn't matter anymore. The poor woman's out of her pain."

How magnanimous, Rebecca thought. "Do you have any idea who killed her?"

Feldberg danced with half-closed eyes as if trying to avoid her questions.

"Do you think it could've been someone from the terror? Maybe someone with a grudge?"

His eyes snapped open; his dancing slowed. "It's all over. The terrorists are in Argentina, most of them pardoned by the new regime. It's not logical for them to risk their lives to come here and finish someone off."

His dancing continued to be slow. "I'd rather not talk about her. I feel so guilty about what happened to her," he said. "Three buildings away and I couldn't help her. I cannot imagine what you must think."

His hypocrisy sickened her. As soon as the music stopped, she excused herself.

Outside, the flashing bulbs of the El Dorado sign lit up the sidewalk on College Street as she headed back to her car. The street was empty. She jumped into the Jaguar waiting quietly in the dark by a meter and locked the door.

Driving east along College she rolled her head on her neck to loosen the kinks. God, she was tired! She turned north up Spadina. Traffic was light. One car ahead, a van behind. As long as there were two, she felt safe. But at Dupont, the car in front made a right turn. The van still followed behind. They were the only ones in sight. The van's headlights were bobbing high off the ground and glared into her mirror. As she approached Davenport, the traffic light turned yellow. She took the chance and sped up to fly through as it changed to red. In her rear-view mirror she saw with relief that the van stopped at the light, its size diminishing as she continued on.

She sailed serenely around the curve heading toward Casa Loma. Maybe some music. She turned on the radio and flipped the channels for something easy to listen to; she didn't want to hear any more news.

She loved this part of town, the colossal folly of Casa Loma, the stone turrets of which shone yellow in the night like ghosts high above. The parking lot was empty at this time of night. She drove across the bridge of Sir Winston Churchill Park, heading toward St. Clair, before headlights disturbed the dark road behind her. She squinted at the too-high headlights. They looked like high-beams. It was the same van. He was lumbering up the hill, probably going home to the wife and kids.

She made it through St. Clair as the light was turning yellow. Nearly home. Glancing in her mirror she saw the van pick up speed at the intersection behind her and barrel through as the light turned red. Now he was behind her, his high-beams reflected in her mirror, stinging her eyes. So he was in a hurry. It was late.

She drove toward Forest Hill Village, a quaint little neighbourhood of old-fashioned shops with benches on the sidewalk and daffodils in wooden planters. Everything lit up for the night, but deserted. No strollers out at this hour on a week night.

She yawned and rubbed one eye. What had she learned at the club? Not much more than she already knew: Goldie's American cousin had asked her to look up a shop in Kensington, possibly based on the missing photo. Goldie found Blue Danube Fish and questioned Vogel about a man. Possibly the man who killed her. Vogel sent Rebecca to the El Dorado to find, presumably, the *Capitán*. But the link between the *Capitán* and Goldie was tenuous since he claimed he didn't know her. He could be lying, though Leo corroborated his story. They could both be lying.

She felt herself floating on a surface that deceived, with crests of icebergs in full sun. Everything she needed to know was submerged; somehow she had to find a way to plumb the depths.

All the traffic lights were green as she continued up Spadina. The street was empty except for a few cars driving the other way. And the van a distance behind her. A few blocks north of the Village, she made a right turn down Kilbarry, a side street that would take her to Avenue Road, then home.

Suddenly, headlights emblazoned the road behind her. The van with its high-beams was speeding after her, closing the distance between them. Alarm bells rang in her head. She pushed her foot to the floor. Her tires squealed and pulled her away. What was she thinking? This was a new universe she found herself in and all the rules had changed. She should have been more paranoid.

Her heart knocking in her chest, she raced by huge brick houses. There would be no help here.

A stop sign! She couldn't *stop*. But with her luck, someone might choose that moment to drive through. She slowed down just enough to glance both ways, then tromped through. To her horror the van didn't even slow down but lurched toward her. His engine was gutsier than he had let on and he heaved the van beside her. Adrenaline pushed through her body. They flew parallel down the side street for a few seconds, then finally he pitched his huge front fender toward the side of her car. She swung away onto the sidewalk and slammed on the brake to avoid crashing into the fence.

Blood pulsed through her ears; she could feel the walls of her veins expanding with the rush, but she had to move — the van door was opening. Someone was getting out. "*No!*" she screamed, and punched her gearshift into reverse. Craning her neck to see out the rear window, she pumped her foot to the floor, then screeched backwards off the sidewalk. She flew in reverse for a block till she could turn around in a driveway and race back toward Spadina. Her heart knocked in her chest. Stupid, stupid! If she got away, she would never be this stupid again.

chapter twenty-three

Rebecca jammed her foot on the gas and watched the asphalt speed up beneath her as she raced up Spadina. The street was empty but she couldn't take her eyes off the rear-view mirror. Where *was* he? Had she really lost him? Her eyes were engaged in the mirror when she felt the thud of her tires against the curb. She swung the wheel wide and veered into the oncoming lane. Take it easy. You don't want to wrap yourself around a pole and do his job for him.

She was fast approaching Eglinton Avenue. Up ahead, the traffic light was red. There was no one behind her that she could see, but she wasn't about to stop. Maybe he'd taken a different way. Maybe he'd camouflaged his van somehow; maybe he was a magician. Slowing down, she checked both sides of Eglinton for cars. There was one coming toward her in the distance but she could make it. She floored it and shrieked into a left turn, heading west.

The light at Bathurst was unavoidable. There was always traffic at that intersection. While sitting impatiently at the red, she kept her eyes on the rear-view mirror. No high beams. No vans. He'd given up. For now.

She pulled her car into the nearly empty parking lot of Thirteen Division for the second time in two days. Looking frantically over each shoulder, she hurried into the building.

At the front counter, the same desk sergeant greeted her. "May I help you?"

"Someone just tried to kill me!" she said, trying to control her voice. She was out of breath as if she'd run all the way.

"Calm down, ma'am," said the sergeant, coming out from behind. "Are you hurt?"

"I'm not injured," she said, realizing she had been lucky.

"Have a seat, ma'am, and I'll get a constable."

"I've got to see Detective Wanless. Is he still here?"

The man craned his neck behind him. "He's working late on a case, but I'll get one of the other men."

"This is about the case he's working on." She hadn't sat down and she wasn't going to.

"The Morelli murder?" he asked.

So Wanless had other fish to fry. She had a sinking feeling about Goldie's case but kept her face determined. The sergeant hesitated, then made for the back corner of the station.

In the distance she could see Detective Wanless pulling on his sports jacket while he strolled toward her.

"What can I do for you, Doctor?" he said, his bullet head tilted and waiting.

"He tried it again, he tried to kill me," she said. "I just barely got away."

"Take it easy," he said. "You're all right now."

Rebecca was taken aback at the soothing tone of

his words, words she had murmured herself often enough to patients. It felt odd being on the receiving end but she was surprisingly grateful for his sympathy and followed him back to his office in the corner.

His desk was awash in clutter, paper piled in organized clumps. Wanted posters decorated his walls. It wasn't until she sat down that she realized her knees were shaking.

"Who tried to kill you?" he asked.

"It was Goldie's killer. He must've followed me all the way from the club. It was a van. Dark blue, I think. It was hard to see because of the headlights. He was very clever, hanging back at first. Then when I turned down a side road and he followed, I knew. He pulled in front of me. I heard his door open. He was going to drag me out of my car...." She took a breath to calm herself, knowing she hadn't explained it well.

Wanless was taking notes behind his desk. "So how did you get away?" His voice was too even.

"I backed up as fast as the car would go. Then I turned and gunned it out of there."

"What did he look like?"

Was Wanless trying to be obtuse? "I couldn't see him," she said. "He was driving behind me with his headlights shining in my eyes."

"What about when he stopped?"

"I wasn't going to hang around to see who it was! I just got out of there fast." She paused, uncertain. "There's a man I've seen a few times. He watches me from a distance. Strange-looking man in a sweatsuit and baseball cap. Couldn't see his face, but it could've been him in the van."

"Height?" Wanless asked. "Weight? Hair colour?"

"I don't know. Slim, I'd say. Average height. I couldn't see his hair."

"What about the car? Did he hit your car at all?"

She thought a moment. "He swung over at me, but I pulled onto the sidewalk."

One of his eyebrows went up but he kept writing in the notebook, his skepticism an aura around his face.

"You say you were at a club." He glanced up from the desk and perused her skirt and modest heels. "Which club?"

"El Dorado," she muttered, suddenly embarrassed.

His face clouded over. "The one on College Street?" She nodded, but said nothing. "Doesn't seem to be your style, Doctor. I would've thought something more upscale, maybe one of the ones near Eglinton and Yonge."

He would get it out of her sooner or later. "I went there to speak to someone who knew Goldie Kochinsky."

"And you did that because...?"

"I wanted to clear something up." She ignored the blank stare that said, "I'm too busy for this crap," and went on.

"The man who runs the club — *Capitán* Diaz — is from Argentina. What if he had something to do with her torture there? What if he had orders to finish the job here?"

"Do you have any evidence?"

She blinked and turned away.

"If I followed every 'what if' in a case, Doctor, I'd need to bring my sleeping bag to the office and my wife would divorce me. Look, we're professionals. Let us do our job."

"Why don't you admit it, Detective. You're already working on a different case. This is obviously more important to me than it is to you."

He sat back in his chair and absently brushed his palm against the side of his head. "All murder cases are important. Some are just more straightforward than others. I went over Mrs. Kochinsky's file today. I go with your first diagnosis, Doctor. Sure looks like the woman was paranoid as hell. Nothing to reproach yourself for there. I'm glad you gave it to me though; helped clear up any doubt I had. See, we couldn't find any evidence of premeditated murder. Everyone who knew her is accounted for. And we have no motive besides the obvious. It isn't final yet, but I'm going to mark it down as a robbery gone bad."

Rebecca opened her mouth to speak but he lifted his hand for her to wait. "Someone, some punk, maybe a few punks, broke in planning to rob the place, probably thought it was empty. Mrs. Kochinsky confronts the guy or guys, they panic. She was an excitable woman, maybe she starts to yell. One of them loses it, knows he has to shut her up, and pulls something around her neck. Maybe some rope he brought with him. I'm sorry, Doctor, but doesn't that make sense to you?"

Her heart plummeted; he was giving up. "It makes perfect sense. Except that someone's trying to kill me."

Wanless observed her more carefully, searching her face with opaque blue eyes as if he would find some clue on the surface of her skin, some hidden message her mouth had not revealed.

"Did you meet anyone at this club? Maybe you had a few drinks?"

At first she was angry at the implication. Then she thought of the wine, the two glasses sipped during her conversation with the *Capitán*. "I met who I intended to meet. And I'm not drunk, if that's what you're insinuating."

Wanless sat back in his chair, the tips of his fingers arched together in a steeple. His voice was softer. "I'm not insinuating anything. You're upset, as you have every right to be. People interpret things differently when they're upset. I don't have to tell you, Doctor. And I'm not saying you weren't followed. But maybe the guy was after something else. Do you have an old boyfriend who might be trying to scare you? A disgruntled patient? You see, there are other possibilities."

"I know it was Goldie's killer after me. I lead a very quiet life and believe it or not, I have no old boyfriends and no patients angry enough to run me off the road." She felt her blood heating up and could barely contain her anger. "I can't believe you're finished with this case. You barely started. Is it because the victim was just an old woman?"

"Now you know that's not fair," he said, sitting forward. "If anything, her being a senior citizen makes the crime more despicable. But I've got to be realistic. Look at my desk. I forget what colour it is. These files just keep piling up. How many homicide detectives do you think there are? It's the same old story: overworked and understaffed."

"So Goldie's killer is going to get away because you don't have the time?"

"Look, Doctor, I know how frustrated you are. If I thought it would do any good, if I had a shred of evidence that it was premeditated or someone she knew did it, I'd keep going. But there's nothing." He lifted a large envelope from under the morass of papers. "You'd better take Mrs. Kochinsky's file back. I'm done with it."

She rose to her feet, her face burning. "You want evidence? You'll have evidence soon enough." Her heels clicked against the floor as she headed to the door. "It'll be my body at the morgue."

chapter twenty-four

Friday, April 6, 1979

Detective Wanless saw to it that a constable followed Rebecca in a squad car as she drove home. The young uniformed officer watched her open the front door with her key and turn on every light, going nervously through the rooms as he waited in the hallway. In the kitchen she turned on the floodlamps that bathed the backyard in artificial light. Even if the driver of the van knew her name, she thought, she was not listed in the phone book. He would have to find her address some other way, like following her home. She had lost him this time. But how did she know he hadn't followed her before?

The constable waited at the foot of the stairs while she climbed to the second floor and wandered from bedroom to bedroom, flicking on the lights. By the time she was finished, the house blazed with lights in every room and closet.

She smiled sheepishly at the constable. "It's all

right," she said. "I'll be fine."

But she wasn't fine. She felt completely alone and without help. Wanless, with his professional sympathy, had made up his mind about her the way she had made up her mind about Goldie. Would Goldie still be alive if Rebecca had believed her? She slunk into bed, feeling the old familiar pang in her heart. *Stop it*! she cried to herself, Goldie's paranoia had precursors; it had been a valid diagnosis for Rebecca to make. Even Wanless saw that. She imagined that he considered his reasoning about the case was sound, too. Her blood froze when she took the comparison to its logical conclusion: Goldie had ended up dead in her own living-room. Rebecca had no intention of submitting to that fate.

Even with the kitchen knife stashed away in the drawer of her nightstand, Rebecca slept fitfully, the glare of the van's headlights piercing her shallow dreams. Sometimes *Capitán* Diaz got out of the van and sometimes it was Feldberg's face she saw coming toward her.

Feldberg. Seeing him at the club was a shock. And the relationship with Isabella. How long had he been cheating on Chana? Before her illness, Rebecca guessed. Was that a motive for murder? How was he involved with Diaz? She seemed to have come to a dead end with the *Capitán*.

If only Chana could talk. There was no one else to ask about Feldberg. She was loath to go to sleep; if only she could keep looking for the killer round the clock. Maybe then she could survive. He knew her; that was his advantage. She had to find him. In that twilight between sleeping and waking, she saw Feldberg in his leather armchair, his legs crossed, one knee pointing toward her. "*Too many letters*," he whispered. "Why should Chana miss Goldie, they wrote and wrote, always writing. She told Goldie everything."

Rebecca opened one eye to check the clock: 7:10 a.m. She told Goldie everything. Rebecca sat up with a start. There would be letters. Goldie might have kept letters from her sister. But would Chana have written anything important in them?

By eight-thirty, in the muted light of a grey morning, she was heading along Eglinton Avenue toward Bathurst. Her eye caught every dark van that passed by. How was she ever going to feel safe again? She parked on a side street south of Goldie's duplex. The yellow police tape flapped in the chill morning breeze, but no police stood guard. Their investigation seemed over. They were giving up.

She ignored the tape strung across the front door and tried to turn the knob. The door was locked. Traffic on Bathurst drifted by as always, people going to work, people going for breakfast. Good God, what was she doing here? She squared her shoulders. Trying to survive, that was what.

She walked down the lane to the side door, looking over her shoulder. Maybe she had missed him in the mirror. Maybe he was watching her right now. She tried the side door. Locked.

She stood a long moment facing Bathurst, scanning the circumscribed view of the street that the lane afforded her. If he were there, she would see him. She had to stay calm, keep her head clear.

She walked further down the lane toward the garage, wondering if Feldberg would see the irony of her asking him for the key. She turned the corner of the house and stopped. In the back the blinkered bedroom window reflected the morning light.

"Argentina too hot," Goldie had said more than once. "In Poland, air was fresh. Canada, too. Air fresh.

Can't sleep with window closed."

Rebecca glanced around at the backs of the houses facing the rear of the duplex. People still minded their own business in a big city. Thank God for small mercies.

She gingerly tried the whitewashed sash of the window on the ground floor. It seemed loose in its place but wouldn't lift. She knew from experience that everything stuck in old houses. That didn't mean it was locked. She braced herself and pushed hard against gravity and old paint and damp-expanded wood. The window moved. Marginally. She was dogged about it and pushed the sash up an inch at a time till there was an opening wide enough. She wondered what the College of Physicians and Surgeons would say if they could see her. One more cursory glance at the blank-eyed windows of the houses opposite, then she heaved herself up one leg at a time, wondering why, at her weight, it was still so hard to lift those bones a few feet. She fought with the drapes inside the room before finding herself crouched on top of Goldie's dresser. Some tubes and jars clattered beneath her.

There was less debris in the room than she remembered, the remainder no doubt divided onto glass slides in the forensics lab. What could she possibly find that they hadn't?

Creeping up the hall — why was she creeping? — she could see there had been no attempt to clean up the apartment. The police had collected their samples, then left without looking back. So much for civic responsibility.

She headed to the living-room, drawn by some ghoulish force. Goldie was gone, there was no blood, no bodily evidence to mark her final resting-place. Nevertheless Rebecca knelt down near the spot, trying to evoke earlier memories of Goldie than the image of her that had imprinted itself on the inside of Rebecca's eyelids.

She had to get on with it. Who was she feeling sorry for anyway? Goldie, or herself?

Rebecca began methodically opening drawers in the dining-room and kitchen, then in Goldie's bedroom and the den. She went through every paper she could find, foraging in the apartment for nearly two hours. So far, she had come up empty.

The last stop was the spare bedroom near the front. She had the least hope for it since it appeared unlived in. The closet had been trashed, its contents helter-skelter on the floor. Nothing of interest: old shoes, sweaters, blankets. The top drawer of the dresser had been left pulled out. She searched it and pulled out the other drawers in a cursory shuffle if only to convince herself she had looked. Then she found them. In the bottom drawer, pale blue against the nightgowns and slips lay a sheaf of airmail envelopes bound with an elastic. The police had found them and hadn't bothered with them.

The top envelope was written in a rounded European hand addressed to Mrs. Goldie Kochinsky in Argentina. Rebecca slipped off the elastic. All the envelopes were the same. The return address from Chana Feldberg on Bathurst Street in Toronto. Rebecca pulled out a letter and sighed. It was written in Polish. At least she assumed it was Polish, the strange dots over letters and strokes through l's. It certainly wasn't Spanish.

Suddenly a noise startled her. A key turned in the apartment door. Someone was stepping in. She held her breath while the blood began to roar in her ears.

chapter twenty-five

Rebecca quickly noted the window in the small room. It would take too long to open and would make too much noise. The closet in the corner. If she could make it to the closet without creaking the floor. A pounding, like a surf, began in her ears.

The intruder had stepped into the hall and stopped. Rebecca turned her body, slowly trying to head for the closet. Clothes lay strewn on the floor. Her feet prodded the ground gingerly before each step. The surf rose in her ears.

The intruder moved through the living-room. Rebecca caught the toe of her running shoe in a sweater on the floor. It made a slight shuffling noise that she hoped would not be noticed. No such luck.

"Is someone there?" said a voice Rebecca recognized. The intruder appeared in the doorway of the small room and turned on the light.

"What are you doing here, Doctor?" asked Feldberg.

He was small, she thought. I'm only in trouble if he has a weapon. "I could ask you the same thing," she said.

His chin rose in a self-righteous thrust. "I wanted to see the condition of the apartment. What needed to be done. I helped her with the maintenance while she was alive. She was my sister-in-law, after all. I have a right."

The beat of the ocean receded from Rebecca's ears. She bridled at his gall. Goldie had dealt with everything herself. He needed a good jolt of reality.

"Perhaps you want to take responsibility for cleaning it up then."

His thin lips twisted as he looked around. "I'm going to call and complain to the police. They'll have to send someone." His eyes moved down to her hands and his expression shifted, resolved at the sight of the letters.

He stepped closer to the door, then held out his palm before her, ready to receive them. "I believe that is my property," he said, the German accent more guttural.

Suddenly the letters took on a new light. She quickly bundled up the envelopes and put them in her purse. "This is something Goldie left for me," she said.

She tried to step past him in the hall. He grabbed her arm and held her fast. "Are those the letters of my wife?"

Size wasn't everything, she realized. His grip was iron hard. She was in pitiful shape in comparison.

"Certainly not. I wouldn't keep letters from your wife." She counted a heartbeat. "My secretary's waiting for me outside." She looked down pointedly at his hand on her arm.

For long seconds he seemed to be weighing his options. Then his iron fingers released her with reluctance. She scooped up her jacket and hurried out the front door.

Rebecca had trouble concentrating that afternoon in the office. She was relieved the problems her patients brought her that day were relatively simple ones. Flus, birth control problems, stomach ailments. Iris had given her an odd look several times and Rebecca wondered if her distraction was showing. She would not compromise the care of her patients. If she had to take off more time, she would.

At the end of the day she eased into a chair near Iris, who was finishing some paperwork. All Rebecca could think of was the sheaf of letters that lay undeciphered in her purse. Who did she know who spoke Polish?

"You must've been out late last night," Iris said without looking up.

Rebecca shifted gears. She hadn't mentioned the trip to the club or the police. "Did you call?"

"Twice. Did you get my message?"

"I didn't check my phone. I just went straight to bed."

Iris finally looked up from her papers. "Are you all right?"

Rebecca was unwilling to drag her friend into her own troubles. She didn't want anyone else on her conscience. "You're always telling me to go out, so I went out."

Iris pulled her glasses down to perch on her nose and observe Rebecca. "You look tired," she said. "Come for dinner tonight. Joe and Martha are coming. They'd love to see you again."

Rebecca wasn't in the mood for company. She stood up. "I know what I need," she said, trying to sound more cheerful than she felt. "It's a good day for a brisk walk."

As soon as she closed the door to her inner office, Rebecca looked up the number of the bakery.

"Could I speak to Rosie?"

"She gone home." A tired woman's voice.

Rebecca peeked at her watch: six o'clock. "Could I have her home number?"

"We don't give up home numbers. Call tomorrow." The woman was finished.

"Wait! Do you happen to know if she speaks Polish?"

There was a surprised pause. "Rosie? Nah. She speak Jewish."

"What about you? Do you speak Polish?"

"Me! You joking? I'm Hungarian. Look, customers are here. I'm busy."

The woman hung up.

Grey vaporous clouds hung over Cecil Street, casting a pall. Rebecca marched smartly along the sidewalk in her sweatpants and leather running shoes, though her heart wasn't in it. She had to clear her mind. Speedwalking was good for that. April smelled of earth and moist clouds. She wanted to take it all in, like someone seeing it for the last time. To die in spring would be too ironic, everything just beginning again. God, she felt morose. A few days ago she could almost hear the new buds twisting in the ground. Now it hardly seemed possible to consider any kind of regeneration on this grey-canopied street.

She needed to feel her pulse rise, get her heart beating like it used to when she felt alive. The light at Spadina turned in her favour as she approached and on impulse she decided to cross to the market side. There was something about disorderly stores and merchandise spilling onto sidewalks that suggested energy, an affirmation.

It wasn't till she reached Baldwin Street that the gathering odour of dead meat and fish negated that promise. She glanced down the street, then stopped. Blue Danube Fish sat sedately in the evening. She wondered whether Vogel knew anyone in the market who spoke Polish. It was Friday; everything was still open. Shoppers strolled along Spadina, some of them peering up at the lowering sky. Rebecca stepped onto Baldwin Street. A misty drizzle cooled her skin.

It was almost too late when she saw him striding toward her from the parking garage across the street. The grey sweatsuit, the baseball cap that shaded his eyes into a dark blur. He was coming straight at her. She gasped at his speed. He was three yards away when she turned around and bolted across Spadina against a red light.

Traffic was slow but two cars had to brake to avoid her. One honked as it streaked by within inches, raising the airborne spray into her face. She turned, looking for her pursuer: the grey sweatsuit weaved between the cars more deftly than she. Nearly across the six lanes, she dived for the curb to avoid a speeding taxi. Her foot slipped on the pavement. She fell down on one knee, stunned for a moment as blood began to appear through her pants.

"Wait! Stop!" someone called out.

She jumped up and began to run again. No looking back, no time left. Down the other side of Baldwin, run to Beverley Street. Her knee began to throb, she wasn't running fast enough, the trusty running shoes couldn't do it alone, they couldn't perform miracles. The office was too far away, she wouldn't make it. She'd have to stand and fight in front of one of those gaudily painted houses. No, her best bet was to find someone at home. There was no one apparent on this side of Baldwin, especially since the drizzle in the air had taken shape and slanted into a soft rain. Her hair hung wet and sticky in her face.

She could barely see where she was going. She couldn't run anymore. This house would have to be it! She pulled herself up two steps at a time onto a veranda, the green door in sight. Just get to the door! He was stumbling up the stairs right behind her.

"Jesus!" he said as they both toppled over an old bike that leaned into a corner of the veranda. The front door of the house was within reach while her body swayed over the bike. She began to bang her fist on the door.

"Listen to me!" he cried, trying to pull her away.

Just then the door opened. An elderly Chinese woman in a brocade blouse stood in the doorway.

"Call the police!" Rebecca cried at her. "911."

The tiny woman looked from Rebecca to the man and back at Rebecca again with expressionless eyes, then uttered a stream of singsong Chinese.

Rebecca tried to make for the open door but the man held her back. "Police! Call the police!" she yelled.

The woman registered a brief exclamation of annoyance, then closed the door.

The man took Rebecca by the shoulders and held her firmly. He was very strong, she couldn't move. He said something to her but she was too frightened to listen. Suddenly adrenaline coursed through her when she remembered. Her office keys were in her pants pocket. Plunging her hand inside, she struggled to arrange the keys between her knuckles. Then, with all her strength, she plucked her hand out of her pocket and aimed at his face. Sharp metal edges scraped at his cheek.

He let go of her then. His hand probed the wound. He looked down at the blood on his fingers. "Are you crazy?" he said in a perturbingly quiet voice. "Why did you do that?"

For the first time she looked at his face. His eyes were not what she expected. They were deep-set and restrained with a perplexing depth to them. And he wasn't big, just a few inches taller than her. But her heart still pumped fiercely and her words gasped out.

"Why are you chasing me?"

"I need to talk to you."

"Talk to me?"

Under the wet visor he watched her. "I'm sorry if I frightened you. I wanted to talk to you about Goldie Kochinsky."

"Just who are you?"

"I was trying to tell you back there but you wouldn't stop. My name is Malkevich. Nesha."

Despite the cap, his face had not escaped the rain and drops of moisture glistened on his tanned cheeks. A piece of puzzle edged into place.

"Look, I'm sorry about back there," he said. "I should've tried...."

"You're the cousin," she said in an instant of revelation.

"She told you about me?" Rain mingled with the blood on his face.

"You didn't have to chase me. You could've tried some other way to communicate." Rebecca felt stupid and embarrassed and, finally, paranoid.

"I said I was sorry...."

"Forget it," she said. "We'd better see to that cut. My office is just around the corner."

chapter twenty-six

They were both soggy as they climbed the stairs to Rebecca's office, their footsteps echoing in the empty building. She found some towels in a storage closet. Thank you, Iris. Handing one to Goldie's cousin, she led him to an examining room, then excused herself. In her private office, she removed the sweatpants and put on her light wool skirt. Her knee had stopped bleeding; she quickly washed it off and applied a bandage.

When she returned to the examining room, she was caught off guard by the change in the man's appearance. He had pulled off his wet sweatshirt and thrown the towel around his shoulders. His upper body was surprisingly muscular. The cap had come off revealing longish, damp grey-black hair that hung over his ears. The rain had washed most of the blood off his face. His melancholy eyes watched her.

"This wouldn't have happened if you'd told me who you were right away, Mr. Malkevich," she said.

"Call me Nesha."

She swabbed the cuts on his face with antiseptic.

He smelled of soap. "When was the last time you saw Goldie?"

"I was seven or eight."

Rebecca stopped a moment, surprised.

"We lived far apart in Poland. They were city girls, we were country cousins. Didn't visit often. Goldie left for Argentina when I was nine. Then the war broke out in September. For five years I was isolated from the world. When I was fifteen, my Uncle Sol found me and brought me to California."

So this was the root of his melancholy. "You were very young. How did you survive?"

"Who says I survived?"

She took in an involuntary breath. "I'm sorry. I didn't mean to intrude."

He watched her face with glazed unseeing eyes. He was disconnected from his body, ignoring her ministrations. "A Nazi patrol pulled into our town. *Ordnungspolizei*, order police, though I didn't know it then. I was playing deep in the woods with a Polish friend. By the time we got back, all the Jews were being marched in this ragged line into the square. I saw my mother in the line holding my little brother's hand, my older brothers were somewhere behind. She was turning around looking for me. I started to run to her, waving my arms, but before I could get close, our eyes met. She shook her head frantically — I didn't know what to do. She had such a look on her face. I'd never seen her look like that, filled with terror. Some women were wailing, and that look on her face — I held back.

"A Nazi officer stood in the centre of the square, directing the chaos. His uniform was clean and pressed, his leather boots shined. He was a giant — immaculate, the handsomest man I'd ever seen. We were all small

218

and dirty in comparison. We were nothing. Even the visor on his cap — it threw a shadow over half his face. Anonymous, mysterious power. I was too far away to see his features, but the aura of fear after all these years — I ran away into the woods. I deserted them. I saved myself. But I realized even then that there was no point being alone without them. So, after a while, I ran back. This is what haunts me forever. They were all in the synagogue when I got back. The soldiers had set fire to the building. Flames rose out of the windows. Screams, screams — I can still hear them. One girl managed to get out of a window. They shot her while she ran. I watched and didn't understand anything. It's still a mystery. What had these people done? Everyone I ever loved went up in smoke. The air was filled with ashes."

Rebecca felt her skin crawl with his darkness. She couldn't leave him there. "Where did you go then?"

He pulled the towel closer around himself, crossed his arms over his chest. "Back into the woods. I found a group of Jewish partisans. Maybe they found me. I stayed with them till we were raided. Somehow I managed to escape. I was young. I could run fast."

She smiled slyly. "You still can."

He pursed his lips, nearly smiled.

"Go on," she said.

"I was alone for a while before I found some more partisans. I constantly had to find new groups because people were always being caught, disappearing. Anyone who managed to survive in the woods was a partisan. We fought with whatever we could find. A few had guns but it was rare. Then one day, I got a gun. I'll never forget because it was the first time I saw a Nazi killed. He must've been on patrol and gotten lost. The partisans I was staying with then, one of them stabbed him, then ran off. A group of us teenagers hid

219

behind trees for twenty minutes watching the body, sure he would get up again. You have to understand, the Nazis were like gods. We were afraid to look at them. They were so far above us. How can I explain? They weren't real. We didn't believe they could die. So when they killed this Nazi, we thought: how can a god die? Finally I got up the courage to approach — I was fifteen then. Up close he looked like all the other corpses I'd seen. I touched him with my foot. He rolled over and I knew he was dead. It was a revelation. I took his gun." He looked askance at her, mischievously. "I still have it."

Rebecca led him down the hall into her inner office. She took the kettle Iris kept near the sink and boiled some water for tea while he watched, ensconced in one of her upholstered chairs.

"You said you went to California?"

"My Uncle Sol, on my father's side. I don't know how he found me. I was fifteen by then. A couple of years later I got a letter from Goldie and Chana. That was the first I knew Chana had survived. Somehow they'd traced me to Uncle Sol's, who was no relation to them. They were very polite, but we hardly knew each other. I grew up. I studied accounting. My life went on. We corresponded off and on for years, mainly on holidays. When Chana moved to Canada she stopped writing. But I still heard from Goldie now and then."

Suddenly Rebecca thought of something. "In what language?"

"What?"

"What language did you correspond in?"

He thought a moment. "Polish."

She jumped up and pulled her purse out of the closet. Taking the top letter out of its envelope, she thrust it under his nose. "Can you tell me what this says?"

220

He took the page and held it out at arm's length. "I should get reading glasses." After a moment, he said with surprise, "This is from Chana." Then in a voice halting in the translation, "'I wish you would come. Even for a visit. The High Holidays will be here soon. Please, please come. I am so lonely here. Leo doesn't like me having friends or going out. He even got angry when I tried to meet someone for lunch.'"

Rebecca handed Nesha a few more letters. He stumbled, reading. "'If only I had children, but as you know, this topic was always forbidden. Once he made up his mind, there was no changing it. I so much wanted children. How is Enrique? It's been so long since I heard from you. We could help you move here if only you would think about it. Please write. You are the only person I can talk to. Leo is always angry with me about something. Sometimes he scares me.'"

Nesha flipped to another letter. "'I had a dream that took me back thirty years. I was in the camp again.'" He dropped the letter down, shaking his head. "Enough," he said.

"Please go on," she said softly. "I'd like to hear."

He observed her for a moment, his brown eyes resigned, as if to say: You really want to know this? Alright, you shall hear it.

"'I was in the camp again. The Ukrainian guard took me from the barracks, walked behind me to the building that I cleaned every day, the officers' quarters. Only, something makes me afraid today and I don't want to go. There's something there I don't want to see, and I resist. So in my dream I'm walking slowly, very slowly down the street. The Ukrainian guard screams to walk faster. And I try, but it's like I'm in water, I cannot make my limbs move faster. I don't want to go inside. But it's not in my control and suddenly, I'm in

the room, the dust rag in my hand and then — then I
see it, what I've been so afraid of. *The Hand*. I don't
want to touch it but I can't help it. I'm drawn to the
shelf where it sits upright, like a silver glove on a glass
base. I remember it perfectly — the little framed glass
windows over the knuckles of the middle fingers. In my
dream I reach for it closer and closer but I know I
mustn't touch it or I'll die. Just like *he* did. I'm about to
touch the silvered fingernails. I'm willing to die to
touch it — then I wake up. Goldele, I'm frightened of
this dream. It's a bad omen. I don't understand why it's
come back to haunt me.'"

Nesha let the letter fall into his lap. They both sat
in a solemn quiet.

"What do you suppose it means?" she said.

He shrugged. "A nightmare. People who lived
through those times always have nightmares."

"But it was so specific."

"Why did you give me these?" he said.

"I'm sorry if they upset you...," she said. "But the
brother-in-law didn't want me to have them."

"So?"

"Maybe he had something to do with Goldie's
death."

Nesha shook his head. "I haven't told you
everything. I didn't come to you right away because I
didn't know if I could trust you. I didn't know what your
role was in this whole thing."

"My role?"

"I saw you come out of Goldie's place the night she
died. Then I saw you go into the store on Baldwin
Street. I thought you might be involved in some way."

"What does the store have to do with anything?"

A minute ticked by before he seemed to make a
decision. Reaching into the pocket of his sweatpants, he

pulled some folded pieces of paper out of a plastic liner.

"I've been after this man most of my life. Last week I got lucky. A trick of fate brought me this." He unravelled one of the pages and held it out to Rebecca.

She recognized the picture that Goldie had waved in her face that last time in the office. A duck running along a sidewalk. But now that Rebecca could study the photo, she saw the Blue Danube Fish shop in the background. Walking past it, emerging from a shadow, was the unmistakable image of Feldberg.

Then came the Shoichet* and slaughtered the ox
That drank the water that quenched the fire
That burned the stick that beat the dog
That bit the cat that ate the goat
That Father bought for two zuzim.
    One little goat, one little goat.

* ritual slaughterer

chapter twenty-seven

"This is the man?" Rebecca said, gaping at the picture.

Nesha, who was about to take a sip of tea, sat up to attention. "You recognize him?"

"It's him," she said. "This is the brother-in-law."

"I don't understand," Nesha said in a flat voice. "Chana's husband?"

"This is Leo Feldberg," she said, incredulous herself.

"Is it possible?" he said, staring at the picture as if for the first time. "Steiner has hidden himself in plain sight all this time by masquerading as a Jew?"

"You lost me," she said. "Who's Steiner?"

"*Oberscharführer* Johann Steiner. The Nazi in the square that day."

"But you said you were too far away to see his face."

"I would never be able to recognize him. That's why it took me so long to find him. He wasn't one of the major ones. Maybe he only killed five hundred instead of ten thousand. Maybe no one was looking for him except me. I had to do research — it was just luck — I found a file with documents, papers with his signature. And this photo." He couldn't take his eyes off it. "Why would the photo be in his file if it wasn't him?"

"Where did you find the file?"

He observed her. "You know, most people don't want to hear this stuff."

"Please, I want to know."

He stared at her another moment, then went on. "As soon as I arrived in America I started looking for him. I didn't know his name; I didn't know what he looked like. Every year on the anniversary of that day in April, I went to the Jewish Congress searching for information. Then the Wiesenthal Center opened and I kept looking. For anything. Names, documents. Anything. Other boys my age played football and lied to their parents about where they took their dates. All I dreamed about was finding the murderer. It was as if...," he struggled to find the words, "as if there was a fire burning in me. Like the fire I'd seen consume my family. It won't be put out until I get him." He pulled the towel tighter around himself.

"They got to know me at the Wiesenthal Center. I always asked for Louis. He showed me whatever they got that year that might've helped. Up till now there was almost nothing. But finally I got lucky. A man named Greenspan, a survivor, died recently and his children sent them his research in boxes. His son said he didn't want it in the house. That he had to listen to it all his life and now he was glad to get rid of it. So the poor schnook spent half his life collecting this stuff, maps, photos, all kinds of goodies, and his children couldn't give it away fast enough. Louis just left me in the room with all these cartons. Most of the stuff was labelled. But this one box I came across, it was some kind of a grab bag: photos, affidavits, old passports. And no labels. It was as if he had things left over he didn't know what to do with. So he threw them into a box until he could get to them. Only he never got to them. And there it was, just sitting and waiting for me after all these years. A very slim file with Steiner's name scribbled across. I photocopied what was in it, two photos and two documents."

He pulled more paper out of the small plastic folder he'd retrieved from the deep pocket of his sweatpants. Unfolding the sheet carefully, he held it up so that she could see the meticulous small script.

"I can't read German," she said.

"Of course," he said. "I'll translate." He took in a quick breath before starting.

"'We entered the village of Dobienk on Sunday, April 6, 1941, where my men rounded up 140 Jews with the help of local informants. Some locals helped us take them into the synagogue, which we set on fire. Also burned down the Jewish quarter. Rescued whatever silver pieces found, as instructed. *Unterscharführer* Johann Steiner.'"

Rebecca had barely grasped the horror of what he'd read when Nesha pulled out a second document from his little folder. She stared at it a few moments, realizing she didn't need a translation to figure it out. It seemed to be a day-by-day report in list form of the activities of Group 3 of the *Ordnungspolizei* for a period of a week in April 1941, beginning with the sixth. The flowing methodical hand of *Rottenführer* Ernst Waldhausen noted the town, date, and number of Jews killed in each, starting with Dobienk. Obviously this sheet represented only a quarter of the month. Somewhere lay the rest of the month, followed by the next month, and the next, all neatly recorded within the lines. A ledger of bones.

"Oh, my God!" she murmured. She looked up, wishing she could say something comforting to him, but he had already taken out the last thing in his plastic folder. She stared at the other photo he had copied from the file. A group shot of men in greatcoats standing in front of a fence of barbed wire. One man wore the peaked hat of an officer, the others cloth caps, his subordinates. Underneath was written "Skarzysko."

"I don't understand," she said. "Is this him, too?"

"I think what happened was that he was given this position at the camp — Skarzysko was a labour camp — as a reward for his services in the *Ordnungspolizei*. Probably promoted to *Oberscharführer* then. It must've been later in the war."

She examined the picture of the man. It had been taken from far away, all the faces blurred with time and distance. It could've been Feldberg. But then it could've been anyone.

All of a sudden Nesha came awake. "Where is he?"

She was startled by his newfound energy. "You don't know it's him."

"I'll ask him."

"Then what?"

He rubbed both eyes with his thumb and forefinger. "That has nothing to do with you."

"Let the police deal with him. If he's a killer."

He leaned his head forward toward her, his jaw set beneath the stubble starting to shade his skin. "Do you have the death penalty in this country?"

She looked away, understanding his drift and uneasy with it.

"Is it enough for him to go to jail?" he said. "You didn't know my family. But you knew Goldie. You know how if feels when someone you care about meets a violent end. Is it enough for that monster to go to jail and sit comfortably watching TV for the rest of his obscene life?"

"I'm only concerned for your safety," she said, impressed with the emotions he was raising in her. No, it wasn't enough.

He sat up stiffly. "I'm sure your concern is admirable, Doctor, but I neither need nor want it."

His attention turned to the letters in her lap. All at once he reached across the space between their chairs and lifted one of the empty envelopes from the top of the pile. His dark eyes travelled from the address on the envelope to her face.

"He didn't have far to go," said Nesha.

He rose abruptly, pulling the towel from around his shoulders, and headed for the examining room.

She stood in the hallway, watching him shuffle something from under the heap of his sweatshirt. Facing her, he took pains to manoeuvre it into his waistband out of her sight. Who did he think he was fooling? He pulled the still damp shirt over top.

"I can't let you go like this," she said alarmed. "Don't you care what happens to you? You could spend the rest of your life in prison."

"It means nothing to me. I've been in one kind of jail or another since I was ten years old."

"You must've had moments of happiness since then."

His full lips curled up in an ironic smile. "I know what you're trying to do, and I almost appreciate it. But it's too late to save me, Doctor. I have nothing to lose."

She stood in the doorway, blocking it. "I can't begin to understand what you've been through. To be honest, I don't want to understand. It's too painful. But that's why I can see the whole picture. You're too close. You can't see that you're about to ruin any chance for peace you may have."

"You're right — you can't begin to understand. It's my fault Goldie's dead. If I hadn't sent her the picture —"

"Don't fall into *that* trap. Let me help you."

"There's nothing you can do." He hovered near her impatiently. "Let me by."

"Let's sit down and talk."

"It's too late for that."

The quietness of his voice belied the turmoil underneath, the rage that fed the fire in his eyes. She was not going to convince him of anything.

She stepped backwards into the hall. He barely glanced at her, then squeezed past her out the door and downstairs. She couldn't call Wanless, there was no time. Besides, what would she say? Someone else believes in the murderer and plans to kill him? That sounded ludicrous, even to her.

She closed up her office and sailed down the stairs. From the front door she could see him getting into a blue car parked on Beverley Street. She lost sight of him for a minute while running to the back lot to get her car. It couldn't have been more than a minute, but by the time she turned north up Beverley, he was gone. That was all right. She knew where he was going. She just had to get there in time.

chapter twenty-eight

Rebecca raced her Jaguar up Beverley Street through the blue twilight. The rain had darkened the sky early as she turned left along College Street. The evening traffic rolled along here too slowly, people relaxed after a day's work with nowhere important to go. Exasperated, she cut into the right lane and turned north on Spadina. It would be faster this way.

She veered in and out of slower traffic, then was caught at a red light. It gave her a minute to think. Why was she in such a hurry? To stop Nesha from what? Killing someone who had been stalking her for two days? Killing Goldie's murderer? From her own personal viewpoint, it wouldn't be such a loss. She might be safe again. Why was she in such a goddam hurry? It couldn't be the democratic process she was rushing to save. Maybe it was Nesha's prospects once he had reduced himself to the level of everything he despised. She couldn't stop him if he had a gun. She was sure it was a gun. Probably *the* gun. She couldn't just watch him throw his life away. He'd been through so much already.

It was probably arrogance to think she knew what was best for him. The weight of that possibility, that perhaps justice was not always straightforward or even easy, held her back for a moment. Feldberg, if he was Steiner, deserved whatever Nesha gave him. But what did Nesha deserve? Better.

She sped the rest of the way, finally climbed the rolling hill of Bathurst Street till the familiar line of duplexes was in sight. She slowed down on approach, keeping an eye out for a blue car in vain. There were other streets he could park on. She passed Feldberg's building, Goldie's empty duplex, then made a right turn into the first side street off Bathurst. She parked, then hurried from her car.

In the dimming light, she sprinted down the block till she reached the front door of Feldberg's duplex. Opening it, she found herself in the entranceway before two apartments, the same layout as Goldie's. The door to Feldberg's apartment was closed. She hadn't noticed it being such a solid door when Feldberg had opened it for her. It had no window like Goldie's, but was made entirely of panelled wood with only a peephole. Better to keep people out.

She listened for shouts, two men arguing. There had been no gunshot; she would've heard that. Something was wrong though; it was too quiet. But she recalled Nesha's low still voice and imagined it recounting its horrors to an unrepentant Feldberg.

She did the ordinary thing. She knocked. Nothing. She knocked again. Not a sound, not a movement. She wasn't leaving without an answer.

"Mr. Feldberg!" she cried through the door. "Mr. Feldberg, it's Dr. Temple. Could I have a word with you?"

Without warning the door flashed part way open

and a leather-clad arm reached out. A strong hand grabbed her by the forearm, pulling her inside. A gasp issued from her throat.

The hall was dark but the reflected light from the living-room showed her Nesha in an old leather bomber jacket, one vexed hand on a hip. "You trying to wake up the whole neighbourhood?" His voice was a hoarse whisper.

"Where's Feldberg?" she murmured.

"Not here." He stood blocking her entrance into the apartment.

"How did you get in?"

"I'm not a burglar. It was open."

She looked over his shoulder at the apartment. "Open?"

"You don't believe me? I knocked. I heard him moving around in the apartment and I waited. Then everything got quiet and I got suspicious. So I tried the door. It was open and he was gone." Then something on the wall behind her distracted him.

She turned to find the keypad of what looked like a fancy burglar alarm. "I'd say you were lucky he hadn't turned the alarm on."

"I ran in. He probably didn't have time. He must've gone out the back door, but I wasn't fast enough to see him."

She turned back to look at the spotless apartment, the baby blue leather sofa, the steel and leather armchair. "Maybe he keeps a lot of cash," she said. "Why else would he need a burglar alarm?"

Then she noticed it. The Corot that had hung over the fireplace was gone.

She pushed her way past Nesha and ran to the spot where two hooks pierced the wall above the mantel. Against one arm of the leather couch leaned a very empty carved gilt frame.

She dove into the dining-room, Nesha on her heels. The Utrillo was missing. The empty frame had been thrown behind the steel and leather armchair. Everything else appeared as she remembered.

"Did you actually see who was in the apartment?" she said.

He shook his head.

"Then it could've been a thief who didn't know any better. That means that Feldberg could come walking in any minute." She stood still, listening. Someone honked outside on Bathurst Street, but the building was quiet.

"Let him come," he said. "I'm ready for him."

"I'd like to avoid a confrontation," she said. "If anyone comes to the door, we run out the back."

He gave her a wry smile. "You run, I'll cover you. What d'you mean the thief didn't know any better?"

"These paintings aren't real. They're good reproductions, but not valuable."

Nesha shrugged. "I don't know anything about art. I'm going to take a look around." He disappeared into one of the bedrooms.

Suddenly tired, she leaned against the small round table in the centre of the dining-room. "I don't understand any of it," she said out loud to herself. Sitting down, she lay one arm along the cool shiny surface of the burled wood. What exquisite taste he had for a man who repulsed her.

She looked up at the drawings she hadn't seen before on the wall opposite. They were religious sketches of saints and angels, possibly studies drawn before a painting in oil. She tried to cross one leg over the other under the table, but there wasn't enough room beneath the wooden apron skirting the tabletop. Her leg had elicited a dull thud from below, making it apparent that a panel closed off the bottom of the apron. Then where was the drawer? There was more than enough room for a drawer, but there *was* no drawer. She poked her head beneath: there were no openings, no latches, no knobs. What was she looking for?

She knocked the flat of her fingers gently against the underside of the table, like somebody's belly. Hollow. She moved her fingers further to the left. Hollow. She moved to the right. Not hollow. She struck it again. The table resonated. Definitely not hollow. Something was inside that section of the table. She bent down on one knee to examine the apron. It was divided into four quadrants, each ending with a seam at one of the legs.

She pulled at the quadrant that echoed with its elusive contents. No movement. Maybe she was wrong. She pried around its edges trying to loosen any joints. She pulled at it again. Nothing. This time she took off her shoe and banged it around underneath the apron.

Nesha emerged from the bedroom. "Are you crazy?" he said under his breath. "There might be people upstairs."

Rebecca tugged at the quadrant of wood once more. To her surprise it pulled out easily. Inside lay an album of some kind. Nesha came closer as she lifted the plastic cover. Each page contained two plastic sleeves for photos, one above the other, set into a wire spiral. The first photo was a likeness of a Claude Monet painting of lilies. A very good likeness, the swirling violets and greens approximating summer in Giverny. Inserted into the sleeve below was a typewritten card: Alfonso Hauptmann, Avenida Arboles, 124, Buenos Aires, 467-9342. She flipped to the next page. A photo of a crowd scene by Renoir. The women in hooped skirts and flounced hats, the men cavalier in their boaters. The card below read: Victor Ocampo, Calle Cordoba, 56, Buenos Aires, 921-0743.

"This is a waste of time," Nesha said impatiently, and returned to his search through the bedrooms.

She kept flipping the plastic-sheathed photos, mesmerized by the beauty of the paintings. What could such a catalogue mean and why was he hiding it? All the addresses on the cards were from South America. Then she came upon an extraordinary picture. It was labelled *Portrait of a Young Man*, by Raphael. Good God, she thought. *Raphael*. They really picked the best ones. The painting was a tease — a young nobleman with dark hair curling over shoulders that blended, in the shadows of the photo, into a rich robe. Wistful eyes beneath perfect feminine brows watched sideways, averted from the viewer. She froze when she read the card below: Max Vogel, 103 Northgate Cres., Toronto, Ontario.

How did Vogel know Feldberg? And what did this picture mean? She pried the photo and address card from their plastic sleeves. Then she replaced the catalogue into the quadrant of wooden apron beneath the table and pushed it back into place as quietly as she could.

She knew a little about Raphael from her undergrad art history courses, that he was overshadowed in the Italian Renaissance by the giants da Vinci and Michelangelo. He was famous for his dewy, graceful Madonnas, but it was his secular portraits that lingered in the memory for the depth of their feeling.

Had she seen this particular portrait before? She approached the oversized art book that lay on Feldberg's coffee table. It was a good compendium of art history from prehistoric times to the present. She looked up Raphael in the index at the back. There was reference to a *Portrait of a Young Man* in chapter eight. She quickly turned to the page where the title was narrowed down to *Portrait of Bindo Altoviti*. The arrogant young man there looked quizzically over his shoulder, his neck adorned with reddish-blonde hair. The elegant narrow shape of the head was similar but the two young men were miles apart in character. This one lived at the National Gallery in Washington. Who knew how many portraits of young men Raphael had painted. What was she looking for anyway? She'd have to wait to speak to Vogel.

She crept into the small bedroom at the front of the flat, listening for sudden noises. A bare clothes dummy stood in one corner, a tiny delicate size that probably suited both Chana and Goldie. There were two dressers, a wooden chair, its seat covered with a home-made cushion, and a table that looked like it had been a stand for Chana's sewing machine.

Rebecca began to open the drawers of one of the dressers, painstaking in her attempt at silence. Cuts of neatly folded fabric lay stored inside, awaiting the seamstress. Each time Rebecca made a noise, she stopped and listened, waiting for someone to come through the door and discover them.

The top drawer of the other dresser was filled with spools of thread of all shades. In one corner of the drawer lay a cookie tin. She opened it, thinking to find sewing paraphernalia. Instead, she found a mound of pale blue airmail envelopes, much like the ones she had confiscated from Goldie's apartment. Only these were from Goldie to Chana. Rebecca pulled out the top letter. No use. She had to find Nesha.

She tiptoed toward the light in Feldberg's bedroom. With each creak, she stopped and waited, adrenaline on alert. The room was empty. The bed floated beneath a down-filled black and blue duvet, its headboard and dresser a rich mahogany. There was very little surface clutter, everything orderly.

She heard a sudden scrape of metal on metal coming from the den. When she got there, Nesha stood near the open drawer of a small desk, absorbed in some kind of ledger. He'd broken the lock.

"Could you read this?" she said, holding a page in front of his face.

When he looked up his eyes were distant, but he took the page from her. His lips began to move silently. "This is an old letter Goldie wrote to her sister," he replied, still reading. "Nostalgic, but not useful, I think."

"Could you...?" Rebecca said.

He glanced at her briefly, then began. "'Chanele, I'm so glad you are still in touch with our cousin in California. Our dear cousin. How strange and wonderful to think of someone who brings to mind our life from so long ago. Memories both painful and happy. Happy because life at home was good; Mother, Father, our sisters and brothers, all happy memories of those poor sweet souls. What I can't bear to think about is leaving them behind, never seeing them again. The grief never goes away. It is good to know there is one last person still living who has some connection to our dear family.'"

Rebecca felt a trembling come over her. She closed her eyes and rubbed her forehead. "It doesn't sound like the same person. She's so articulate in Polish. I never knew that side of her. I never really knew her at all. It was always such a struggle for her to communicate in English." She felt her eyes tear over, quickly forced herself past the moment, unwilling to lose control in front of a stranger.

"What about the others?" she said, pulling out a few of the letters.

He scanned them quickly. "Same kind of thing.

Domestic details. Goldie telling her she was lucky to be in Canada. Sympathizing with her about the husband. And so on." He handed the sheets back to her.

A car door closed somewhere nearby. Both their heads snapped up. Nesha carefully replaced the books in the desk. Rebecca's body stiffened from the effort of listening. Someone had just parked outside in the back. A man's voice disturbed the quiet. A key turned in the lock of the side door.

Nesha grabbed Rebecca's hand and pulled her toward the closet in the corner. The side door of the duplex slammed and a woman's voice joined the man's. Nesha pushed her inside the closet, then squeezed in front, closing the door. She was pressed tightly against his back; she had to turn her face to the side. She was gagging on the overpowering smell of mothballs. His breathing was remarkably even as his shoulder blades moved softly against her chest. Even if they weren't discovered, how would they get out? In another second, noisy footsteps began to pound up the stairs. The other apartment. They both let out their breath but waited until the steps sounded overhead. She realized she was leaning her head against the back of his neck.

"Good God!" she whispered, when he opened the door. She couldn't breathe amid the mothballs. The tenants were moving around in their apartment upstairs.

"Why don't you go?" he said, once they were back in the den. "It'll be safer." His eyes seemed softer when he looked at her.

"If you come."

He smiled with resignation. "You're a stubborn woman."

They headed down the hall. Near the phone on the kitchen counter lay the day's mail, mostly bills and junk mail. However, one envelope bore an official-looking return address from Germany. Without hesitation, she pulled out the letter on official stationery, heavily typed in German. All she could tell was that Feldberg was being notified about something that involved money.

She thrust the sheet in front of Nesha's face. "How's your German?"

He screwed up his eyes and began to move his lips silently.

"The bastard!" he said finally. "He's getting paid for his so-called suffering. Incredible! This letter says his restitution — he's getting restitution from Germany! — will go up because of his incarceration at a labour camp in Poland. Which camp was he in?"

Nesha's eyes shifted quickly along the page. "*Skarzysko Kamienna.* That's it!" he cried. "That's the link. Steiner was in *Skarzysko* — he was promoted to the labour camp. It's *him*!"

She shook her head. "How could he have lived all these years as a Jew? Even fooling his wife?"

"Everything fits. Do you have a better explanation?"

Rebecca was pushing the letter back into the envelope when a ring exploded from the phone less than two feet away, making her jump. Nesha lurched toward her protectively. They stood watching each other, waiting through three rings, then four. Suddenly a machine clicked on. Feldberg's raspy voice told the caller to leave a message.

"Leo, pick up the phone. I know you're there." Rebecca recognized Isabella's low Hispanic voice. "Please, Leo, I need you tonight. I can't go on. I called Teresa to take my place at the club but I can't stand it, can't stand being alone here." She'd had something to drink. Probably numerous somethings. "You must forgive your Isabelita if I said something. I can't remember, did I say something bad? Where are you, I've been calling for hours! Please don't be angry, pick up the phone, please Leo, please."

When the phone finally clicked off, Rebecca said, "We've got to get out of here." She turned to look into his face. "Now."

He blinked once, expressionless, but he didn't argue. "Just a minute," he said. He vanished into the den and came out a minute later with Feldberg's ledger and a few bankbooks.

"You're taking those?" she said.

"I'm an accountant. I'm going to do his books."

chapter twenty-nine

Nesha, carrying the ledger under his arm, walked Rebecca back to her Jaguar which she had parked on a side street off Bathurst. She was the one looking over her shoulder at the empty street. The people in the houses whose tidy lawns and ornamental trees breathed quietly in the dark were no doubt sunk in front of their TVs by now and paid no attention to two shadows navigating the sidewalk.

"Nice car," he said. The red coat beamed beneath the street lamp.

"Want a ride to yours?" she asked.

He got in and she drove him one street over to his rental car. He was in no hurry to get out.

"Are you hungry?" she asked. It was nearly nine.

He smiled. "Got any Jewish delicatessens here?"

"Follow me," she said.

They drove in tandem along Eglinton Avenue, she leading in her Jaguar, he following in his rented Olds. She shifted lanes around slow cars and kept an eye on Nesha in her mirror. Close to Avenue Road, she signaled that she was parking. They were two blocks away from her house. Across the street was Yitz's Deli, a long-standing Toronto fixture where the robust fragrance of corned beef had decades ago settled permanently into the sidewalk in front of the store.

On their way to their table they passed a cooler filled with jars of dill pickles and pickled red peppers. Nesha flipped the over-long pages of the laminated menu and grinned. "This is my kind of place. We don't have anything like this in San Francisco. I guess we've assimilated too well."

He ordered a pastrami sandwich on rye and a kishka. She watched him eat in wonder as she nibbled at her salad. She would've been up all night with such fare.

"What's it like in San Francisco?"

The food had relaxed him. His black eyes gleamed in the soft light of the booth. "The most beautiful place on earth," he said. "Not just the city itself. The bay. All the little towns around it. I can see the Golden Gate Bridge in the distance right outside my window. It's like a misty piece of art. There's something new each time the light shifts. I read somewhere there was an artist who painted a haystack a hundred times, each time in a slightly different light. That guy would've loved the Golden Gate Bridge."

"Monet," she said. "It was Monet." She was reminded of David and the connection made a piece of lettuce stick in her throat.

"I'm a little disoriented here because of the flatness. My house is set into the side of a hill and the eye is constantly moving up. Very exciting, really. You've heard of 'sea legs'? Well, a few times I've had to catch myself from keeling over here because I keep expecting a hill where there isn't one."

"I don't believe that for a moment," she said, smiling.

"Well, I invite you out west to check it out. Come visit me and I'll take you up all the good hills."

"What about your family?"

"My son's away at college. I'm alone in the house." Then, "Who's at your house?"

"I'm a widow. My husband died last fall."

Nesha shrunk back in his seat. "I'm sorry. Then you're still in mourning. That's the sadness I saw."

"Is it that obvious?"

He crossed his arms over his chest. "Only to someone else in pain."

Tears stung her eyes without warning and she turned away. "I promised myself I wouldn't cry in front of people."

He reached out a hesitant hand. "I'm flattered that you feel safe enough with me."

He pulled back when the waiter approached. "Would you like some coffee?" Nesha asked.

"You know, my house is just around the corner," she said. "I can make us some coffee."

She unlocked her front door and felt him follow her in. It was an odd feeling, bringing a strange man into the house after ten.

She turned on the light in the kitchen. "I only have decaffeinated coffee."

"You're too young for your diet," he said. Suddenly he yawned.

"You must be tired," she said.

She led him into the den and turned on a lamp. "Make yourself comfortable and I'll bring in the coffee."

"Black," he said and sat down heavily on the L-shaped sofa.

She was carrying the cups into the den when she stopped in her tracks: he was fast asleep on one L of the sofa, lying with his knees up toward his chest, hand under his head. He had taken off his shoes. The gun lay nearby on a coffee table. His face had softened, the eyebrows dark and finely formed against the skin. There was something touching about the shape he had taken. Something vulnerable and young that was hidden while he was awake. It was probably self-defence after all he had been through. Suddenly she saw him ten years old, thin and dirty, spinning through the indifferent Polish woods, eyes filled with terror and grief, too preoccupied trying to stay alive to mourn for his family. She had the inexplicable urge to take that boy in her arms and stroke his hair, tell him everything would be all right. Only she knew it wouldn't be. It would never be all right again.

She covered him with an afghan that lay nearby and turned the lamp off in the den. In the kitchen she poured the coffee back into the pot. She was dead tired herself but something was nagging at her. She knew what she had to do, but dreaded doing it. It was her own fault for putting the art books in the basement.

She opened the door that led downstairs and turned on the light. Her heart shrank as she stepped down the carpeted stairs. Without looking at David's paintings stored upright in the unfinished part of the basement, she approached the bookcase. She pulled out a thick volume on the Renaissance and plopped down on the nearby sofa with it. The old tweedy couch had been in their first apartment when they got married and Rebecca felt a twinge in her chest.

Checking the index references on Raphael she began to look up page numbers. She pushed past Madonnas and the St. George and the Dragon motifs that Raphael had been so enamoured of. She flipped pages impatiently and finally lost hope. Too many Renaissance artists to include more than a token of each. Then all of a sudden, there it was.

The nobleman with averted eyes beneath a perfect brow and the sensuous mouth of a girl. Below: *Portrait of a Young Man*, formerly in Krakow, Czartoryski Collection. She searched for elaboration in the text but the author was more interested in playing the profound art critic than imparting any practical knowledge:

> There has been a tendency to recognize Francesco Maria della Rovere, up to 1516 the Duke of Urbino, in the Czartoryski portrait of a young man of a beauty that is almost feminine, but cruel. But even if the identification is rejected today it is still the typical image of a lord of the *cinquecento*, refined and ethically insensible, in this face that looks at us contemptuously from the chromatic glory of the rich vestments....

Krakow, Rebecca thought. Her mother-in-law had grown up in Krakow. And hadn't been back since the war. Understandably, since most of her family had been killed in the vicinity. But Sarah was a resilient person, well-read and cultured, and it was just a little question she had for her. As long as they didn't talk about David.

Rebecca checked her watch. Just ten-thirty. She wouldn't tell Sarah she had a stranger sleeping on her den sofa. She picked up the old phone extension they kept downstairs and dialed Sarah's number.

"Hello dear, is anything wrong?" Sarah asked in her dramatic, scrupulous accent when she heard Rebecca's voice. Rebecca usually called her weekly on Sundays.

"No, no. Everything's fine." Yeah, sure. Rebecca pictured Sarah's slightly waved auburn hair, chin length and perky for a woman of sixty-one. "I just had a question I thought you might be able to answer."

"Yes?"

"Have you heard of the Czartoryski Collection in Krakow?"

"Oh, *Czartoryski*." She pronounced the *cz* like *ch*. "Yes, of course. They were an old aristocratic family in Poland. They collected art. All kinds of art. So what can you do when you have a mansion full of paintings and tapestries and beautiful furniture? You graciously open your doors and show everyone. So that's the museum."

Sarah had a lively critical mind and had picked up an impeccable English during her years in Canada. She was always studying something. "Why do you ask?"

"I'm trying to find out about one particular painting. My source says that a Raphael painting, a portrait of a young man, used to be there."

"Ah, one of the big three. Everyone knew there were three important paintings at the Czartoryski. The most famous one is *Lady with an Ermine*, by Leonardo da Vinci. They came from everywhere to see that. And a so-so Rembrandt landscape. Those two were recovered after the war. Not the Raphael."

"What happened to it?"

"Oh, that is the big question. First you have to know that the Germans were fond of art. They saw it as their rightful booty in war. Wherever they went they stole the best pieces. So when they invaded Poland, Hans Frank — he was the Nazi governor of Poland — confiscated those three famous paintings and hung them in his apartment in the castle. You know about the castle in Krakow? Wawel?" She pronounced it *Vavel*.

"Uh... no."

"Doesn't matter. When the Nazis realized they had lost the war, they ran with whatever they could carry that was valuable. I heard Frank grabbed those three paintings when he fled to Bavaria at the end of the war. When the Americans caught him he had the da Vinci and the Rembrandt with him. But not the Raphael."

"And it was never found?"

"You have to keep in mind the chaos at the end of the war. Everybody was on the move. The people who were lucky enough to survive roamed around in shock. Suddenly their Nazi captors had fled. As for the Germans, if they knew where to look and they kept their heads, they could pick up stolen pieces their comrades had left behind. There were many, many stolen pieces." A slight pause. "What's your interest in this, dear?"

"It's a long, involved story. Maybe I'll be able to unravel it by the time you come over on Passover."

Rebecca slowly climbed the stairs from the basement. She was not only exhausted, but bewildered. Could Vogel actually have in his possession the genuine Raphael? And if so, what about the other pieces in Feldberg's catalogue? She couldn't think anymore.

Leaving only a night-light on in the kitchen, she crept into the den where Nesha still slept on the sectional sofa. He had barely moved, his breathing rhythmic. She lay down on the adjoining L of the sofa. David's watercolour of her reclining by the river hung mutely above her like a remnant of another life. A street lamp sent a blue shaft of light through the window onto the floor. The triangle of light floated toward the ceiling and grew into a blinding horizon that loomed before her. The sun glanced off the river into her eyes. She squinted as she jogged along the shore. When she got closer, the line of the horizon wiggled and took on a familiar shape. It settled into the outline of David painting at an easel.

David. She could feel the fuzzy flannel of his shirt, the
orange hair between her fingers though he was fifty feet
distant, his back turned to her. She also knew, without
seeing the canvas, that he was painting a self-portrait.
Which struck her as odd, since he'd never expressed any
interest in doing one. She quickened her pace, prodded
by the urgency of reaching him before he disappeared.
She called out to him but he was intent on his work and
didn't turn. He must be alive, she thought, or he
wouldn't be so casual about seeing her again. The whole
thing in the hospital was a nightmare and he's alive. Her
chest expanded with such relief — when she reached him
she flung her arms around him, weeping in her throat.
He lost no time directing her to the painting on the easel.
She tore herself away to stare into the dark melancholy
eyes of Nesha reproduced on the canvas, the deft brush
strokes rendering his sculpted mouth open in an
expression of surprise.

"Rebecca..."

Her eyes shot open. Nesha crouched before her,
one knee resting on the floor. The light from the
kitchen slanted off his face. "You were calling out," he
said shyly.

"I'm sorry." She sat up, embarrassed, tears still in
her throat. "I was dreaming about my husband."

He was still crouching. "Then I'm sorry," he said.

Now that she was sitting, he had to look up at her.
He observed her openly without speaking. To her
surprise she wasn't self-conscious; rather, she felt
comfortable with him.

"You're not as strong as you make out," he said.

"Are you?"

He reflected for a minute, then stood up. "I am
when I swim."

This was something new, she thought.

"When I feel really bad, I find the nearest pool and swim and swim till I can't breathe anymore. I feel strong in the water; it keeps me afloat." His hands were curled into loose fists. "But in the end it doesn't matter. When your heart is dead, you can be strong. Mine's just a lump in my chest. You can do almost anything if you don't have to feel."

She stood up beside him. There was no expression in his eyes as she brought the fingers of one hand together and pressed them flat against his chest. She tilted her head, played at listening to the ailing heart but the warmth of his body beneath her hand distracted her, the gentle breathing.

"I'm sorry to be the bearer of bad tidings," she said at last, feeling his eyes upon her. "But as a doctor, I can say with confidence that your heart is alive and well — and lodged firmly in your chest."

He seemed to be looking at her from beyond some gulf of distance or time. His gaze made her feel awkward and she began to pull her arm away. He caught her gently and clasped her hand to his chest with his own. She stopped breathing. His hand warmed hers against the delicate movement of his breast.

"It's been a long time since I let someone get this close," he whispered.

That seemed remarkable to her since her arm was almost fully extended. She stepped forward, insouciant. "How close?"

The line of his mouth relaxed, his eyes softened with bemused surprise as he watched her face, ten inches away. "Doctor —" he began.

"Rebecca."

"I don't think you understand. You can't save me."

"I don't give up as long as there's hope," she said.

His full lips parted, she was close enough to see the

sculpted line of his upper lip. "So where can you possibly see hope?" He asked this while still clasping his hand over hers, tight against his chest.

She squeezed his fingers and said, "Here." She lifted her face to his, whispering. "And here." Then she pressed her lips lightly against his wide sculpted mouth.

She pulled away, staggered by the silken warmth. He hadn't let go of her hand though his eyes were closed, his brow creased in some distress. The last thing she wanted was to cause him more pain. "I'm sorry," she murmured.

He opened his eyes and stared at her face a full minute, as if finding something there he had missed before. Then slowly, purposefully, he slid her hand from his chest up around his neck and drew her close. His soft mouth enfolded hers, burned with heat. She was melting into it, disappearing from the world gladly, dissolving into a lump of flesh and everything was gone except the arms pressing her waist strongly to his.

For two years she had forgotten how to feel desire. On the sectional couch in the den, Nesha reminded her. He probed her body like an explorer without maps, without compass, only instinct and passion to guide him. Nesha. His name was like the sound water made splashing over stones. Her head swam with his heat, with the tautness of his body arched against hers, the firm round muscles of his shoulders and thighs. His lips searched her breasts, her belly. She felt his bewilderment become hunger and she rejoiced in her victory over death. Hers as well as his. She rejoiced in the fever of her skin that burned where his hand touched. They made love in the hazy dark, the light of the street lamp splitting the night.

chapter thirty

Saturday, April 7, 1979

Why is it so cold? Isn't it spring? Why am I shivering under the cover, a duvet filled with enough silky down to clothe a flock of geese? Rebecca opened one eye and became disoriented. There was no duvet, there were no bedclothes, indeed there was no bed. She was lying stark naked under the afghan she usually kept folded on the den sofa. A thin light filtered into the room. Dawn. The highlights of last night played out before her eyes: Nesha's muscular body, his mouth sweetly pressing.... She craned her neck, still squinting from the light, to peer up at the other side of the sectional. Empty. Flown the coop. A one-nighter. He seemed more reliable than that. She looked over at the coffee table. There was a note.

Her arm reached out through the cold air. "Sorry to run. Call you later." He must've taken down her number from one of her phones.

She wrapped the afghan around herself and started upstairs. No, check the front door first. He couldn't have locked the deadbolt without a key. She hobbled down the hall to the door and clicked the deadbolt down. How long had he been gone? One hour? Two? The killer had missed his chance. Eyes screwed up against the incipient light, she hiked upstairs to bed and set her alarm for 8:45. Every new sound roused her as she drifted in a shallow sleep. The alarm woke her with a start. Exhausted, but awake. She had scheduled two hours of patients this morning, starting at ten.

After quickly showering, she pulled on a pair of beige linen trousers and a loose cotton sweater. She scrunched up her damp hair in her fingers, squeezing the curls into place. A bit of foundation on her skin, a bit of mascara, her cotton spring jacket, and she was out the door.

She drove down Avenue Road until it became Queen's Park, then all the way down to College Street. Traffic was light Saturday morning and allowed her the opportunity of mentally reliving last night's lovemaking. She was ashamed she had enjoyed it so much. *Sorry to run. Call you later.* Maybe Nesha hadn't felt the same.

She parked in the back lot beside Iris' Buick, the only car there since Lila Arons didn't work on Saturdays. She unlocked the back door of the building and stepped in. Approaching the staircase that led to her office she knew something was wrong — the door was ajar. She stopped cold half way up, listening for every sound. Iris never left the door open. What if he were up there? She listened. Nothing but the sound of her own heart. Iris. Rebecca ran the rest of the way until a few steps before the top, when her eyes were level with the office floor. All she could see was Iris' blonde head on the carpet.

"Oh, God," Rebecca whispered. Iris' large legs stretched out below her skirt, which bunched around her thighs. She lay face down on the grey carpet.

"Oh, God," Rebecca murmured at the blood on the coiffed blonde hair. Please be alright, she thought, her stomach lurching in her mouth. She thought of David, who had died despite her; she thought of her medical degree on the wall, a blind piece of parchment that guaranteed nothing, especially not the safety of loved ones.

Do something, she screamed at her paralyzed body. What was the order? *Think!* Breathing, Bleeding, Brain, Bladder, Bone. It would all come back automatically if she could only lose the panic. She knew what to do; she just had to do it. She forced herself to move, almost watched from a distance as that other Rebecca rolled Iris gently onto her side and listened for her breathing. She brought her face close to Iris' and watched her chest: slight but steady movement. Rebecca smiled. Okay, she thought. Okay. The pulse at her neck was weak but rapid. She lifted Iris' eyelids: her pupils responded to light. Good. Iris' hands were cold. She was in shock.

She ran to a small cabinet for gauze and pads. Crouching over Iris she applied pressure to the back of her head with a pad, wrapping long pieces of gauze around to keep it tight. That was when she noticed the wooden stool lying on its side behind her. It was kept in one of the examining rooms for her to sit on when she spoke to patients. It could have landed a crushing blow. Taking a closer look at one side, she could see blood on the wooden seat. She ran to one of the examining rooms for a blood pressure cuff and a scalpel.

"Sorry, Iris," she murmured under her breath and carefully pushed the scalpel through the sleeve of Iris' tailored jacket. She tore off the heavier fabric, then the silk of the blouse. Wrapping the blood pressure cuff around Iris' upper arm, she listened for her pulse through the stethoscope. Too low. She found a blanket to cover her with, then called 911. It would probably take them ten minutes to respond to the call.

Meanwhile she went to her emergency supplies and found a prepackaged intravenous preparation that would combat shock. Pumping a dextrose solution through her constricted blood vessels would increase volume, keep the network going. It was so simple, yet so essential. Such a little thing. She found Iris' vein and injected the syringe into her arm. Since she had no IV stand, Rebecca had to hold the bag of liquid above Iris until the paramedics came.

What had he wanted, she thought, looking around. There were files on the counter; had Iris taken those out? Or was he already here, looking for whatever, when Iris arrived? It was Goldie's file, she thought with a start. Goldie had told her about a man who had followed her. No names had been mentioned, but he didn't know that. He was looking for Rebecca's notes to see if Goldie had given him away. How could he know that she hadn't put Goldie's file back after Wanless had returned it? It was still in her house.

She sat down on the floor and brought her face close to Iris'. The larger woman's breathing was shallow and irregular, her colour grey. Rebecca knew that the brain could survive interruption of its blood supply for only a few minutes. A neuron, once destroyed, was lost forever. How much damage had there been? Was Iris going to be Iris when she awoke? If she awoke?

She stroked Iris' exposed arm softly with her free hand. "Hold on, Iris," she whispered in her ear. "Hold on."

Rebecca rode in the ambulance with Iris. Once she had explained to the paramedic her treatment thus far, there was nothing further to say and they rode the rest of the way in silence. She hoped none of her patients had arrived with emergencies that morning. She had taped a note to her office door announcing that all appointments were cancelled.

Toronto General was the hospital of choice for trauma, though it didn't look the part. Small dingy windows poked out of a dun-coloured brick facade that rambled along a city block. Compared to the modern Mount Sinai Hospital across the street, where she had admitting privileges, it might have been mistaken on the outside for a nineteenth-century factory. The surgical resident on call looked barely old enough to shave. None of the surgeons were available and the resident — he had to be over twenty-one, didn't he? — assured her that he had handled head trauma in the O.R. and he would do everything he could for Iris. What he was more worried about was the extra bulk she was carrying.

"I don't have to tell you that overweight patients are more at risk under the knife. How old is she? Fifty-one, fifty-two? Her heart should be okay. And this anaesthetist knows his business."

The chairs in the surgical waiting room were dark green vinyl but roomy and not uncomfortable. Rebecca sat down in the empty room, suddenly numb. More at risk under the knife. She had always found surgical specialists cold. Maybe they had to make themselves aloof from patients who might die on the table. There was also the theory that they were sublimating their fierce aggression into the positive act of cutting up people. Whatever it was, this young pup resident hadn't made her feel confident about his skill or Iris' chances.

She was surprised at how little she wanted to know about what was happening to Iris on the operating table. She didn't want to imagine her beautiful blonde hair shaved in a large shape around the wound. She didn't want to picture any of it, the cleaning of fractured bone and debris, the drilling of burr-holes, maybe two centimetres in diameter, to locate the damage. The procedure was too frightening to consider when the brain inside that skull was Iris'.

All she could think of was the lovely blonde hair gone. She pushed from her mind all the various possibilities of brain damage. All the many ways things could go wrong. She sank further into the skin-warm vinyl chair and wondered if it was worth trying to sleep, considering the dreams she would have.

By 12:40 she wandered out of the room to stretch her legs. The kitchen staff, their hair in spidery nets, were collecting patients' trays after lunch and stacking them in high-wheeled metal stands. They looked as if they wanted to be doing anything else.

The young resident, still in green gown, found her down the hall. "We've done everything we can for her. All we can do now is wait. She'll be in recovery for a while before you can see her."

"How much damage is there?" she asked.

"Hard to tell. We stopped the bleeding. Blood pressure's still low, but I'm hoping she'll stabilize."

Rebecca used the phone at the nurses' station to call her answering service. Two patients had called with pressing medical problems. Nesha had left several messages with a number where he could be reached. Her heart lifted a little.

She called the mother of a feverish little patient, told her to sponge her daughter with lukewarm water, give her Tylenol, and call Dr. Romanov. The second patient was suffering menstrual cramps and needed a renewal of a prescription for painkillers. Then she called Nesha.

He arrived at the nurses' station in twenty minutes, wearing his antique leather jacket, a gym bag on his shoulder. His eyes softened when he caught sight of her. He presented such a mask to strangers but she had seen beneath it. "I'm so sorry about your friend," he said, embracing her. He smelled of soap and leather.

He told her he had gone to Feldberg's early in the morning in an attempt to catch him, but the door had been open just as they had left it and no one appeared to have visited in between. Then he'd gone to the hotel to shower and change and tried in vain to reach her.

"I've got something to show you," he said lifting the bag. "Is there anywhere we can talk?"

The waiting-room was occupied by a family whose grandfather was being operated on. She led him down the hall to the doctor's lounge. It was empty.

After they sat down on one of the brown leather couches, Nesha pulled Feldberg's books from the gym bag. "The ledger seems straightforward, based on my limited knowledge," he said. "But the bankbooks. I took these two, but he had at least four others with similar figures in them. Look at the numbers. He's constantly depositing and withdrawing large sums of money, but each under $10,000. That's the magic number the banks have to report. As long as he keeps moving sums of money under $10,000 — that's why he's got so many bank accounts — he won't be investigated."

"I don't get it."

"He's got illicit money that he's probably brought from out of the country."

"Argentina," she said. "It's an Argentine club."

"He's operating some shady business. It could be anything."

"Art," she said, surprising herself.

"Art?"

"Those paintings we saw at his place. The photos of paintings in the catalogue. They're real. They have to be. It's the only explanation. I don't know quite how, but I think Feldberg is dealing in stolen art."

Nesha stared at her a moment, thinking, then continued. "They have to bring in the money without reporting it, maybe get it wired to different banks in relatively small amounts. But they can't bring in a huge sum into any one bank, so Feldberg distributes it among six. Or eight. Then it's invested in a legitimate business."

"Let me see that ledger," she said.

In an upper corner of the first page were written the initials E.D. El Dorado. Expenses starting January, 1979, listed tickets of admission, liquor receipts, and restaurant receipts. She flipped to the end for the latest entry, Thursday, April 5; two days before. The business had taken in one hundred and eighty tickets of admission, grossing $1,800, $3,800 worth of liquor from the bar, and $6,500 from the restaurant. Did Feldberg have *another* club? Thursday was the evening she had stopped in. There were maybe forty people there, in a generous estimate. By no stretch of the imagination could another hundred and forty have stampeded in after she'd left. And when she'd arrived downstairs, the restaurant had been nearly empty.

"This is all wrong," she said. "I was there just on Thursday and the numbers here don't add up."

"You were there?"

"Feldberg's inflating his numbers, inventing customers he doesn't have."

"It's a front," he said. "Classic money laundering

operation."

"Where does Goldie fit into all this?" She glanced down the list of businesses that supplied the club. Suddenly her eye was caught by a familiar name. Blue Danube Fish. Another connection to Vogel. He was the one who'd sent her to the club. It seemed he was selling El Dorado enough fish to start their own school, lots more than they could ever hope to fry up. She had a lot of questions to ask him.

They heard sudden male voices outside in the hall. Rebecca opened the door and saw two men in trench coats speaking to a nurse at the station. One of them was Wanless. She turned back to Nesha.

"The police are here."

He jumped up and shut the door in her face, but quietly. "Don't tell them anything!"

She hung back, flabbergasted. "But they can help. I was on their backs before to stay on the case."

"If they start, we'll lose control. If they find him first — it'll be in the courts for years. Canada doesn't punish war criminals. He'll have three meals a day, TV, he'll be laughing at us. At *them*. I won't let that happen."

"But if he killed Goldie, surely...."

"The system doesn't work. How many times have you seen evil rewarded? There is no justice."

She had nothing to counter with. She could call Wanless later.

He listened at the door. "We've got to get out of here."

She opened the door a crack and saw the nurse lead the two men to the door of the recovery room. The nurse was strict and did not allow them in, but let them examine Iris from the distance. Then the nurse said something to them and turned to guide them toward the surgical waiting-room. Probably in search of her.

As soon as their backs were turned she pulled Nesha into the hall toward the rear exit. She tread quietly in her loafers not to make any sound. She dared not turn around, knowing the group would need only to open the door of the waiting-room to see she wasn't there. Time was short. They turned the corner and rushed out a side entrance of the building.

University Avenue was cold in the windy shade of the hospitals and government buildings that lined the street. The sun was struggling to assert itself this April, making Rebecca shiver in her gabardine jacket. Nesha took her elbow and led her down the street like an old-fashioned man at a dance. She managed to steer him west along Elm toward Kensington Market. They were two blocks away from her office, then another two blocks to Spadina. The rain the night before had soaked the lawns and trees along Baldwin Street, leaving a damp earthy fragrance in the air.

They reached the rushing torrent of Spadina Avenue, that line of demarcation between the calm east side, reaching back to Beverley Street, and the chaotic west side which slid into the market. She felt awkward in the hand-on-elbow position and had taken his arm. He seemed content to have her lead.

The street light turned red before they finished crossing. Saturday shoppers filled the sidewalks of the market as far as she could see. She hated crowds. On Baldwin Street, a few stores past Spadina, she stopped. He said nothing. The ancient Blue Danube Fish sign reflected the paltry afternoon light. In the window lay a greying fish with hard dull eyes, possibly once a trout, displayed on a newspaper.

She took a deep breath, braced herself against the smell. He followed her hesitant step through the door of the shop. Any hint of spring vanished inside the shadows of the store. The awful smell of old fish washed over her. Mona stood behind the counter, wrapping fish for a woman customer.

Beneath the same bloodied apron, Mona wore a brilliant red cotton top. Rebecca thought she would've had enough of the colour in the shop without adding it to her wardrobe. Mona's black-pencilled eyes showed a spark of recognition when they turned to Rebecca. Noticing Nesha, her cheeks lifted in an attempt at a smile. A few bangs wisped down from her widow's peak.

She nodded. "Can I help you?"

"I'd like to ask you some more questions," Rebecca said.

"I don't know anything."

Rebecca held out the news photo over the loathsome counter. "You know this man?"

Mona squinted at the photo. "Fuzzy picture. Oh, it's our store! And this is one of our customers. Mr. Feldberg. He has a restaurant."

"When was the last time you saw him?"

"Not for a while. He usually phones to order."

"What do you know about him?"

Mona tilted her head observing her. "He's a good customer."

"Do you know anything about him personally?"

Mona shrugged beneath the blood-red sweater. "He's a good dresser. Classy looking, you know? But what a ladies' man. Always flirting." Her hand whisked a loose strand of hair off her face. She peeked at Nesha, who was playing coy near the carp basin. "His wife came once. Probably checking on him."

Chana had been there. Rebecca made a mental note of that. "What do you know about his restaurant?"

"Not much. It's on College Street somewhere."

"It's a Spanish club called El Dorado. It's a front for money laundering."

Mona stood there, absently wiping her hands on her apron. "I don't know anything about that. We just sell them fish."

"Max said you're the one who takes care of the store."

Her face went blotchy red. "I know fish!" she cried. "I don't know business. He does the business!"

Rebecca pulled back. She made a point of looking around at the shabby walls, the rickety carp tank. "How is business?"

She looked at Nesha, who was no longer pretending disinterest. "We get by."

"According to Feldberg's books, you're selling him enough fish to restock Lake Ontario. You're making an awful lot of money."

Mona's black-limned eyes grew wide. "What are you talking about?" she rasped. "Look at this place. Does it look like we're making money?"

Either Mona was a good actress, or she was being duped. Rebecca glanced toward the door of the partition. There was a muffled sound in the back, someone moving.

"Let me put it this way. If you'd actually sold Feldberg all the fish he shows on his books, you'd have retired to Florida long ago. But you *are* getting a cut for being involved."

Mona stared at her, bewildered. "A cut?"

Her eyes turned toward the partition. "Max and Mr. Feldberg knew each other from before. I didn't tell you but — they were in the same camp during the war. Max told me."

Nesha snapped to attention. He shuffled closer.

"I'd better talk to him," Rebecca said, edging

toward the side counter.

All at once an invisible door slammed. Rebecca knew just which one. She remembered a rear door leading outside from the study into a laneway. She pictured Vogel running down the alley and disappearing into the market.

Before the women could move, Nesha swung open the door to the study. While he was orienting himself, Rebecca pushed past him and quickly opened the back door that led to the alley. Nothing. He would disappear quickly in the market.

Nesha stepped out and peered around. "Who am I looking for?"

"He never mentioned being in a camp," Rebecca said.

Nesha came back in and closed the door.

Mona stared at the empty chair. "He told me he was making passports for Jews and some guy found out and turned him in. He was sent to a camp."

"Then, how did he keep his collection?"

"Hmm?"

"He must've been given these things before he ended up in the camp. He couldn't take them with him."

Mona shrugged. "Maybe he hid them."

Rebecca pushed past Mona toward the display of antiques, the filigreed spice box, the delicately wrought menorah. Her eyes swiftly scanned the bookcase. Did he? Didn't he? He did. She yanked out a slender volume on Raphael and flipped through. A full-page photo of the right *Portrait of a Young Man* made her catch her breath. The face was alive, the coy expression in the eyes, the careless self-confidence of youth that cannot foresee death.

"What do you know about this painting?" Rebecca asked her.

Mona stared with fish eyes. "It's very nice," she said.

"Have you seen the rest of Mr. Vogel's collection?"

"You mean at home?" she said. "Once. A while ago. He's a very private man."

"Did you see this painting there?"

Mona's eyes clouded with confusion. "A painting? I — I don't know. It was a long time ago. I mostly remember silver things. Why are you asking this?"

Outside the store, Rebecca and Nesha strode past the food stalls, searching the streets for a hint of Vogel. The newly-killed ducks and chickens still hung upside down, their necks dangling. Smells fought with each other as they passed a butcher's, a bakery, another fish shop. They struggled through the shoppers down one street, then another.

What were they to make of the new information Mona had tossed out, that Vogel and Feldberg had been in the same camp during the war? If Feldberg was a Nazi, what did that make Vogel? His prisoner?

Further into the market, people jostled them on all sides as they headed toward eggplants and five different kinds of lettuce. Surprising even herself, she halted in the middle of the sidewalk like a stone in a stream, prompting the flow of irritated traffic to swirl around them and onto the road.

"We're not going to find him here," she said. "It's his territory. I've got to go back to the hospital to check on Iris."

"I'll meet you later, then. I'm not going back there."

By the time Rebecca returned to the hospital, Iris was in intensive care. When she opened the door, Joe and Martha stood on either side of their mother. Martha, the larger of the two, was a stout, unglamourous though blonde version of Iris in baggy jeans and a sweatshirt. Her older brother, his hair a dark contrast, hid a smaller, more delicate frame under a navy sports jacket and tie. Both their faces were drained of colour and carried that glazed distant look she recognized in people confronted by the possible loss of a loved one.

Joe acknowledged her with a slight nod. Martha barely looked up. "What's going to happen to her? Will she be all right?"

"We won't know till she wakes up," said Rebecca.

She stepped to the foot of the bed and gazed at Iris. Her head was tightly wrapped in white bandages. She looked not at all like Iris without the uplifted waves of blonde hair to soften her round face. Her skin was transparent; Rebecca could almost see the workings of the bones beneath. The human being reduced into body parts. The IV bag hung in the air above the bed, the solution silently dripping, dripping down the tube into her arm. A plastic tube snaked into her nose and down to her stomach, a precaution against aspiration.

"We'll be outside," Martha said, moving toward the door, motioning to her brother to follow.

She was her mother's daughter, after all, sensing Rebecca's need, she thought. Once they were gone, she covered Iris' hand with her own and watched the closed eyelids. "Iris," she said leaning closer. "You hold on, Iris. You're strong and you can do it. You're going to come out of this, Iris. I need you to get better."

It wasn't until she was walking away down the hall that she realized how much she needed Iris. She wiped her eyes quickly, hoping Joe and Martha could no longer see her.

She had barely reached the waiting-room when her pager went off. Her answering service passed on a message from Nesha to call him. The number was unfamiliar.

"Yitz's Deli," said a man's voice.

"Could I speak to Nesha?"

"Hold on."

She had to smile.

"How do you like my new office?" he said when he had pulled himself away from his kishka platter or whatever morsel he was dispatching.

"You must be paying with American money. They're not usually that compliant."

"Don't be cranky. You're probably hungry. You want to come up and have a bite before we go to Isabella's?"

"You're going too fast for me."

"Feldberg hasn't come back. I've checked. I also checked his machine while I was there. Isabella left three messages. Very weepy. It seems he hasn't called her and she's worried. He must've skipped. That's what I was afraid of. That something would scare him off. She's our best lead."

"But if she doesn't know where he is...."

"Maybe she knows something she doesn't realize she knows."

"Alright," Rebecca said, checking her watch. It was almost five. Isabella wouldn't have left for work yet. "But we should also talk to the *Capitán* at the Spanish club I told you about."

"Will they let me in without a tie?"

chapter thirty-one

The stretch of Bathurst Street north of Eglinton must have had the most traffic lights per inch of roadway in the city, one suspended like a winking eye over each block. Staid brick apartment buildings lined both sides of the main street while tonier highrises, chaste in the white brick beloved of the early sixties, towered over the narrower side roads, throwing shadows. According to the address Nesha had found at the back of Feldberg's ledger, Isabella Velasco occupied one of the apartments on Mayfair Avenue, an elbow of a side street between Eglinton and Bathurst that Rebecca sometimes used as a shortcut.

Rebecca was walking toward the highrise after parking her car when she came upon Nesha leaning against his rented Olds. With his cracked leather jacket and lean insouciant pose, he looked like a character out of *West Side Story*, only twenty-five years later. He held a paper bag out to her. The deli-grease aroma of french fries wafted on the air. She kept away from fried foods as a rule, but the gesture, the smell, were seductive.

"Live dangerously," he said when she hesitated.

She took the bag, which held a carton of vinegar-soaked fries, and speared them with the plastic fork he gave her.

"I didn't think you were a ketchup girl," he said, watching her wolf down the potatoes.

Apart from some sugarless ginger ale and an apple from the market, she hadn't eaten that day.

He grinned as she finished the box. "I knew I should've brought you a hamburger."

With her mouth full she said, "I never eat hamburgers."

He reached through the open window of the car and brought out a can of Coke. "Here," he said.

"I never drink Coke," she said smiling as he popped the tin. She took a swig.

They stood inside the front vestibule of a genteel-shabby apartment building. She found Isabella's name on the list displayed beneath a sheet of glass. There was no suite number, just a dial-in code. Rebecca tried the inside door. It was locked. She picked up the in-house phone and was about to dial the code.

"Wait," Nesha said, taking the receiver from her hand and replacing it. He pulled her back out the front door.

Taking her arm, he strolled her down the pavement. When a young couple turned to go into the building, he steered Rebecca around and followed them. He waited until the couple was buzzed in by the people they were visiting, then casually caught the door before it closed.

"I'd rather surprise her," Nesha said.

"I'm assuming you have her apartment number."

"Follow me," he said.

The foyer must have been grand once, marble floor and rounded columns. But the weave of the two chesterfields was smooth where it should have been nubbly and the Chinese area rug had been crunched under by too many feet.

They took the elevator to the fourth floor. The geometric broadloom in brown and blue triangles felt prickly with static. Rebecca followed him down the hall with misgivings. What could they possibly say to Isabella that would convince her to let them in? Nesha stopped in front of Isabella's door. Voices were barking inside. Glancing around, he brought his ear to the wood.

He didn't need to; she could hear them from two feet away. A man and woman were bellowing at each other in Spanish.

"Those messages she left on his machine were fake," he whispered. "She's a good actress. Why didn't I think of it before? He's here! He's really here!"

His eyes widened and his mouth turned down; Rebecca hardly recognized him.

He began to pound his fist on the door. "Open up! Open the door!"

The voices inside stopped. Isabella, still combative, asked, "*¡Quien es!* What do you want?"

"Open up now! You can be charged with harbouring a fugitive. We'll call the police if you don't let us in now!"

The door flew open. Isabella, reeking of liquor, wavered in the doorway in red silk pyjamas and bare feet. Without her heels she was much smaller than Rebecca remembered.

"Who are you?" she said looking at Nesha.

Rebecca pulled her attention away. "We met at the

club a few nights ago." It was enough for him to push past Isabella into the apartment.

"Where is he?" Nesha cried.

Isabella stared at him, dumbfounded. Her oily black hair hung thin and limp around her shoulders. Old mascara smudged the skin beneath her eyes. "Who?"

"Who do you think? Your boyfriend. We heard you outside." He began to head toward a closed bedroom when the door opened. A man stepped out.

"I think we are all looking for the same person," said the *Capitán*.

"Who the hell are you?" said Nesha, poking his head into the empty bedroom.

"Capitán Diaz, at your service."

Nesha observed his well-oiled dark hair and suavely-cut suit. "You're the guy who runs the money-laundering operation."

A shadow passed over the *Capitán*'s eyes. "You are mistaken, sir. I run a legitimate establishment. Leo would tell you so if he was here." He stepped toward Isabella.

"But he isn't here. So where exactly is Leo?"

"If I knew where he was, would I come here? I have a business to run. People want to get paid. He must write the cheques. But he doesn't come in for two days on a weekend, when everyone is standing at my door with their hands out."

He reached into an inside pocket of his jacket.

Nesha, wound up like a coil, swung his arm around his back and whipped out the gun.

Diaz froze. He held the pose in a tableau, one arm fixed across his chest like a street-corner mime, fingers curled around a package of cigarettes.

They all watched the gun, waiting.

"A smoke!" said Diaz. "I just wanted a smoke."

Isabella stood precariously, one hand gripping the frame of the red velvet sofa, the other holding a cigarette that threatened to nosedive into the carpet.

"As you can see," said Rebecca, "my friend's a little irritable. It might help if you told us what you know about the paintings."

"If he puts away the gun."

Rebecca caught Nesha's eye. He lowered the gun but held it at his side.

"May I...?" Diaz lowered his gaze toward the mannequin arm.

Nesha gave an impatient nod.

"What do you want to know?" said Diaz, taking out a cigarette.

"Where's the money coming from?" Rebecca asked.

"What money?"

"The money that the club is a front for. The money you're laundering at the restaurant."

Diaz stared sullenly at her. "I just run the club. It's Leo's place. Leo's business."

"What business?"

Nesha's hand began to rise slowly.

"Art," he said finally. "Stolen. You wouldn't believe how big it is. Even the Mafia's doing it."

"Stolen from where?" she asked.

"Anywhere. Galleries, private collections. Museums are harder, unless they're small. Most of the big museums have modern safeguards. You'd be surprised how casual most people are about paintings hanging in their homes."

"The club isn't just a front, is it?" Rebecca said, "He also finds clients there, Argentinians who came with money, or maybe something to sell...?"

"Business is where you find it."

"What about the paintings in his apartment?"

"A lucrative sideline. Leo only deals with people he knows for those."

"He must have a hot little black book," Nesha said. "What do you know about the Edelweiss Club?"

Diaz sighed. "Sometimes he meets clients there. It's a small place and they respect his privacy."

Rebecca questioned Nesha with her eyes.

"They wouldn't give me his number," he answered. "And I wouldn't give them mine. It was a stand-off."

"Why do all the people selling the paintings live in Argentina?" Rebecca asked.

"Those are his connections. They trust him, he knows them. The paintings are very valuable. They can't sell them to galleries because they were stolen. From before."

"They're looted, aren't they?" she said. "From the war."

"This is an old story," he said. "Everyone steals during war."

Nesha said, "A lot of Nazis went to Argentina after the war. These people selling the art are Nazis, aren't they? Selling art they stole from Jews."

Diaz blew smoke out of his nose, but he was thinking. He seemed surprised at the turn of the questioning. "Nazis, yes. Maybe they're Nazis. Nazis are respected in Argentina."

"You don't care, do you?" said Nesha. "As long as you make your money, you don't care who you're dealing with."

"I'm a businessman, sir. I must make my money where I can. I must live, like everybody else. You have no idea how hard...."

"I don't give a rat's ass about your business. Your partner is a murderer, a war criminal. Your partner murdered my family. That's all I care about."

"Leo is many things, but he is not what you say. You are mistaken."

"Does the name Johann Steiner mean anything to you? *Oberscharführer* Johann Steiner?"

Diaz shrugged, shook his head.

"All the SS had their blood type tattooed under their arm." He turned to Isabella who had fallen into the Spanish sofa. "Have you seen a tattoo like that?"

"You are *loco*!" she said. "He was in a camp during the war. He's a Jew and he suffered like all of them. And I can prove it." She closed her kohl-stained eyes to emphasize the point. "I happen to know he's circumcised." She picked up a glass of whiskey that had been sitting on the coffee table and took a delicate sip.

Rebecca and Nesha looked at each other. "That doesn't prove anything," he said.

"Leo is a gentle and generous man," Isabella said. "But strong, too. He has to be strong for business. And what he has with that wife, he has to be strong. He suffers because of her."

"What happened to her?" Rebecca asked. "Why did she break down?"

Isabella had found another cigarette and was trying to light it with shaking hands. "She couldn't understand that he had to make a living. She's a weak woman, a selfish woman. She found out what he was doing and she couldn't take it. She called it blood money. But it paid for the food in her mouth. He told her if he didn't sell the paintings, somebody else would. The Jews who owned them were dead anyway. What difference did it make?"

Was that really it?

"Is that why he killed Goldie," Rebecca asked. "Because she found out?"

Isabella gaped at Rebecca. "He is not a killer. You don't comprehend him."

"Where is he? Did he run back to Argentina?"

Diaz grimaced a no. "He made too many enemies there. He would never go back."

"Was he involved in the terror?" Rebecca said to Diaz. "Did he have anything to do with Goldie's abduction? Did you?"

Nesha watched, not giving away his surprise but she sensed it.

"You are accusing without proof. Where is your proof?" said Diaz.

"The police would be very interested in the way you run your business," she said. "We've got your expense book. It reads like a novel. All fiction."

He leaned on the arm of an upholstered chair, subdued for the moment. "I had nothing to do with Goldie. I only knew her son because he was a friend of Isabella's boy and Leo was involved with Isabella. Carlos helped us sometimes. We had a different business then. Drugs. He helped with exchanges. You know. But the boy didn't understand how it worked. He thought if he kept a little for himself, no one would know. Sometimes he kept some money, sometimes some drugs."

Rebecca made a wild stab. "*You* were the one who informed on them." He didn't deny it, only stared into space, puffing on his cigarette. "You were losing money so you told the death squad where they were hiding. You didn't care if they killed Goldie's son, too. He had nothing to do with your business."

Diaz glanced uneasily at Isabella. "Many were killed. For less reason."

Isabella exploded out of her seat. She threw the glass of whiskey into his face with vehemence. He appeared stunned, wiping the liquor from his eyes. But before he could move she launched him from his perch on the chair arm and sent him flying onto the floor.

"¡*Asesino!*" she screamed. The red silk arms flew around her body, unattached to reason or will.

Without warning she leaped toward Nesha and snatched the gun from his hand. Diaz had barely enough time to lift himself onto his elbows when she positioned herself above him. Holding the gun with two hands she pointed it at his head.

"My boy died because of you! All this time I blamed her..." Her hands began to shake and she appeared to take aim.

"Isabella ...," said Rebecca, who started toward her.

Nesha held his hand up like a traffic cop. "Excuse me, lady," he began. "I agree with you one hundred percent. The bastard deserves whatever he gets. But I'm sorry to say it won't be with that gun. Take a closer look. It's just for show. It's an antique."

Isabella looked down at the Luger as if for the first time. That was when Nesha stepped forward and gently but firmly plucked it from her hands.

Then came the Angel of Death and killed the Shoichet
That slaughtered the ox that drank the water
That quenched the fire that burned the stick
That beat the dog that bit the cat
That ate the goat
That Father bought for two zuzim.
    One little goat, one little goat.

chapter thirty-two

The white pavement curved through mountains of highrises on either side of Mayfair Avenue as Rebecca and Nesha walked wordlessly back to the car, each lost in thought. Their arms bumped intimately while they moved, each one's trajectory slightly overlapping the other.

She had phoned the hospital from the lobby of the apartment building and spoken to Martha. Iris' vital signs were hopeful, but she hadn't regained consciousness.

"So what's the deal with the gun?" Rebecca asked, though that wasn't what had been on her mind.

"Oh. You mean, is it just for show? Let's say I was hoping I'd get to it before she tried out the trigger."

Rebecca put her arm around his waist so that she could feel the gun beneath the jacket. "Do you always live this dangerously?" she asked.

He unfurled her arm like a belt and deftly pulled it through his elbow, fitting his hand over hers. "Just when I'm with you."

His full upper lip curved into a bow and she wished

she could forget everything else. "I think there's more to Chana's breakdown than Isabella told us," she said.

"What difference does it make?"

"I'm not sure. But I think it might be important. If Chana was so upset about Leo dealing with Nazi loot, it's not very likely she'd knowingly marry a Nazi. And they were in the camp together, so she knew who he was." They approached Nesha's rented blue Oldsmobile. "If only she would speak."

Rebecca stopped in mid-stride. Opening her shoulder bag, she pulled out the sheaf of letters. "Maybe she will speak!"

They climbed into the back seat of the Olds. She spread the letters out on both their laps, checking the postmarks and placing them in order of date. There wasn't much daylight left.

"These are the letters Chana wrote to Goldie in 1977. Then she came to Toronto and they didn't need to write to each other anymore. So we don't have anything written around the time she actually had her breakdown. Still, I'd like to read through some of them to see if she says anything that'll help us."

Nesha picked up one of the letters. His lips moved silently till she bumped her knee against his. "'He goes out every night and I'm alone. I can't complain about my surroundings, he keeps bringing home the most beautiful paintings. He says friends of his have asked him to sell them, but I've never met any of his friends. I can't wait till you're here.'"

Nesha took out a sheet from another envelope. "'Maybe we couldn't have children as punishment for what I did during the war. Children are the innocents. I often think about that boy who died because of me. Do you think God has punished me by taking away my children?'"

Nesha stared stonily outside the window as Rebecca handed him a letter dated September 25, 1977. "This was the last one written before Goldie came to Toronto. It's longer than the others."

A full minute went by before he took the sheet from her and began to read. "'It's almost Yom Kippur. Though I don't go to *schul* I must again ask forgiveness from the soul of the boy who died because of me. Also this is the time of year I think of him because he died in the camp soon after the holiday in 1943. He showed up one day at the machine near mine on the factory floor. A religious boy, pale with thick dark sideburns where his forelocks used to be. I imagined his mother cutting them off before being led to the gas chamber. Orthodox Jews were the first to die. His hands large and smooth like baby's skin. Probably never used those hands for anything but turning pages of religious books. I saw him struggling on the machine. Those long fingers trying to fit into the mechanism and cut the metal pieces. They had to be precise. I tried to show him how but he just couldn't. He tried, but impossible. People who didn't reach quota didn't survive. Beaten to death, or taken to *Werk C* where the yellow powder for the explosives killed them. Skin turned yellow after a few weeks. I feared for him and did work for two. Thank God my hands were fast enough from the sewing. One day we got word about Yom Kippur prayers in the next barracks. After work we ate our watery soup and crust of bread quickly before sunset so we could fast next day. Even in the camp we felt we had to fast on the Day of Atonement. Next door was filled with people, but very quiet, everybody listening to a beautiful pure voice singing *Kol Nidre*. I looked to see who. It was my young orthodox friend (can't remember his name) in a spot cleared in the middle between bunks, singing from memory, everyone in a trance. The song so sad and pure, surely God must've heard. Even the SS guard came to listen, and like jungle animals at the waterhole, we stood together listening. And the guard's face — I can't explain, he looked human for the first time. Soon after, I got the job cleaning officers' quarters so I left the factory. I saved myself without thinking about the boy. When he couldn't do the quota they transferred him to *Werk C.* He worked with the yellow powder but not for long. Something went wrong, it always did, and an explosive blew up in his hands. Pieces of him everywhere, what gruesome stories they told. He wasn't more than sixteen. One day I went to clean the SS guard's room and there it was. The Hand, encased in silver like a relic from a saint. I knew it was his. Recognized the shape of the long fingers, the silver melted over the hand, outlining even the nails. Little glass windows framed in gold over the knuckles so you could see through. A work of art. They said the guard had found a local silversmith. I was sick in the toilet. I had to look at it every day when I went to clean."

Nesha's voice had become increasing lower while reading. Closing his eyes, he leaned his head back on the seat. Rebecca took his hand in hers.

"We have to speak to her again," she said softly. "Maybe if we ask her the right questions...."

Rebecca drove the Olds up Bathurst Street while Nesha slouched in the passenger seat, eyes glazed over, staring out the side window. Bathurst was lined with senior's buildings, which often meant that old men in plaid hats held up traffic driving big cars too slowly. She manoeuvred around them in the fast-falling dusk past Lawrence, past Wilson, past Sheppard, past Finch. In twenty minutes she pulled into the parking lot of Sunnydale Terrace.

They approached the front desk. A semi-circle of

people waited to speak to the pudgy blonde who had taken Rebecca up to Chana's room the other day. Pulling Nesha by the hand, she skirted the crowd and headed for the stairs.

Nesha seemed to come awake once they were on the second floor. He strode to Chana's room and knocked quietly, then opened it. Rebecca knew something was wrong when he turned on the light and stopped on the threshold. Chana was lying on her back, one eye open, one closed. An IV dripped into her arm and the metal sides of the bed had been raised up as a restraint. The open eye saw nothing; she was unconscious. Her mouth hung partly open, her skin a paper-thin white.

Nesha approached the bed, his eyes large with fear. "*Meema Chana*!" he murmured. "*Meema Chana*, it's me! I've come back."

Rebecca fought the urge to pull him away and picked up the chart at the foot of the bed. The attending physician, Dr. Chan, had written "Provisional Diagnosis — CVA," cerebral-vascular accident, and had prescribed blood thinners. Blood samples had been sent out to a lab for testing but Rebecca knew by looking at her that it was serious. She put the chart down and lifted Chana's wrist to take her pulse. The rate was high and irregular. Chances were she'd thrown off an embolus. Rebecca checked her pupils: they were fixed and dilated, a bad sign. Drawing back the covers at the bottom, she pinched her leg. No response.

She turned reluctantly to Nesha. "I'm sorry," she said. "It looks like she's had a stroke."

He took her small immobile hand. "*Meema Chana*, I'm here. Wake up."

Rebecca couldn't bear it and left them alone. She stepped outside and breathed in the nursing home smell of stale urine. Down the hall a few rooms away, the frail old man she had seen last time hovered as if waiting. At once he began a quirky waddle toward her, punctuated with his cane. Curious, she met him part way.

"Do you know what happened to Mrs. Feldberg?" she asked.

"Here today, gone tomorrow," the little wisp of a man muttered. "Weren't you here the other day?"

"Has her husband come to visit in the last few days?"

He peered up at her through thick bifocals and fluttered a hand in the air. "He don't come no more. That's what happens. You come here, people forget about you. It's no good."

"Did she have *any* visitors yesterday?"

The old man leaned on his cane, nodding, a satisfied smirk on his face. "That's what I wanted to tell someone. No visitors, no. But a workman came late last night."

"Workman?"

"Plumber or something. Wore overalls and carried a toolbox. Saw him come out of her room."

"What time was that?"

"Couldn't sleep last night. I'm a bad sleeper, too old you know. I got up for a glass of water and heard something outside. So I opened the door and saw him come out. Maybe midnight."

"Isn't that unusual, a plumber coming here at midnight?"

"That's what I thought."

"Did you see what he looked like? Hair colour? Age?"

"Had a cap on. Just an average fella. All I know was he was younger'n me." He chuckled. "Maybe a young fella of sixty."

"This is important: do you think it could've been her husband?"

The man squinted at her through his thick lenses. "Now that's an interesting question. Sorry I can't answer it."

"Did you tell someone downstairs?"

He waved the suggestion away. "Aw, they're idiots. Don't listen to a word I say."

Rebecca excused herself and went downstairs. The blonde was still being monopolized by visiting relatives. Rebecca approached the reception desk and spotted, further back, a woman wearing a nurse's cap busy with some papers.

"Excuse me," Rebecca said, "I'd like some information about Mrs. Feldberg." When the woman stared back at her without moving, she added, "Am I not speaking English? I'm a doctor and I want information on one of your patients." Damn she was riled. If this woman didn't watch out, Rebecca would take everything from the past three days out on her.

The middle-aged nurse rose heavily and trudged toward the desk.

"When was Mrs. Feldberg found in her present condition?"

The woman's grey eyes observed her with barely concealed anger. "Night nurse found her going off her shift this morning. Maybe seven."

"Did she mention anything unusual? Something that didn't look right?" The woman tilted her head. "For instance, did it look like she'd been in any kind of a struggle?"

Her eyes grew into circles. "What do you mean?"

"I mean that in Mrs. Feldberg's condition a stroke could've been caused by undue stress, a threat perhaps. Did you know that a workman went into her room at midnight? Possibly a plumber?"

"I ... I don't understand...."

"Can you check if a workman was called to fix something in Mrs. Feldberg's room last night?"

The nurse flipped the large lined page of a book on a nearby desk. Scowling, she approached the buxom blonde and whispered something in her ear. The blonde looked over at Rebecca and disengaged herself from her entourage.

"Now what's this about someone coming into Mrs. Feldberg's room at night?" Her lips were tight and nervous, her eyes waiting.

"So there was no workman called last night?"

"Where are you getting your information?" asked the blonde in a too-pleasant voice.

"The small thin man on the cane two doors down from Mrs. Feldberg. He says he saw a man coming out of her room."

The taut lines that had stiffened the blonde's round face relaxed. She smiled. "Oh, Duncan! I should've known. He says he's an insomniac but he really falls asleep and has vivid dreams that he thinks are real. You should hear some of them! Well, I think you already did."

On her way back upstairs Rebecca asked herself why Feldberg would dress up and come late at night to do something he could easily have managed on a regular visit. If he wanted to make sure Chana didn't tell anyone what she knew, he could've visited legitimately during the day and if she happened to have a stroke — well, she was fragile and no one would have been surprised. Maybe he was a perfectionist and wanted to be certain no one connected him to her deterioration. Or maybe the hefty blonde was right and the old man couldn't tell a dream from the real thing.

When she got back to the room, Nesha was

standing at the window. She approached Chana, getting close enough to search for petechiae, tiny broken blood vessels around the eyes that occurred with strangling or choking. There were none. There were no bruises visible on her upper body, no signs of a struggle. She looked at Chana's hands. No broken nails. Nothing beneath them, like maybe a killer's skin. Yet Rebecca had an uncomfortable feeling about this. It was too convenient. If her husband had entered her room to silence her, would she have resisted?

"What are you looking for?" Nesha asked.

"I don't know."

He stepped over to a cardboard box near the table. Bending over, he picked out one of the rag dolls Chana had sewn. "I thought I'd have another chance to talk to her. This is all that's left of her," he said.

Rebecca approached. Someone had unceremoniously dumped the dozen or so dolls into the box on the floor. She took them out and lined them up on the tabletop. A crude uneven lot fashioned from coarse grey cotton, their faces a few stitches of yarn. All but one wore slapdash striped skirts and trousers. The exception was dressed in a little black jacket with matching pants and cap. Three of the dolls' heads were sheathed in red gauze: the uniformed one, and two prisoners. The last time she had visited, Chana had made a fuss about Rebecca picking them up. But now that she could examine the three of them closely, she wondered if they mattered at all.

"What do you suppose this means?" she said to Nesha. "These three who have red gauze covering their faces."

He took the uniformed doll from her and turned it over in his hand. That was when she took note of the irregular grey object sewn onto the end of its arm. Last time she had seen it, she'd assumed it to be a gun. That went along with the uniform. Her father's words echoed in her ear: "assume" makes an ass out of "u" and "me."

"It isn't a gun," she said out loud.

Nesha held the tiny grey appendage away from the doll's body. Up close she saw the fingers sewn around in wobbly grey thread.

"It's the Hand," she said breathlessly.

"The *Hand*?" he said.

"The silver hand from the camp. In the guard's room."

They both stared at the doll. "Creepy," he said.

"These dolls represent something," she said. "Only three have red faces. One officer and two prisoners, one male, one female. The officer is the SS guard in her letter. What if she was the female and the young orthodox boy was the male?"

"Why are their faces red?" he said.

"When I was here before, she called the dolls *kinder*. But then when I tried to hold one of these, she shouted "*Nisht kinder!*" You know, maybe it just means innocent. She said in her letter, children are the innocents. Maybe these three are not. Red is for blood. They're guilty of something."

"That makes sense for the SS and even her, considering she felt responsible for the boy's death. But the boy, himself. She wouldn't consider him guilty of anything."

"There's another thing," she said. "If the guard has the hand, that means the boy's dead already."

"So who's the third doll?"

"What about Vogel?" she said.

"The guy in the fish store?"

"He's involved in Feldberg's business. From both ends. He's supplying fish to the club and he's selling a painting he has no business owning. And we know they were in the camp together." She dug the catalogue card with Vogel's home address out of her purse. "And I know where to find him."

Before they left, Nesha approached Chana's bed. "You should've seen them when they were young. Knock-outs, both of them. Shiny brown hair, trim figures, stylish, always stylish. And full of energy. I followed them around when they came to our house that time. I was just a *pisher*. They were like movie stars."

He stroked the pale downy hair, bent forward, and whispered something in her ear. He pressed his lips to her forehead, then stepped away.

chapter thirty-three

Rebecca once again got behind the wheel of Nesha's rented Olds. Night had fallen and brought with it a brisk clear sky whose stars were invisible above the canopy of street lamps. Nesha stared out the windshield as she pulled out of the parking lot and drove down Bathurst Street to Wilson Avenue. She turned west. Murky fields ranged on both sides, the landing area for a military airport somewhere in the distance. Here some stars winked out of the high black sky.

One of the stars up there had Iris' name. A ray of hope. Rebecca had reached the hospital again, this time from a pay phone at the nursing home. Martha said Iris had opened first one eye, then the other. The doctor was optimistic.

Past Dufferin Street an endless series of strip plazas lined Wilson Avenue. Metal signs loomed in shadow above Italian restaurants, dress shops, and fabric stores set back from cracked asphalt parking lots. She turned north at Keele Street where a ragtag of small family stores and houses had been erected with no obvious plan, before the building code separated commercial from residential and some Einstein realized it was cheaper to build queues of stores joined at the hip. An architecturally interesting old church stood on a corner, but in the company of frame houses the government had constructed after the war for soldiers returning from duty.

She found the street she was looking for and turned left. The neighbourhood became very suburban with hills of lawns and chain-link fences. Vogel's house sat on a corner across from the backyards of two other houses whose fronts faced away. The third corner was an empty lot. High cedar hedges lined his driveway. Very private.

Lights were on inside though the curtains were drawn across the front window. The brick house was modest in width but deep, with a garage attached near the back. They climbed what seemed an inordinate number of concrete stairs leading up to the small porch. She knocked, Nesha standing behind her.

The door opened sooner than she expected and Vogel greeted her with an unsurprised smile. "Ah, Doctor, how nice to see you again. I hope you've come to look at my collection."

"You're too kind," she said. "My friend's visiting from out of town and he's very interested in art. I hope you don't mind my bringing him."

Vogel gave Nesha a cursory glance. "Not at all. My pleasure."

He ushered them in through a small entryway and up a short flight of stairs that led up to the living-room, all carpeted in robin's egg blue.

When Vogel turned, she said, "This is Nesha Malkevich. Max Vogel."

They shook hands. The navy cardigan Vogel wore deepened the blue in his eyes.

"Take off your jackets," he said, "while I put the kettle on." He vanished into the kitchen.

Neither of them went to remove their jackets, but stood staring at the royal blue oriental rug lying over the blue broadloom. A pale blue French Provincial sofa and chairs bearing curved white arms and legs stood on the carpet. Instead of soothing her like it was supposed to, the undulating blue pulled at her feet, made her feel like she was drowning. It had been a long day.

While noises came from the kitchen she noted the broadloomed steps that led downstairs off the dining-room. The house was a backsplit, a style known for its surprising nooks and crannies.

When he emerged from the kitchen, Vogel said, "I keep the collection in a special room on the lower level."

He led them downstairs where the floor was a gleaming parquet that smelled of wax. The hallway led to two doors, both closed. He stopped in front of one of them and pulled out some keys. She glanced at Nesha while Vogel unlocked a deadbolt. Once the door opened, she could see it was steel-layered with a wood veneer.

They followed him into a room panelled in rich mahogany. It was like stepping into another century, lights sparkling off the glass fronts of wooden display cases that filled the room. The ceiling was full height; a chandelier hung in the centre, its crystal teardrops shimmering in circles. Some framed drawings hung on the walls, but no paintings. There were no windows in the room.

A black leather armchair stood in the centre of the room beside a heavy desk with carved legs and leather-embossed top. Brass bookends shaped like lions held up several large volumes on one end. One book lay open. Vogel leaned on the desk, hands in the pockets of his cardigan, waiting, it seemed, for the compliments that must follow.

She approached the cabinet closest to the door. Candlesticks, mostly silver, some brass, stood arrayed on glass shelves. She could hardly believe how many. She stopped mutely before them, remembering the silver candlesticks her grandmother had brought with her from Poland to Toronto in the 1920s. When Rebecca was growing up, her family went to her grandmother's most Friday evenings to eat the Sabbath dinner. The old lady threw a shawl over her head, passed her hands over the candles twice, then covering her eyes, mumbled the prayer as if she were on familiar terms with God. The candlesticks were in her mother's dining-room now, of more sentimental value than anything else; no one lit candles Friday night anymore.

Sentimental value. Vogel's candlesticks were all someone's sentimental value. Many someones. Whose candlesticks were these that she was staring at? Where had they been murdered? The women who faithfully lit the candles every Sabbath, where were their final resting places? There were no tombstones anywhere with names engraved, only memorials bearing lists of the dead. But she hadn't come to mourn.

"I must admit," she began carefully, "I was hoping you would have the painting out, a valuable painting I was told you had."

Vogel blinked twice, his face blank. "I beg your pardon?"

"Leo told me about the Raphael. Don't be modest. We won't tell anyone about it. But you must let us look."

The blood had drained from his face. "I see how hard it is to keep a secret. Well, then. But Mr. Malkevich must come upstairs and help me retrieve it from its wooden crate. Why don't you stay and enjoy my collection while we men get to work."

While they marched upstairs, she pretended to examine a cabinet in the corner. Three glass shelves held a dozen or so silver pointers of varying lengths and styles. Tiny ornate index fingers pointed from silver fists into some mysterious distance as if an answer might be found if only one looked in the right direction. The cards adjoining each artifact bore typed designations of country of origin and time period. Very professional.

When they were out of sight, she skulked to the desk and opened the top drawer. Pens, pencils, paper, scissors, tape. She tried the larger drawer beneath; it was locked. Opening the top drawer again she rummaged through, poking her hand near the back. Nothing. She glanced around the desk, checking beneath the open book. No. Her eye fell on the lion bookends. She lifted one up and there it was: a key. Taking a breath, she turned it in the lock below. The drawer pulled open. Inside lay an oblong wooden box. Just another silver goblet or pointer, she thought. She listened for voices or footsteps. Safe for the moment. She swung the top of the box open and gasped. Nestled in red velvet was the silver reliquary, the hand from Chana's nightmare that had crossed the boundaries of time and space to land at Rebecca's feet. There were the tiny gold-framed windows over the knuckles through which the bones were visible. The sheet of silver seemed to have been melted on, curves and lines profiling the skin, the very fingernails rendered.

She shut the box in horror. Her heart was leaping in her chest. With quivering fingers she replaced it in the drawer. How could she have been so blind? Leo was the third rag doll. Vogel was the uniformed doll. The head guard who had become human for a few minutes listening to the young orthodox boy singing *Kol Nidre. Oberscharführer Steiner.* The monster who had rounded up villages of Jews. Who had killed Goldie. She heard footsteps approaching and jumped toward one of the cabinets.

Vogel entered the room alone, his wavy greying hair somewhat ruffled, falling in strands around his ears. Rebecca's heart throbbed.

"Where's Nesha?" she said in a voice strange to her ears.

His head motioned toward the door. "He was so enthralled with the painting I couldn't get him away."

What had he done with Nesha?

"Why didn't you mention you were in a concentration camp?" she said.

The expression went out of his eyes. "What makes you think I was?"

"Mona told us."

"Mona." He grimaced.

"She also said that's where you met Leo."

He sniffed as if there were a bad smell. "Leo was no innocent. I don't know what he told you. Did he say he was a *kapo?* Oh, yes. He was responsible for the deaths of his own people. You know who were chosen to be *kapos?* Sadists. Thugs. People who liked to see others suffer."

"Why don't you tell the truth?" she said, trembling. "Leo wasn't the murderer."

A pained smile creased his mouth. He drew himself to his full height, taller than she remembered, and pulled the Luger out from beneath his cardigan. "You know nothing!" he spat. "Have you ever starved? Did you ever go to school in rags and have to sit beside children who whispered about you behind their hands? It's easy to be self-righteous when you have enough to eat."

"Lots of people grew up poor and didn't become murderers." He stood between her and the door.

"Nothing is that simple. You put ordinary people in the same circumstances — yes, we were ordinary.... I've seen it time and again: every man is a potential killer under the right conditions. Sometimes we must kill in order to survive."

"You didn't have to murder children to survive."

"I was there to do a job. I was told what to do and I did it. It was nothing personal. At first it disgusted me. But then, after a while, I would squint my eyes at the lines of people — especially from the distance — and they wouldn't be quite people anymore ... they looked like ... ants ... columns of ants.... It's very easy to step on ants, you hardly notice, they're so small...."

"You profited from murder...." She waved her arm at the room, the glittering glass cabinets. "All this.... It's not a collection — it's a graveyard."

His mouth turned down, the gun steady in his hand. "What do you think would've happened to these things if I hadn't taken them? You should've seen the warehouses full of goblets and candelabra. They never even missed what I took. At least I study and appreciate them."

"How did you get the Raphael?"

He tilted his head watching her. "How did you find out about it?"

"Does it matter?"

He shrugged. "It was just a stroke of luck, as most things were then. We had lost the war and I was driving as far away from the camp as I could in a jeep. I was the first to come upon a wrecked truck — the driver was killed. In the back was a crate of paintings, untouched. Some General was probably waiting for them somewhere. Raphael was the best by far, but the five others were nothing to sneeze at. My income has depended on them over the years. I saved the Raphael for last. It was always my favourite, the precious young man in the velvet robe, the eyes so sure ... with a wave of his hand he could have anything.... But now I find my finances need an injection of cash...."

"Where is it?

"Where no one will ever find it."

"Why did you kill Goldie?"

The animation in his face dropped. "Your questions are getting tedious. This is the last one. She was a crazy woman. She came to the store while Mona was out. She had this picture.... And she made these wild accusations, screaming — completely unreasonable. She knew who I was. She said she was going to the police.... I couldn't talk to her, she wouldn't listen. She ran out and I followed her. To your office."

So he *had* been there.

"Goldie was paranoid; she accused *everybody*. Couldn't you tell she was ill?" Rebecca considered trying to make a run for the door. Maybe she could get him off his guard.

"She knew who I was. I had to ... take care of her...."

"You don't understand. She wasn't a threat to you. You made a terrible mistake. She couldn't know who you were because she was in Argentina during the war. You killed her for nothing."

He shook his head, unconvinced. "Leo warned me about her. She showed him the picture and he got nervous. He didn't want any connection between us. He was afraid people would still remember he was a *kapo*. The old woman must've been with Leo's wife in the camp. She *knew* me...."

Rebecca was trying to inch sideways, but he had noticed. He lunged forward and grabbed her arm with brute strength, twisting it round her back.

"What, no more questions?" he cried as he pushed her forward toward the other closed door.

"Where's Nesha?"

"You win the prize, Doctor! Here he is. All you have to do is open the door."

She turned the knob with her left hand. A gust of cold air blew into her face along with a sickly, fetid smell. It was a cold-storage room. Maybe he stored his garbage there. In the shadows, she spotted the rubber tip of a running shoe. Nesha lay on his side on the concrete, the back of his head bloody, hair tossed across his face. She screwed up her eyes — his chest was moving. He was alive. As her eyes adjusted, she saw another body behind him: Feldberg, his eyes bulging, his mouth open, surprised by death. He had to have been dead for at least a day, judging from the smell. He must have guessed about Vogel killing Goldie. It was probably too much for him to resist the temptation for blackmail.

Vogel breathed on the back of her neck, wresting her arm till it became numb. "I'm going to let go of you. And when I do, you're going to drag Mr. Feldberg outside for me."

He stepped back, freeing her arm. She massaged it through her jacket sleeve to get the blood flowing again.

"Let's go, Doctor. We have work to do."

She stepped over Nesha and bent to collect Feldberg under the arms. The smell was unbearable. Vogel closed the door of the cold room. Feldberg was not a big man, but he was a dead weight. While she struggled to pull the body to the side door, she could see the purple impression of a ligature around the neck. The back of his head had taken a blow, no doubt to stun him first.

Thank God the door was on the basement level;

she couldn't have dragged him up any stairs. She followed Vogel, who was walking backwards with the gun, out the side door of the house. A three-foot walkway was all that separated it from the side door of his garage. Nobody would see them. There was no point in screaming. She hauled the body inside the garage then dropped it with a thud. Then she looked up. There in the shadows loomed the van of her nightmare. Vogel lifted the back gate open. Finally she believed she was going to die. The blackness of the interior transfixed her.

"Go on!" he rasped. "Jump up."

She had no chance as long as he had the gun. She jumped.

Still pointing the Luger, he raised the body into a sitting position with one hand. His cardigan sleeve pulled away, revealing a bandage encircling his forearm. Rebecca remembered the broken glass in Goldie's door.

"Lift him up!" he growled.

She bent down and grappled with shoulders and head to get a grip beneath the arms. Tugging with all her energy she yanked him up, falling backwards further inside. Here the odour of the decomposing body competed with the putrid smell of last week's fish.

"Okay, your friend next."

He prodded her back inside at the end of the gun. She supposed she should have been grateful that he wasn't going to kill them in the house. Where was he taking them?

She stooped and pressed her fingers to Nesha's neck to feel a pulse.

"It's academic, Doctor," said Vogel. "It'll all be over soon."

This time, carefully, she lifted Nesha under his

arms and pulled him along the parquet floor. She didn't know where she found the strength. He moaned as she bumped him along, adding some of his blood to the dirt soiling her linen trousers. She wished he would come to; she could really use the help. Her mind was trying to work, but she was so tired. For a second she considered: what if she just *ran*? He would shoot her before she reached the street. At this range it would be a piece of cake. Even if she managed to escape somehow, Nesha would be a dead man.

She gently let Nesha drop to the garage floor behind the van. Her heart pounded in her mouth, whether from exertion or fear she didn't know. She had to think of something before Vogel drove them to their final destination. She would have to find an opportunity to go for the gun while his attention was on the road.

Vogel waved the gun toward the back gate of the van. She would have to find a way. She was just raising her leg to climb back in when she felt him lunge behind her.

"Help!" she screamed into the night. "Someone help me!"

A searing pain exploded in her head. Then the asphalt floor came up to meet her.

Then came the Holy One, blessed be He,
and slew the Angel of Death,
That killed the Shoichet that slaughtered the ox
That drank the water that quenched the fire
That burned the stick that beat the dog
That bit the cat that ate the goat
That Father bought for two zuzim.
   One little goat, one little goat.

chapter thirty-four

There were no shouts at the door this time, no fists on wood. He came quietly treacherous and while she slept, pulled her, deaf and mute, through the unfamiliar dark. Though her hands were not bound, she couldn't move them. She was paralyzed. The dark became black.

She lay on a grooved metal floor that moved beneath her. No, not just *her*. Her uncooperative body bumped against another, also inert. Was it David? Had she somehow found David again? The stench of decomposing flesh, animal and human, inhabited the air. Fish-encrusted, slimy. I must open my eyes, she thought, I must stand up. The nightmare wheels whined under her ear, a groove dug into her cheek yet she couldn't move. Her head throbbed, throbbed, distracting her, confusing her. She was being taken somewhere but was it to be tortured in some derelict basement, or to be strangled in some wood? Were they heading out of Buenos Aires or some highway north of Toronto? Black sedans rose in Argentine scenarios that faded in and out. She opened her mouth, or thought she opened it, but nothing came out. "¡Abra la puerta!" she screamed to herself. Only where *was* the door?

An uneasy calm began to spread over her. A floating beneath consciousness. She couldn't fight it. He had won. She was going to just slip away. The way Chana had, without a fight. She was too tired to fight. Is that how Chana had felt when he had slunk into her room? Had she expected him — is that why she began to pull away from everyone? Last year. Her mind had turned inward last year. July. Like the duck. The duck waddled along the sidewalk last June. How'd she remember that? What if Chana had seen it in the paper? Recognized her own husband? Found the store? Found *Steiner*? Vogel. A stone masquerading as a bird. The *smell*! The smell was unbearable.

The wheels bumped, bumped beneath her ear. A grid of streetcar tracks? If only she could wake up, if only she could fight back. With what? She struggled to remember where she had been and what she had on her. Almost from above she saw herself wearing the gabardine jacket. The jacket. She had put something in the pocket in what now seemed like another life, but she couldn't remember what. It didn't matter what was in her pocket. If she couldn't make herself wake up, the police would find whatever it was on what remained of her body. And the other body. No, not David. David was dead. But this other body, it would die too if she didn't do something.

She was still floating, but rising somehow, rising to some surface. What if Chana confronted Leo? Light shining in through a window. Rebecca could almost see something. The cloudy window in the back door of the van. Noisome bacteria, slimy mildew. What if Chana asked him the right questions? It might have amused him to tell her the truth, that he was in business with the Nazi. Profiting from the murderer. What unspeakable crimes had she seen him commit that wouldn't allow her to accept this final degradation? That's what had destroyed Chana, the memory of the dead. It was blood money. The red gauze heads of the three dolls.... When Steiner-Vogel had walked into her room last night, he pulled what was left of her into oblivion. Only the shell remained.

The light diffused — were Rebecca's eyes open? Her nose was certainly awake. The stench! Then she felt her body sway into a turn, someone else's turn, out of her control. She rolled slightly and nudged something next to her. Then a bump in the road lifted her head up and dropped it back. Like a mound of flesh, she thought in her dream, helpless and inert. But a mound of flesh couldn't open its eyes. And suddenly she was opening her eyes. She wished she'd kept them closed. In a light that seemed dimmer than the one she'd seen behind her eyelids, she found, not more than a foot away, the wry face of Feldberg, his eyes bulging, his hair matted. With the force of will, she turned the other way. Nesha, head on his chest, his breath shallow. The three of them stretched full length like sardines. With great effort, she moved one hand and touched Nesha's chest. She gave a pathetic little push. He moaned without moving. She hoped Steiner hadn't heard.

The bumpy ride flattened into an elongated line, a rolling, rolling, a monotonous tremulo down endless road. No more street lights. Hadn't there been street lights behind her lids? She was sure it had been brighter. Now there was a sudden humidity in the air. She twisted her head back trying to look out the front windshield: there he was, Steiner driving in shadow, lit only by the phosphorescent reflection from the dashboard. From the floor of the van, all she could see out the front was black sky. But the dampness, the vague presence of ... water. That was it. He was taking them to the lake. Somewhere east of the city along the waterfront. He could stop where the lake was deep at the shore, and push their bodies into the water.

She had to start moving, she had to gain her strength back. And how would she do that, short of a miracle? She didn't believe in miracles anymore. Not since David. God may have split the sea once and saved the Israelites, but He had since disappeared. She knew she was alone, could count only on herself. The Angel of Death would not pass over if she didn't act. She lifted her head with effort. Hammers bounced at her temples. Who was she kidding? She didn't have a chance. He had a gun. She strained her eyes to examine the area around him. The dashboard — no. The passenger seat — no.

Then she spotted it: a bulge of black against the dark floor beside him. Almost under the dashboard. It wasn't far. In her other life she could've just reached out and it would be hers. But her head felt like an overripe melon and her legs were rubber. She was moving in slow motion, wedged between two bodies. She couldn't get to the gun before he would grab it.

Without making a conscious decision, she turned slowly onto her side, then her front, trying to dislodge herself silently from the floor. She lifted herself up on her forearms. Her head ached as she pulled herself to her knees, then crouched on rubber legs. The movement sent a shot of fresh blood to her brain. All of a sudden, something flashed in her memory. The thing in her pocket. The something she couldn't remember. She had deposited it there when the young cop had responded to her 911 call.

She reached in with her hand and felt the familiar

shape. It had waited there quietly for her, through everything. She closed her fingers around the scalpel, flicked off the protective cover. It was up to her. She had to be strong. Her heart thundered in her ears.

She gripped the scalpel in her fist. The motion of the van made her sway. Adrenaline surged through her body as she rose behind him like a shadow. She wasn't going to die without a fight.

She steadied herself. With her left hand she reached out and firmly grabbed a fistful of Steiner's hair, pulling back his head in the tightest grip she could summon. The scalpel in her right hand scraped at his throat.

"Stop the van!" she screamed.

His face contorted with pain but his foot stayed pressed on the gas. The van kept rolling, a bit slower.

"*Stop!*" she shrieked, pressing the scalpel harder. "This is a fresh, new blade. It'll go through your throat like butter!"

His icy eyes watched her through the pain. She could tell he was weighing his options. If he slammed on his brakes he could send her flying. He could also send the scalpel into his throat. He brought the van to a gentle stop. She glanced out the windshield: everything was dark. Water lapped against a shore somewhere.

Now her problem was how to get the gun without losing her grip on him. If she reached down with her right hand, she'd have to take the scalpel away from his throat for a second. Instead, she let go of his hair to free up her left hand, then snaked it round the other side of his head. With a deft flick, she switched the scalpel into her left hand. So far so good. The gun was still not within her reach as long as she stood behind him holding the blade at his throat. She stretched her right arm out blindly, unwilling to take her eyes off him, but it was no good. She needed fifteen more inches of arm. She loosened her grip for a second — a heartbeat — to lean over and reach for the gun. That's when he made his move.

He kicked the Luger out of her reach. It slid along the grooves toward the back into the dark. A bolt of fear gave her the strength — she plunged the scalpel home into his neck. She felt it enter the flesh but she missed what she was aiming at. He took his foot off the brake and the van careened off the road. She was thrown onto the ground between the seats. The phosphorescent dashboard illuminated his face. His mouth opened in the effort as he reached for the scalpel lodged in his neck, not fatal as she had hoped, no artery severed. He made a gagging sound as he pulled the scalpel from his throat. He was bleeding but not enough to make a difference, not enough to stop him from turning on her with her own weapon.

She was more dazed than hurt by her fall when she saw him bring the scalpel up at a murderous angle. He thrust it down toward her chest. With all her strength, she caught his forearm on its way down. God, he was strong! She couldn't hold it. Still seated, he stabbed wildly into the air, cutting her hands, ripping her jacket. Her blood began to flow.

His eyes blazing, he kept thrusting the scalpel at her. She couldn't hold him off any longer. He was too strong. If only she could get the gun. She heard someone screaming and realized it was her. She was out of time, out of ideas.... Then suddenly — the *noise*! The noise swelled in her ears, its echo resonated in her body.

Steiner had stopped slashing and looked up in shock. Still holding the scalpel, he brought his fingers to touch his left arm. They came away red with blood.

She scrambled to the back where Nesha crouched, wild-eyed and dazed, pointing the gun at Steiner. "We've got him," she said. "Let's take him to the police."

Nesha shook his head. "No police."

Steiner held his fist, still gripping the scalpel, to his arm while perched on the side of the driver's seat. "She's right. I'm just an old man now. I was young and stupid during the war. I did what I was told. Everybody did. Should I be punished for that?"

"Shut up!" said Nesha. "You've been alive thirty-eight years longer than my family...."

"I'm sorry...," Steiner began, "... it wasn't personal ... we did our job...."

Nesha breathed irregularly, pressed his other hand to his brow. He lifted himself from the crouch, trying to stand, but had to steady himself holding onto the side of the van.

"You need to get to a hospital," Rebecca said.

Steiner used the moment of distraction. He dove into the back, pouncing on Nesha. He stabbed the scalpel at Nesha's hand until the gun dropped once more. Steiner slashed at him with a fury.

She crawled along the grooves feeling for the gun. It wasn't so much pain as numbness that slowed her down. It was simply hard to move. She found the gun near Feldberg's shoulder. She needed both hands to pick it up.

Nesha was shielding his body from the ripping scalpel with his arms. The leather jacket protected him. But Steiner began to aim for his neck and head.

Rebecca had never fired a gun before. Crooking her finger around the trigger, she pulled. Nothing. Maybe it was too old. Maybe Steiner had the only weapon between them. *Try again.* She pulled harder this time.

The shot cracked in the air, the report filling the van. Her heart roared in her ears. Steiner stopped. Just like that. Bent over, gripping the scalpel, his mouth strangely open. He raised the scalpel again tentatively, unconvinced of his mortality. But a worm of blood trickled from his mouth. His breathing became laboured. His eyes stared but saw nothing. He fell backwards over Feldberg's body, the two merging in shadow.

She couldn't move, the weight of the gun pulling her hands down. Was he really dead? She waited for the undefined mass to move. She stepped toward it, holding the gun at the ready.

"He's dead," Nesha said, crouched on his knees to one side. "I felt the weight lift off my chest when he died."

She took one last look into the dark, but discerned no movement. She breathed deeply, both relieved and appalled. She had taken a life, she, who had dedicated herself to preserving it. How had the world turned so far upside down that she had found herself in the role of killer? No, not killer. Executioner. But that implied some kind of moral right. And moral right to kill belonged only to God. At least, the God she had once relied on. The God that had failed her.

"Are you all right?" she asked Nesha.

She knelt down and took his bleeding hands in hers. One side of his hair was caked with dried blood. She realized she was shivering.

Pulling him to his feet, she led him toward the rear of the van where she opened the gate. A cool spring wind rushed through her hair. They jumped down onto the grass where the van had landed. They were both trembling.

I didn't die, she thought. *It's spring and I'm still alive.* Beyond a field to their right, an ink-black basin stretched toward the lowering sky. The lake. She had just lived through a parting of the waters. Hallelujah.

She probed the wound on his head. "You took quite a blow," she said, moving aside his hair. "There's

a lot of blood, but no real damage. You were lucky."
She couldn't stop shivering.

He put his hand up to the wound. "I have a hard head." His sad soft eyes took in her face. "I'm so sorry you had to go through this. I should've done things differently... too many people got hurt... good people..." He closed his eyes, swayed as if he might fall over. "There is no justice ... God always waits too long ... we suffer and die and He comes too late...."

She took him gently in her arms. He was a rag doll, limp and tractable. "At least, you feel He still comes." She stroked his back beneath the leather jacket.

They stood for a long time, the water-fragrant breeze wafting off the lake, cooling their skin. They listened to it head inland like a vast breath and rouse the shadowy leaves of nearby trees. Finally she felt his arms tighten around her. He would be all right now. He began to shake, and she held onto him until his body was still.

She gazed at the black sky over his shoulder, the black shadow of water. She didn't tell him that she envied his belief, or that she no longer thought about forgiving God because He had stopped being part of her universe. There was a hole in her heart where God used to live and when she peered into it, all she saw was her own reflection looking back. She had not only lost David; she had lost the sense of her place in the world. God had failed David, but *she* had failed David, too. How was she ever going to believe in herself again? Somehow she would have to start with herself, then, in time, she might be able to consider God again, some wary day when the hurt finally flattened into the kind of dull ache one only noticed in the silence of the night. But for now, she was alive, that was all she knew. The Angel of Death had passed over. Her heart was still beating and it was April and the sun would come up tomorrow. Was there anything sweeter than spring?

author's note

Raffaello Sanzio — Raphael — painted the *Portrait of a Young Man* in oil on a wood panel, 28 by 22 inches, around 1512. The clear-eyed face of the nobleman looks down on the viewer from the elongated neck. Fine dark eyebrows, the long curly hair beneath the rich cap are pretty enough to be feminine. Prince Adam Czartoryski, the Polish aristocrat who bought the painting in 1807 in Venice, regarded it as Raphael's self-portrait.

The Czartoryski family, possessing both wealth and taste, acquired a large collection of antiquities, porcelain, graphics, and paintings, the stars of which were the Raphael, Leonardo da Vinci's *Lady with the Ermine*, and Rembrandt's *Landscape with the Good Samaritan*. The collection opened to the public in 1876 in Krakow's old City Arsenal.

During the Second World War, Hans Frank, the Nazi governor of Poland, confiscated the Czartoryski "Big Three" paintings to hang in his baronial apartments in Krakow's Wawel Castle. The paintings had already been earmarked by other high-ranking Nazis: Herman Goering had whisked them away to the Kaiser Friedrich

Museum in Berlin, while Hitler's art deputy coveted them for the Führer's personal collection in Linz, Austria. In 1942, however, the paintings were shipped out of Berlin by train to escape the bombing. They were returned to Dr. Frank in Krakow with the understanding that they would go to Linz after Germany won the war. In January 1945, with the war lost and the Russians closing in, Dr. Frank ordered an assistant to drive a truck loaded with art to his villa at Neuhaus, just south of Munich, two days ahead of Frank himself.

In June 1945, while examining the art cache that had been taken from Dr. Frank's house, the allies opened one of the cases to find a dozen paintings including da Vinci's *Lady with the Ermine* and Rembrandt's *Landscape*. There was no sign of the Raphael. In 1955 the Czartoryski family tried to trace the missing painting but with no success. There is conjecture that the painting may be lying unidentified in some attic or cellar.

Perhaps because Hitler was a failed painter, works of art acquired a rare importance in the Third Reich. The confiscation of art became a priority of war and was carried out by numerous branches of government. Official looters had at their disposal the necessary staff for the job, as well as clearance to commandeer the trucks, trains, and fuel required to transport warehouses of art out of their country of origin and back to Germany. With one country after another falling to the Wehrmacht, the Nazis had access to an ever-expanding supply of booty. Not only government agencies profited. German officials and SS officers regularly travelled as diplomats to Switzerland where dealers bought paintings and artifacts stolen from private homes all over occupied Europe. The Nazi plunder of European art during the Third Reich stands unprecedented in history. Fifty-five years after the war, many important works of art are still missing.